Jane Bowles in New York City, 1946, by Karl Bissinger

Two Serious Ladies

A NOVEL

Jane Bowles

INTRODUCED BY

Lorna Sage

WITH A MEMOIR BY

Truman Capote

Forthcoming from Sort Of Books

Everything is Nice: Jane Bowles' Collected Stories

Two Serious Ladies © Jane Bowles 1943
Introduction © Lorna Sage, 2000

Photo credits
Inside cover photos © Cecil Beaton, Courtesy of the Cecil Beaton Studio Archive at Sotheby's
Page 3: Jane Bowles in New York © Karl Bissinger
Page 11: Jane and Paul Bowles © The Estate of Paul Bowles
Page 16: Jane Bowles with Cherifa © Terrence Spencer/Getty Images
Page 22: Jane Bowles in Mexico © The Estate of Paul Bowles
Page 278: Truman Capote with Jane and Paul Bowles © Emilio Sanz de Soto
Page 283: Jane Bowles © Emilio Sanz de Soto
We are grateful to the Archivo de la Residencia de Estudiantes, Madrid, for use of the Emilio Sanz de Soto images.

No part of this book may be reproduced in any form without permission from the publisher except for the quotation of brief passages in reviews.

This edition first published in 2010 by
Sort Of Books, PO Box 18678, London NW3 2FL.

Typeset in Goudy and Gill Sans to a design by Henry Iles.
Printed in Italy by Legoprint.

288pp.
A catalogue record for this book is available
from the British Library

ISBN 978-0-95600-385-0

Contents

TOWER HAMLETS LIBRARIES

91000000500124

Bertrams	02/08/2010
AF	£7.99
THBET	TH10001329

Cover of the first American edition of *Two Serious Ladies*, published by Alfred A. Knopf, New York, 1943

Introduction

by Lorna Sage

There were originally three serious ladies, but the story of the third, Señorita Córdoba, was never finished. From the passages about her that survive, however, you can tell that she was as wonderfully unpredictable as Miss Goering and Mrs Copperfield:

> The traveller and Señorita Córdoba were seated together having a chat.
>
> "Doesn't love interest you?" the traveller was asking her . . . "Deep down in your heart, don't you always hope the right man will come along some day?"
>
> "No. . . no. . . no. . . Do you?" she said absentmindedly.
>
> "Who, me? No."
>
> "No?"
>
> She was the most preoccupied woman he had ever spoken with.

One source of the comedy of Jane Bowles's serious ladies is their anarchic, deadpan style. They never take other people's natures for granted. After all, their own impulses are mysterious to them. Nothing is natural, anything is possible. The Señorita makes this American traveller in Guatemala look like a mere tourist. Soon he'll be packing his case, 'with the vivacity of one who is in the habit of making little excursions away from the charmed fold to return almost immediately'. Serious ladies, by contrast, embark on their perverse adventures without return tickets. Señorita Córdoba, like other Bowles characters, is probably bisexual, and prefers women – but that is only the beginning of the story.

The book was written in the late 1930s and early 1940s and published in 1943, and parts were inspired by Jane's honeymoon trip to Central America with her husband, Paul. They married in 1938, the day before her twenty-first birthday, and although both chose same-sex sex it wasn't at all merely a marriage of disguise or convenience. They would often live apart, but they always kept in close touch, and only her death divorced them.

They proved well suited. They were card-carrying members of the American avant-garde and (briefly) of the Communist Party, and even lived for a short while in the famously queer household at 7 Middagh Street in Brooklyn Heights, where W. H. Auden made the house rules and queenly striptease artiste Gypsy Rose Lee had written *The G String Murders*. It was in 1940–41 that the Bowleses took over Gypsy Rose Lee's rooms; from 1947 they lived on and off in Morocco, mostly in Tangier.

Wherever they lived, Paul seemed more at home than Jane. She envied and sometimes teased him for being

Jane and Paul Bowles, New York, 1944

such a well-adjusted misfit, and once declared to him that 'Men are all on the outside, not interesting. They have no mystery. Women are profound and mysterious – and obscene.' As Millicent Dillon showed in her excellent biography *A Little Original Sin*, Jane made a kind of private mystery religion out of her fascination with women's hidden lives.

Her character Christina Goering (named after Jesus Christ and Hitler's aviation minister) as a girl invents a grotesque ceremony in which she subjects her sister's meek best friend Mary to a mock baptism: "If you don't lie down in the mud and let me pack the mud over you and then wash you in the stream, you'll be forever condemned." Mary is duly dirtied and drenched, but emerges no more mystically one with Christina than she was before:

> "The three minutes are over, I believe," said Christina.
>
> "Come darling, now you can stand up."
>
> "Let's run to the house," said Mary. "I'm freezing to death."

Sensible Mary doesn't die or undergo a conversion, all that happens is that Christina is confirmed in the loneliness of her calling. In her adult life the same 'promptings' lead Miss Goering first to adopt at random various ungrateful and unattractive hangers on, and then (to their disappointment and indignation) to sell the comfortable house she has inherited and renounce middle-class life: "I really believe that it is necessary for me to live in some more tawdry place. . . " Taking her entourage with her, she settles in a cramped four room house on an island not far from the city, which she has chosen for its squalor 'one can smell the glue factories'. Once there, she takes the ferry to a godforsaken town on the mainland, where she continues to search out her destiny in encounters with strangers in a gloomy bar. Miss Goering disinherits herself, in short, and becomes an adventuress, and a serious lady. That is, a woman who turns her true character into an open question. Perhaps the most bizarre thing about Bowles's women is that the object of their quests is to lose themselves, to fall, to find glory in the mud.

They may seem to belong in the company of decadents enchanted by the glamour of the gutter. Traditionally, poetical prostitution à la Baudelaire had symbolised the hell-tinged happiness of hitting bottom. Bowles's serious ladies are certainly drawn to poverty, and they are warmed by the idea of prostitution. But the working girls she writes about are almost never imagined as abject or sublime, instead they have volatile moods, are often gay, and improvise moment to moment in a quite practical fashion. Mrs Copperfield, the second serious lady, on her own separate adventure in Panama, where she rents a room in the same sleazy hotel as her new-found friend, the prostitute Pacifica, whispers to herself: ". . . what an angel a happy moment is – and how nice not to have to struggle too much for inner peace! . . . No one among my friends speaks any longer of character – and what interests us most, certainly, is finding out what we are like." Mrs Copperfield is in love with Pacifica's life, and wants to share it. Miss Goering is obscurely flattered when a 'big man in an overcoat' who is some sort of gangster picks her up. Like Señorita Córdoba and the traveller, Miss Goering and 'the heavy-set man who owned the hearse-like car' engage in one of those crossed-purpose conversations between straight men and dubious women that Bowles finds so hilarious:

> "Well," he said to her after they had been sitting there for a little while, "do you work here?"
>
> "Where?" said Miss Goering.
>
> "Here, in this town."

> "No," said Miss Goering.
>
> "Well, then, do you work in another town?"
>
> "No, I don't work."
>
> "Yes, you do. You don't have to try to fool me, because no one ever has."
>
> "I don't understand."
>
> "You work as a prostitute, after a fashion, don't you?"
>
> Miss Goering laughed. "Heavens!" she said. "I certainly never thought I looked like a prostitute merely because I had red hair; perhaps like a derelict or an escaped lunatic, but never a prostitute!"

True to her promptings, however, she decides to play along with his mistake. Sexual relations with men will never be 'profound and mysterious', but being taken for a prostitute will put you in touch, perhaps, with a world of women that is endlessly strange.

The serious ladies want to live outside themselves. And that is a want they share with their author, who is herself the third, invisible, serious lady of the book. Like them, Jane Bowles had fled the prospect of a respectable middle-class life. She was born in New York in 1917, the only child of second generation immigrants, a Jewish Hungarian mother and a German Jewish father, Claire and Sidney Auer. They lived on Long Island, but Jane returned to the city with her possessive and ambitious mother when her father died in 1930. She'd had a limp as a child, and after a riding accident in her teens developed tuberculosis in her knee joint; she spent 1932–34 having treatment in a Swiss clinic, and in 1936, back in New York, the leg was fixed so that it would never bend.

This didn't cramp her style rather, it confirmed it. In moods of raucous defiance she'd call herself 'Crippie, the Kike Dyke'. Already in 1936, still in her plaster cast, she was keeping louche company in Greenwich Village bars and being deplored by her mother and her aunts. She reported to a crony, another middle class drop out and would be writer, George McMillan, an emergency family conference:

> 'They all sat down and said . . . that I was a grand normal girl and that this Lesbian business was just an adolescent phase . . . and that if only I didn't have such an analytic mind I certainly would throw it off – and if I really were a Lesbian they'd get up a fund for me and send me down to the village in my own private bus.'

In fact, her travels, and her love affairs, seem to have been driven by a desire for release not only from her parents' world, but from an American-Bohemian counterculture that too much resembled a little excursion from the charmed fold. Years after she wrote *Two Serious Ladies*, her quest culminated in Tangier, in her pursuit of the elusive Arab market-women Tetum and Cherifa. She wrote about this in a notebook with uncharacteristic and sad directness:

> I don't know which one I like best, or how long I can go on this way, at the point of expectation, yet knowing at the same time that it is all hopeless. Does it matter? It is more the coming home to them that I want than it is they themselves. But I do want them to belong to me, which is of course impossible . . . If

Jane Bowles with Cherifa, Tangier, 1967

> I have broken through my own prison – then at the same time I have necessarily lost what was my place of rest . . .

Here the wit of *Two Serious Ladies* has deserted her. In the early 1950s Bowles discovered saintly, self-destructive Simone Weil's book *Waiting on God*, and found in it a mirror of her own sense of apartness. 'There are some human beings', Weil wrote, '. . . separated from ordinary folk by their natural purity of soul. As for me, on the contrary . . . I have the germ of all possible crimes . . . within me . . . It is the sign of a vocation, the vocation to remain in a certain sense anonymous.' We should aspire, she said, 'To empty ourselves of our false divinity, to deny ourselves, to give up being the centre of the world in imagination, to discern that all points in the world are equally centres.'

Weil believed in a deity outside the world, though whether He was the Jewish or the Christian God was never quite clear, and took imaginative refuge in the beauty of nature. Bowles by contrast portrayed the natural world as alien and uncanny. In *Two Serious Ladies* Mrs Copperfield takes a trip with her husband to a deserted beach in Panama:

> She watched him picking his way among the tiny stones, his arms held out for balance like a tight-rope walker's, and wished that she were able to join him because she was so fond of him . . . She threw her head back and closed her eyes, hoping that perhaps she might become exalted enough to run down and join her husband. But the wind did not blow quite hard enough, and behind her closed eyes she saw

Pacifica and Mrs Quill standing outside the Hotel de las Palmas.

For Bowles, other people – other women – were the only hope of salvation (Pacifica will lead Mrs Copperfield into the water, and for once the blasphemous baptism will work). Perhaps art could save, too – but Bowles found it harder and harder to write, and her experiments in living were fraught with tension. She did set up house with Cherifa in Tangier, but it certainly wasn't a 'place of rest', since although liaisons between Western men like her husband Paul and Arab men were relatively accepted, even traditional, homosexual relations across the two cultures between women were entirely outside the rules, off the map. Such was the stormy atmosphere of scandal Cherifa and Jane generated that when Jane suffered a stroke, Tangier expatriate gossip speculated that Cherifa had poisoned her (though some said it was with a love potion).

But even in the later years when, thanks to illness and obsession, the daily details of living absorbed more and more of her energy, there were frequent flashes of mirth. In 1958, for instance, the Beat poet Allen Ginsberg called Paul in Tangier, and got Jane instead: 'Then this complete madman asked me if I believed in God. "Do you believe in God, Jane?" I told him: "I'm certainly not going to discuss it on the telephone."'

So singular was Bowles's sensibility, and so exiguous her output – only the play *In the Summer House* and a handful of stories apart from *Two Serious Ladies* – that it's always been tempting to see her as one of a kind, writing in isolation when she did write. But the work does have precedents. Not in the soulful lesbian tradition associated with Radclyffe Hall (a red herring), but in the polished, modernist, mocking-and-despairing line of Katherine Mansfield, Djuna Barnes and the young Jean Rhys, who are all drawn to freaks and outlaws. When Ford Madox Ford wrote in his Preface to Rhys's first collection of stories *The Left Bank* (1927) of her profound knowledge of 'many of the Left Banks of the world', and her 'bias of . . . sympathy with . . . lawbreakers', he was describing this *demi mondaine* heritage. Djuna Barnes's 'wise-cracking, elliptical newspaper interviews from the century's teens and twenties, featuring stars of burlesque, rabble-rousing preachers and dubious politicians, hit the same note. Here she is talking with actress Helen Westley, a member of the Washington Square Players, in 1917:

> '. . . I say, go to life, study life. Sit on a sidewalk and contemplate the sewer, the billposters, the street-cleaners, the pedestrians, anything – but go there before you go to Chinatown to buy embroidery.'
>
> 'Do you often sit on the sidewalk, Miss Westley?'
>
> 'I do. If doctors would prescribe sidewalks instead of pills and hot water, how much better off we should be.'
>
> 'Really, you have a dirt complex, as Freud would say.'

Barnes's modernist mistresspiece *Nightwood* (1936), inspired by the expatriate Parisian underworld, featured a narrative procession of freakish 'originals' – one of whom, Mademoiselle Basquette, 'a girl without legs' ('She used to wheel herself through the Pyrenees on a board'), seems to have inspired the grotesque story of Belle, who hasn't any arms either, and has been left behind by the circus, in *Two Serious Ladies*. It is Andy, another of the outsiders Miss Goering meets in the bar, who tells her about Belle:

> "I began to notice her mouth. It was like a rose petal or a heart or some kind of a little shell. It was really beautiful. Then right away I started to wonder what she would be like; the rest of her, you understand – without any legs . . . It grew and grew, this terrible curiosity . . . "

The stigma of deformity is for these writers, doubtless, a way of exploring their own estrangement as authors even from the world of the male avant-garde. At the same time it reflects their defiant conviction that the writer's vocation is a marvellous act, a performance brought off against the odds.

Closest to Bowles in her own generation was the Southerner Carson McCullers. They were born in the same year, and their careers had an eerily similar shape – almost all their real work done in their twenties, followed by years of writer's block, excesses and devastating illness, and early death. Both loved women and shared friends and fans among gay men, particularly Truman Capote and Tennessee Williams. In the McCullers bestsellers, *The Heart is a Lonely Hunter* (1940) and *The Ballad of the Sad Café* (1943), the grotesque is the order of the day. In a 1940 *Vogue* article, titled 'Look Homeward, Americans', McCullers wrote:

> We are torn between a nostalgia for the familiar and an urge for the foreign and strange. As often as not, we are homesick most for the places we have never known.

> All men are lonely. But sometimes it seems to me that we Americans are the loneliest of all . . . Our literature is stamped with a quality of longing and unrest, and our writers have been great wanderers . . .
>
> So we must turn inward. This singular emotion, the nostalgia that has been so much a part of our national character, must be converted to good use . . . We must make a new declaration of independence, a spiritual rather than a political one this time

This is close to the ethos of Bowles's writing, and yet its sentimental and elegiac tone, the very ease with which McCullers can say 'we', marks a parting of their ways. Writing to Paul in 1947, Jane mulled over the difference: 'Certainly Carson McCullers is as *talented* as Sartre or Simone de Beauvoir, but she is not a serious writer. I am serious but I am isolated and my experience is probably of no interest at this point to anyone.' In the same letter she goes on to draw a distinction between herself and Paul, too. He may also be 'isolated', but his loneliness is somehow representative, unlike hers:

> Not only is your isolation a positive and true one but when you do write from it you immediately receive recognition because what you write is in a true relation to yourself which is always recognizable to the world outside. With me who knows? When you are capable only of a serious and ponderous approach to writing as I am.

She attached a special, semi-private meaning to the word 'serious'. For her, being serious meant risking the

Jane Bowles in Mexico, 1941, at the time of writing *Two Serious Ladies*

possibility that you were meaninglessly weird, an existential Calamity Jane – 'my kind of isolation I think is an accident and not inevitable'. It also, however, meant writing with panache, hilarity and devastating insight on the very edge of that particular abyss. McCullers could say, 'When I write about a thief, I become one.' It's hard to imagine Bowles feeling so readily identified with her characters: when she writes about pariahs she only partly reclaims them for the imaginable world. She said in this same glum, stock-taking letter, 'I realize now . . . that really "Two Serious Ladies" never was a novel . . . ' She was right, but in fact its improbability was its genius. With it she joined the small company of women modernists who celebrated their freakishness in the highest style.

Two Serious Ladies

Jane Bowles

1

CHRISTINA GOERING'S FATHER was an American industrialist of German parentage and her mother was a New York lady of a very distinguished family. Christina spent the first half of her life in a very beautiful house (not more than an hour from the city) which she had inherited from her mother. It was in this house that she had been brought up as a child with her sister Sophie.

As a child Christina had been very much disliked by other children. She had never suffered particularly because of this, having led, even at a very early age, an active inner life that curtailed her observation of whatever went on around her, to such a degree that she never picked up the mannerisms then in vogue, and at the age of ten was called old-fashioned by other little girls. Even then she wore the look of certain fanatics who think of themselves as leaders without once having gained the respect of a single human being.

Christina was troubled horribly by ideas which never would have occurred to her companions, and at the same time took for granted a position in society which any other child would have found unbearable. Every now and then a schoolmate would take pity on her and try to spend some time with her, but far from being grateful for this, Christina would instead try her best to convert her new friend to the cult of whatever she believed in at the time.

Her sister Sophie, on the other hand, was very much admired by everyone in the school. She showed a marked talent for writing poetry and spent all her time with a quiet little girl called Mary, who was two years younger.

When Christina was thirteen years old her hair was very red (when she grew up it remained almost as red), her cheeks were sloppy and pink, and her nose showed traces of nobility.

That year Sophie brought Mary home with her nearly every day for luncheon. After they had finished eating she would take Mary for a walk through the woods, having provided a basket for each of them in which to carry back flowers. Christina was not permitted by Sophie to come along on these walks.

"You must find something of your own to do," Sophie would say to her. But it was hard for Christina to think of anything to do by herself that she enjoyed. She was in the habit of going through many mental struggles—generally of a religious nature—and she preferred to be with other people and organize games. These games, as a rule, were very moral, and often involved God. However, no one else enjoyed them and she was obliged to spend a great part of the day alone. She tried going to the woods once or twice by herself and bringing back flowers, in imitation of Mary and Sophie, but each time, fearing that she would not return with enough flowers to make a beautiful bouquet, she so encumbered herself with baskets that the walk seemed more of a hardship than a pleasure.

It was Christina's desire to have Mary to herself of an afternoon. One very sunny afternoon Sophie went inside for her piano lesson, and Mary remained seated on the grass. Christina, who had seen this from not far away, ran into the house, her heart beating with excitement. She took off her shoes and stockings and remained in a short white underslip. This was not a very pleasant sight to behold, because Christina at this time was very heavy and her legs were quite fat. (It was impossible to foresee that she would turn out to be a tall and elegant lady.) She ran out on the lawn and told Mary to watch her dance.

"Now don't take your eyes off me," she said. "I'm going to do a dance of worship to the sun. Then I'm going to show that I'd rather have God and no sun than the sun and no God. Do you understand?"

"Yes," said Mary. "Are you going to do it now?"

"Yes, I'm going to do it right here." She began the dance abruptly. It was a clumsy dance and her gestures were all undecided. When Sophie came out of the house, Christina was in the act of running backwards and forwards with her hands joined in prayer.

"What is she doing?" Sophie asked Mary.

"A dance to the sun, I think," Mary said. "She told me to sit here and watch her."

Sophie walked over to where Christina was now twirling around and around and shaking her hands weakly in the air.

"Sneak!" she said and suddenly she pushed Christina down on the grass.

For a long time after that, Christina kept away from Sophie, and consequently from Mary. She had one more occasion to be with Mary, however, and this happened because Sophie developed a terrible toothache one morning, and her governess was obliged to take her to the dentist immediately. Mary, not having heard of this, came over in the afternoon, expecting to find Sophie at home. Christina was in the tower in which the children often gathered, and saw her coming up the walk.

"Mary," she screamed, "come on up here." When Mary arrived in the tower, Christina asked her if she would not like to play a very special game with her. "It's called 'I forgive you for all your sins'," said Christina. "You'll have to take your dress off."

"Is it fun?" Mary asked.

"It's not for fun that we play it, but because it's necessary to play it."

"All right," said Mary, "I'll play with you." She took her dress off and Christina pulled an old burlap sack over Mary's head. She cut two holes in the burlap for Mary to see through and then she tied a cord around her waist.

"Come," said Christina, "and you will be absolved for your sins. Keep repeating to yourself: 'May the Lord forgive me for my sins'."

She hurried down the stairs with Mary and then out across the lawn towards the woods. Christina wasn't yet sure what she was going to do, but she was very much excited. They came to a stream that skirted the woods. The banks of the stream were soft and muddy.

"Come to the water," said Christina; "I think that's how we'll wash away your sins. You'll have to stand in the mud."

"Near the mud?"

"*In* the mud. Does your sin taste bitter in your mouth? It must."

"Yes," said Mary hesitantly.

"Then you want to be clean and pure as a flower is, don't you?"

Mary did not answer.

"If you don't lie down in the mud and let me pack the mud over you and then wash you in the stream, you'll be forever condemned. Do you want to be forever condemned? This is your moment to decide."

Mary stood beneath her black hood without saying a word.

Christina pushed her down on the ground and started to pack the burlap with mud.

"The mud's cold," said Mary.

"The hell fires are hot," said Christina. "If you let me do this, you won't go to hell."

"Don't take too long," said Mary.

Christina was very much agitated. Her eyes were shining. She packed more and more mud on Mary and then she said to her:

"Now you're ready to be purified in the stream."

"Oh, please no, not the water—I hate to go into the water. I'm afraid of the water."

"Forget what you are afraid of. God's watching you now and He has no sympathy for you yet."

She lifted Mary from the ground and walked into the stream, carrying her. She had forgotten to take off her own shoes and stockings. Her dress was completely covered with mud. Then she submerged Mary's body in the water. Mary was looking at her through the holes in the burlap. It did not occur to her to struggle.

"Three minutes will be enough," said Christina. "I'm going to say a little prayer for you."

"Oh, don't do that," Mary pleaded.

"Of course," said Christina, lifting her eyes to the sky.

"Dear God," she said, "make this girl Mary pure as Jesus Your Son. Wash her sins away as the water is now washing the mud away. This black burlap proves to you that she thinks she is a sinner."

"Oh, stop," whispered Mary. "He can hear you even if you just say it to yourself. You're shouting so."

"The three minutes are over, I believe," said Christina. "Come darling, now you can stand up."

"Let's run to the house," said Mary. "I'm freezing to death."

They ran to the house and up the back stairway that led to the tower. It was hot in the tower room because all the windows had been shut. Christina suddenly felt very ill.

"Go," she said to Mary, "go into the bath and clean yourself off. I'm going to draw." She was deeply troubled. "It's over," she said to herself, "the game is over. I'll tell Mary to go home after she's dried off. I'll give her some colored pencils to take home with her."

Mary returned from the bath wrapped in a towel. She was still shivering. Her hair was wet and straight. Her face looked smaller than it did ordinarily.

Christina looked away from her. "The game is over," she said, "it took only a few minutes—you should be dried off—I'm going out." She walked out of the room leaving Mary behind, pulling the towel closer around her shoulders.

AS A GROWN WOMAN Miss Goering was no better liked than she had been as a child. She was now living in her home outside New York, with her companion, Miss Gamelon.

Three months ago Miss Goering had been sitting in the parlor, looking out at the leafless trees, when her maid announced a caller.

"Is it a gentleman or a lady?" Miss Goering asked.

"A lady."

"Show her in immediately," said Miss Goering.

The maid returned followed by the caller. Miss Goering rose from her seat. "How do you do?" she said. "I don't believe I've ever laid eyes on you before this moment, but please sit down."

The lady visitor was small and stocky and appeared to be in her late thirties or early forties. She wore dark, unfashionable clothing and, but for her large gray eyes, her face might on all occasions have passed unnoticed.

"I'm your governess's cousin," she said to Miss Goering. "She was with you for many years. Do you remember her?"

"I do," said Miss Goering.

"Well, my name is Lucie Gamelon. My cousin used to talk about you and about your sister Sophie all the time. I've been meaning to call on you for years now, but one thing and another always got in the way. But then, we never know it to fail."

Miss Gamelon reddened. She had not yet been relieved of her hat and coat.

"You have a lovely home," she said. "I guess you know it and appreciate it a lot."

By this time Miss Goering was filled with curiosity concerning Miss Gamelon. "What's your business in life?" she asked her.

"Not very much, I'm afraid. I've been typing manuscripts for famous authors all my life, but there doesn't seem to be much demand for authors any more unless maybe they are doing their own typing."

Miss Goering, who was busy thinking, said nothing. Miss Gamelon looked around helplessly.

"Do you stay here the greater portion of the time or do you travel mostly?" she asked Miss Goering unexpectedly.

"I never thought of traveling," said Miss Goering. "I don't require travel."

"Coming from the family you come from," said Miss Gamelon, "I guess you were born full of knowledge about everything. You wouldn't need to travel. I had opportunity to travel two or three times with my authors. They were willing to pay all my expenses and my full salary besides, but I never did go except once, and that was to Canada."

"You don't like to travel," said Miss Goering, staring at her.

"It doesn't agree with me. I tried it that once. My stomach was upset and I had nervous headaches all the time. That was enough. I had my warning."

"I understand perfectly," said Miss Goering.

"I always believe," continued Miss Gamelon, "that you get your warning. Some people don't heed their warnings. That's when they come into conflict. I think that anything you feel strange or nervous about, you weren't cut out to do."

"Go on," said Miss Goering.

"Well, I know, for instance, that I wasn't cut out to be an aviator. I've always had dreams of crashing down to the earth. There are quite a few things that I won't do, even if I am thought of as a stubborn mule. I won't cross a big body of water, for instance. I could have everything I wanted if I would just cross the ocean and go over to England, but I never will."

"Well," said Miss Goering, "let's have some tea and some sandwiches."

Miss Gamelon ate voraciously and complimented Miss Goering on her good food.

"I like good things to eat," she said; "I don't have so much good food any more. I did when I was working for the authors."

When they had finished tea, Miss Gamelon took leave of her hostess.

"I've had a very sociable time," she said. "I would like to stay longer, but tonight I have promised a niece of mine that I would watch over her children for her. She is going to attend a ball."

"You must be very depressed with the idea," said Miss Goering.

"Yes, you're right," Miss Gamelon replied.

"Do return soon," said Miss Goering.

The following afternoon the maid announced to Miss Goering that she had a caller. "It's the same lady that called here yesterday," said the maid.

"Well, well," thought Miss Goering, "that's good."

"How are you feeling today?" Miss Gamelon asked her, coming into the room. She spoke very naturally, not appearing to find it strange that she was returning so soon after her first visit. "I was thinking about you all last night," she said. "It's a funny thing. I always thought I should meet you. My cousin used to tell me how queer you were. I think, though, that you can make friends more quickly with queer people. Or else you don't make friends with them at all—one way or the other. Many of my authors were very queer. In that way I've had an advantage of association that most people don't have. I know something about what I call real honest-to-God maniacs, too."

Miss Goering invited Miss Gamelon to dine with her. She found her soothing and agreeable to be with. Miss Gamelon was very much impressed with the fact that Miss Goering was so nervous. Just as they were about to sit down, Miss Goering said that she couldn't face eating in the dining-room and she asked the servant to lay the table in the parlor instead. She spent a great deal of time switching the lights off and on.

"I know how you feel," Miss Gamelon said to her.

"I don't particularly enjoy it," said Miss Goering, "but I expect in the future to be under control."

Over wine at dinner Miss Gamelon told Miss Goering that it was only correct that she should be thus. "What do you expect, dear," she said, "coming from the kind of family you come from? You're all tuned high, all of you. You've got to allow yourself things that other people haven't any right to allow themselves."

Miss Goering began to feel a little tipsy. She looked dreamily at Miss Gamelon, who was eating her second helping of chicken cooked in wine. There was a little spot of grease in the corner of her mouth.

"I love to drink," said Miss Gamelon, "but there isn't much point to it when you have to work. It's fine enough when you have plenty of leisure time. I have a lot of leisure time now."

"Have you a guardian angel?" asked Miss Goering.

"Well, I have a dead aunt, maybe that's what you mean; she might be watching over me."

"That is not what I mean—I mean something quite different."

"Well, of course . . ." said Miss Gamelon.

"A guardian angel comes when you are very young, and gives you special dispensation."

"From what?"

"From the world. Yours might be luck; mine is money. Most people have a guardian angel; that's why they move slowly."

"That's an imaginative way of talking about guardian angels. I guess my guardian angel is what I told you about heeding my warnings. I think maybe she could warn me about both of us. In that way I could keep you out of trouble. Of course, with your consent," she added, looking a little confused.

Miss Goering had a definite feeling at that moment that Miss Gamelon was not in the least a nice woman, but she refused to face this because she got too much enjoyment from the sensation of being nursed and pampered. She told herself that it would do no harm for a little while.

"Miss Gamelon," said Miss Goering, "I think it would be a very fine idea if you were to make this your home—for the time being, at least. I don't think you have any pressing business that would oblige you to remain elsewhere, have you?"

"No, I haven't any business," said Miss Gamelon. "I don't see why I couldn't stay here—I'd have to get my things at my sister's house. Outside of that I don't know of anything else."

"What things?" asked Miss Goering impatiently. "Don't go back at all. We can get things at the stores." She got up and walked quickly up and down the room.

"Well," said Miss Gamelon, "I think I had better get my things."

"But not tonight," said Miss Goering, "tomorrow—tomorrow in the car."

"Tomorrow in the car," repeated Miss Gamelon after her.

Miss Goering made arrangements to give Miss Gamelon a room near her own, to which she led her shortly after dinner was over.

"This room," said Miss Goering, "has one of the finest views in the entire house." She drew the curtains apart. "You've got your moon and your stars tonight, Miss Gamelon, and a very nice silhouette of trees against the sky."

Miss Gamelon was standing in semi-darkness near the dressing-table. She was fingering the brooch on her blouse. She wished that Miss Goering would leave so that she could think about the house and Miss Goering's offer, in her own way.

There was a sudden scrambling in the bushes below the window. Miss Goering jumped.

"What's that?" Her face was very white and she put her hand to her forehead. "My heart hurts so for such a long time afterwards whenever I'm frightened," she said in a small voice.

"I think I'd better go to bed now and go to sleep," said Miss Gamelon. She was suddenly overcome by all the wine that she had drunk. Miss Goering took her leave reluctantly. She had been prepared to talk half the night. The following morning Miss Gamelon went home to collect her things and give her sister her new address.

Three months later Miss Goering knew little more about Miss Gamelon's ideas than she had on the first night that they had dined together. She had learned quite a lot about Miss Gamelon's personal characteristics, however, through careful observation. When Miss Gamelon had first arrived she had spoken a great deal about her love of luxury and beautiful objects, but Miss Goering had since then taken her on innumerable shopping trips; and she had never seemed interested in anything more than the simplest necessities.

She was quiet, even a little sullen, but she seemed to be fairly contented. She enjoyed dining out at large, expensive restaurants, particularly if dinner music accompanied the meal. She did not seem to like the theater. Very often Miss Goering would buy tickets for a play, and at the last moment Miss Gamelon would decline to go.

"I feel so lazy," she would say, "that bed seems to be the most beautiful thing in the world at this moment."

When she did go to the theater, she was easily bored. Whenever the action of the play was not swift, Miss Goering would catch her looking down into her lap and playing with her fingers.

She seemed now to feel more violently about Miss Goering's activities than she did about her own, although she did not listen so sympathetically to Miss Goering's explanations of herself as she had in the beginning.

On Wednesday afternoon Miss Gamelon and Miss Goering were sitting underneath the trees in front of the house. Miss Goering was drinking whisky and Miss Gamelon was reading. The maid came out and announced to Miss Goering that she was wanted on the telephone.

The call was from Miss Goering's old friend Anna, who invited her to a party the following night. Miss Goering came back out on the lawn, very excited.

"I'm going to a party tomorrow night," she said, "but I don't see how I can wait until then—I look forward to going to parties so much and I am invited to so few that I scarcely know how to behave about them. What will we do to make the hours pass until then?" She took both Miss Gamelon's hands in her own.

It was getting a little chilly. Miss Goering shivered and smiled. "Do you enjoy our little life?" she asked Miss Gamelon.

"I'm always content," said Miss Gamelon, "because I know what to take and what to leave, but you are always at the mercy."

Miss Goering arrived at Anna's looking flushed and a little overdressed. She was wearing velvet and Miss Gamelon had fastened some flowers in her hair.

The men, most of whom were middle-aged, were standing together in one corner of the room, smoking and listening to each other attentively. The ladies, freshly powdered, were seated around the room, talking very little. Anna seemed to be a little tense, although she was smiling. She wore a hostess gown adapted from a central European peasant costume.

"You will have drinks in a minute," she announced to her guests, and then, seeing Miss Goering, she went over to her and led her to a chair next to Mrs. Copperfield's without saying a word.

Mrs. Copperfield had a sharp little face and very dark hair. She was unusually small and thin. She was nervously rubbing her bare arms and looking around the room when Miss Goering seated herself in the chair beside her. They had met for many years at Anna's parties and they occasionally had tea with each other.

"Oh! Christina Goering," cried Mrs. Copperfield, startled to see her friend suddenly seated beside her, "I'm going away!"

"Do you mean," said Miss Goering, "that you are leaving this party?"

"No, I am going on a trip. Wait until I tell you about it. It's terrible."

Miss Goering noticed that Mrs. Copperfield's eyes were brighter than usual. "What is wrong, little Mrs. Copperfield?" she asked, rising from her seat and looking around the room with a bright smile on her face.

"Oh, I'm sure," said Mrs. Copperfield, "that you wouldn't want to hear about it. You can't possibly have any respect for me, but that doesn't make any difference because I have the utmost respect for you. I heard my husband say that you had a religious nature one day, and we almost had a very bad fight. Of course he is crazy to say that. You are gloriously unpredictable and you are afraid of no one but yourself. I hate religion in other people."

Miss Goering neglected to answer Mrs. Copperfield because for the last second or two she had been staring at a stout dark-haired man who was walking heavily across the room in their direction. As he came nearer, she saw that he had a pleasant face with wide jowls that protruded on either side but did not hang down as they do on most obese persons. He was dressed in a blue business suit.

"May I sit beside you?" he asked them. "I have met this young lady before," he said, shaking hands with Mrs. Copperfield, "but I am afraid that I have not yet met her friend." He turned and nodded to Miss Goering.

Mrs. Copperfield was so annoyed at the interruption that she neglected to introduce Miss Goering to the gentleman. He drew up a chair next to Miss Goering's and looked at her.

"I have just come from a most wonderful dinner," he said to her, "moderate in price, but served with care and excellently prepared. If it would interest you I can write down the name of the little restaurant for you."

He reached into his vest pocket and pulled out a leather billfold. He found only one slip of paper which was not already covered with addresses.

"I will write this down for you," he said to Miss Goering. "Undoubtedly you will be seeing Mrs. Copperfield and then you can pass the information on to her, or perhaps she can telephone to you."

Miss Goering took the slip of paper in her hand and looked carefully at the writing.

He had not written down the name of a restaurant at all; instead he had asked Miss Goering to consent to go home with him later to his apartment. This pleased her greatly as she was usually delighted to stay out as late as possible once she had left her home.

She looked up at the man, whose face was now inscrutable. He sipped his drink with calm, and looked around the room like someone who has finally brought a business conversation to a close. However, there were some sweat beads on his forehead.

Mrs. Copperfield stared at him with distaste, but Miss Goering's face suddenly brightened. "Let me tell you," she said to them, "about a strange experience I had this morning. Sit still, little Mrs. Copperfield, and listen to me." Mrs. Copperfield looked up at Miss Goering and took her friend's hand in her own.

"I stayed in town with my sister Sophie last night," said Miss Goering, "and this morning I was standing in front of the window drinking a cup of coffee. The building next to Sophie's house is being torn down. I believe that they are intending to put an apartment house in its place. It was not only extremely windy this morning, but it was raining intermittently. From my window I could see into the rooms of this building, as the wall opposite me had already been torn down. The rooms were still partially furnished, and I stood looking at them, watching the rain spatter the wallpaper. The wallpaper was flowered and already covered with dark spots, which were growing larger."

"How amusing," said Mrs. Copperfield, "or perhaps it was depressing."

"I finally felt rather sad watching this and I was about to go away when a man came into one of these rooms and, walking deliberately over to the bed, took up a coverlet which he folded under his arm. It was undoubtedly a personal possession which he had neglected to pack and had just now returned to fetch. Then he walked around the room aimlessly for a bit and finally he stood at the very edge of his room looking down into the yard with his arms akimbo. I could see him more clearly now, and I could easily tell that he was an artist. As he stood there, I was increasingly filled with horror, very much as though I were watching a scene in a nightmare."

At this point Miss Goering suddenly stood up.

"Did he jump, Miss Goering?" Mrs. Copperfield asked with feeling.

"No, he remained there for quite a while looking down into the courtyard with an expression of pleasant curiosity on his face."

"Amazing, Miss Goering," said Mrs. Copperfield. "I do think it's such an interesting story, really, but it has quite scared me out of my wits and I shouldn't enjoy hearing another one like it." She had scarcely finished her sentence when she heard her husband say:

"We will go to Panama and linger there awhile before we penetrate into the interior."

Mrs. Copperfield pressed Miss Goering's hand.

"I don't think I can bear it," she said. "Really, Miss Goering, it frightens me so much to go."

"I would go anyway," said Miss Goering.

Mrs. Copperfield jumped off the arm of the chair and ran into the library. She locked the door behind her carefully and then she fell in a little heap on the sofa and sobbed bitterly. When she had stopped crying she powdered her nose, seated herself on the window-sill, and looked down into the dark garden below.

An hour or two later Arnold, the stout man in the blue suit, was still talking to Miss Goering. He suggested to her that they leave the party and go to his own house. "I think that we will have a much nicer time there," he said to her. "There will be less noise and we will be able to talk more freely."

As yet Miss Goering had no desire at all to leave, she enjoyed so much being in a room full of people, but she did not quite know how to get out of accepting his invitation.

"Certainly," she said, "let's be on our way." They rose and left the room together in silence.

"Don't say anything to Anna about our leaving," Arnold told Miss Goering. "It will only cause a commotion. I promise you I'll send some sweets to her tomorrow, or some flowers." He pressed Miss Goering's hand and smiled at her. She was not sure that she did not find him a bit too familiar.

AFTER LEAVING ANNA'S PARTY, Arnold walked awhile with Miss Goering and then hailed a cab. The road to his home led through many dark and deserted streets. Miss

Goering was so nervous and hysterical about this that Arnold was alarmed.

"I always think," said Miss Goering, "that the driver is only waiting for the passengers to become absorbed in conversation in order to shoot down some street, to an inaccessible and lonely place where he will either torture or murder them. I am certain that most people feel the same way about it that I do, but they have the good taste not to mention it."

"Since you live so far out of town," said Arnold, "why don't you spend the night at my house? We have an extra bedroom."

"I probably shall," said Miss Goering, "although it is against my entire code, but then, I have never even begun to use my code, although I judge everything by it." Miss Goering looked a little morose after having said this and they drove on in silence until they reached their destination.

Arnold's flat was on the second floor. He opened the door and they walked into a room lined to the ceiling with bookshelves. The couch had been made up and Arnold's slippers were lying on the rug beside it. The furniture was heavy and some small Oriental rugs were scattered here and there.

"I sleep in here," said Arnold, "and my mother and father occupy the bedroom. We have a small kitchen, but generally we prefer to eat out. There is another tiny bedroom, originally intended for a maid's room, but I would rather sleep in here and let my eye wander from book to book; books are a great solace to me." He sighed heavily and laid both his hands on Miss Goering's shoulders. "You see, my dear lady," he said, "I'm not exactly doing the kind of thing that I would like to do . . . I'm in the real-estate business."

"What is it that you would like to do?" asked Miss Goering, looking weary and indifferent.

"Something, naturally," said Arnold, "in the book line, or in the painting line."

"And you can't?"

"No," said Arnold, "my family doesn't believe that such an occupation is serious, and since I must earn my living and pay for my share of this flat, I have been obliged to accept a post in my uncle's office, where I must say I very quickly have become his prize salesman. In the evenings, however, I have plenty of time to move among people who have nothing to do with real estate. As a matter of fact, they think very little about earning money at all. Naturally, these people are interested in having enough to eat. Even though I am thirty-nine years old I still am hoping very seriously that I will be able to make a definite break with my family. I do not see life through the same pair of eyes that they do. And I feel more and more that my life here with them is becoming insupportable in spite of the fact that I am free to entertain whom I please since I pay for part of the upkeep of the flat."

He sat down on the couch and rubbed his eyes with his hands.

"You'll forgive me, Miss Goering, but I'm feeling very sleepy suddenly. I'm sure the feeling will go away."

Miss Goering's drinks were wearing off and she thought it high time that she got back to Miss Gamelon, but she had not the courage to ride all the way out to her home by herself.

"Well, I suppose this is a great disappointment to you," said Arnold, "but you see I have fallen in love with you. I wanted to bring you here and tell you about my whole life, but now I don't feel like talking about anything."

"Perhaps some other time you'll tell me about your life," said Miss Goering, beginning to walk up and down very quickly. She stopped and turned towards him. "What do you advise me to do?" she asked him. "Do you advise me to go home or stay here?"

Arnold studied his watch. "Stay here by all means," he said.

Just then Arnold's father came in, wearing a lounging-robe and carrying a cup of coffee in his hand. He was very slender and he wore a small pointed beard. He was a more distinguished figure than Arnold.

"Good evening, Arnold," said his father. "Will you introduce me, please, to this young lady?"

Arnold introduced them and then his father asked Miss Goering why she did not take off her cloak.

"As long as you are up so late at night," he said, "and not enjoying the comfort and the security of your own bed, you might as well be at ease. Arnold, my son, never thinks of things like this." He took Miss Goering's cloak off and complimented her on her lovely dress.

"Now tell me where you have been and what you have done. I myself don't go out in society, being content with the company of my wife and son."

Arnold shrugged his shoulders and pretended to look absently around the room. But any person even a little observant could have seen that his face was decidedly hostile.

"Now tell me about this party," said Arnold's father adjusting the scarf that he was wearing around his neck. "*You* tell me." He pointed at Miss Goering, who was beginning to feel much gayer already. She had instantly preferred Arnold's father to Arnold himself.

"I'll tell you about it," said Arnold. "There were many people there, the majority of whom were creative artists, some successful and rich, others rich simply because they had inherited money from some member of the family, and others with just barely enough to eat. None of these people, however, were interested in money as an objective but would have been content, all of them, with just enough to eat."

"Like wild animals," said his father, rising to his feet. "Like wolves! What separates a man from a wolf if it is not that a man wants to make a profit?"

Miss Goering laughed until the tears streamed down her face. Arnold took some magazines from the table and began looking through them very quickly.

Just then Arnold's mother came into the room carrying in one hand a plate heaped with cakes and in the other a cup of coffee.

She was dowdy and unimpressive and of very much the

same build as Arnold. She was wearing a pink wrapper.

"Welcome," said Miss Goering to Arnold's mother. "May I have a piece of your cake?"

Arnold's mother, who was a very gauche woman, did not offer Miss Goering any of the cake; instead, hugging the platter close to her, she said to Miss Goering: "Have you known Arnold for long?"

"No, I met your son tonight, at a party."

"Well," said Arnold's mother, putting the tray down and sitting on the sofa, "I guess that isn't long, is it?"

Arnold's father was annoyed with his wife and showed it plainly in his face.

"I hate that pink wrapper," he said.

"Why do you talk about that now when there is company?"

"Because the company doesn't make the wrapper look any different." He winked broadly at Miss Goering and then burst out laughing. Miss Goering again laughed heartily at his remark. Arnold was even glummer than he had been a moment before.

"Miss Goering," said Arnold, "was afraid to go home alone, so I told her that she was welcome to sleep in the extra room. Although the bed isn't very comfortable in there, I think that she will at least have privacy."

"And *why*," said Arnold's father, "was Miss Goering afraid to go home alone?"

"Well," said Arnold, "it is not really very safe for a lady to wander about the streets or even to be in a taxi without an escort at so late an hour. Particularly if she has very far to go.

Of course if she hadn't had so far to go I should naturally have accompanied her myself."

"You sound like a sissy, the way you talk," said his father. "I thought that you and your friends were not afraid of such things. I thought you were wild ones and that rape meant no more to you than flying a balloon."

"Oh, don't talk like that," said Arnold's mother, looking really horrified. "Why do you talk like that to them?"

"I wish you would go to bed," Arnold's father said. "As a matter of fact, I am going to order you to go to bed. You are getting a cold."

"Isn't he terrible?" said Arnold's mother, smiling at Miss Goering. "Even when there is company in the house he can't control his lion nature. He *has* a nature like a lion, roaring in the apartment all day long, and he gets so upset about Arnold and his friends."

Arnold's father stamped out of the room and they heard a door slam down the hall.

"Excuse me," said Arnold's mother to Miss Goering, "I didn't want to upset the party."

Miss Goering was very annoyed, for she found the old man quite exhilarating, and Arnold himself was depressing her more and more.

"I think I'll show you where you're going to sleep," said Arnold, getting up from the sofa and in so doing allowing some magazines to slide from his lap to the floor. "Oh, well," he said, "come this way. I'm pretty sleepy and disgusted with this whole affair."

Miss Goering followed Arnold reluctantly down the hall. "Dear me," she said to Arnold, "I must confess that

I am not sleepy. There is really nothing worse, is there?"

"No, it's dreadful," said Arnold. "I personally am ready to fall down on the carpet and lie there until tomorrow noon, I am so completely exhausted."

Miss Goering thought this remark a very inhospitable one and she began to feel a little frightened. Arnold was obliged to search for the key to the spare room, and Miss Goering was left standing alone in front of the door for some time.

"Control yourself," she whispered out loud, for her heart was beginning to beat very quickly. She wondered how she had ever allowed herself to come so far from her house and Miss Gamelon. Arnold returned finally with the key and opened the door to the room.

It was a very small room and much colder than the room in which they had been sitting. Miss Goering expected that Arnold would be extremely embarrassed about this, but although he shivered and rubbed his hands together, he said nothing. There were no curtains at the window, but there was a yellow shade, which had already been pulled down. Miss Goering threw herself down on the bed.

"Well, my dear," said Arnold, "good night. I'm going to bed. Maybe we'll go and see some paintings tomorrow, or if you like I'll come out to your house." He put his arms around her neck and kissed her very lightly on the lips and left the room.

She was so angry that there were tears in her eyes. Arnold stood outside of the door for a little while and then after a few minutes he walked away.

Miss Goering went over to the bureau and leaned her head on her hands. She remained in this position for a long time in spite of the fact that she was shivering with the cold. Finally there was a light tap on the door. She stopped crying as abruptly as she had begun and hurried to open the door. She saw Arnold's father standing outside in the badly lighted hall. He was wearing pink striped pajamas and he gave her a brief salute as a greeting. After that he stood very still, waiting apparently for Miss Goering to ask him in.

"Come in, come in," she said to him, "I'm delighted to see you. Heavens! I've had such a feeling of being deserted."

Arnold's father came in and balanced himself on the foot of Miss Goering's bed, where he sat swinging his legs. He lit his pipe in rather an affected manner and looked around him at the walls of the room.

"Well, lady," he said to her, "are you an artist too?"

"No," said Miss Goering. "I wanted to be a religious leader when I was young and now I just reside in my house and try not to be too unhappy. I have a friend living with me, which makes it easier."

"What do you think of my son?" he asked, winking at her. "I have only just met him," said Miss Goering.

"You'll discover soon enough," said Arnold's father, "that he's a rather inferior person. He has no conception of what it is to fight. I shouldn't think women would like that very much. As a matter of fact, I don't think Arnold has had many women in his life. If you'll forgive me for passing this information on to you. I myself am used to fighting. I've fought my neighbors all my life instead of sitting down and having tea with them like Arnold. And my neighbors have fought me back like tigers too. Now that's not Arnold's kind of thing. My life's ambition always has been to be a notch higher on the tree than my neighbors and I was willing to admit complete disgrace too when I ended up perching a notch lower than anybody else I knew. I haven't been out in a good many years. Nobody comes to see me and I don't go to see anybody. Now, with Arnold and his friends nothing ever really begins or finishes. They're like fish in dirty water to me. If life don't please them one way and nobody likes them one place, then they go someplace else. They aim to please and be pleased; that's why it's so easy to come and bop them on the head from behind, because they've never done any serious hating in their lives."

"What a strange doctrine!" said Miss Goering.

"This is no doctrine," said Arnold's father. "These are my own ideas, taken from my own personal experience. I'm a great believer in personal experience, aren't you?"

"Oh, yes," said Miss Goering, "and I do think you're right about Arnold." She felt a curious delight in running down Arnold.

"Now Arnold," continued his father, and he seemed to grow gayer as he talked, "Arnold could never bear to have anyone catch him sitting on the lowest notch. Everyone knows how big your house is, and men who are willing to set their happiness by that are men of iron."

"Arnold is not an artist, anyway," put in Miss Goering.

"No, that is just it," said Arnold's father, getting more and more excited. "That's just it! He hasn't got the brawn nor the nerve nor the perseverance to be a good artist. An artist must have brawn and pluck and character. Arnold is like my wife," he continued. "I married her when she was twenty years old because of certain business interests. Every time I tell her that, she cries. She's another fool. She doesn't love me a bit, but it scares her to think of it, so that she cries. She's green-eyed with jealousy too and she's coiled around her family and her house like a python, although she doesn't have a good time here. Her life, as a matter of fact, is a wretched one, I must admit. Arnold's ashamed of her and I knock her around all day long. But in spite of the fact that she is a timid woman, she is capable of showing a certain amount of violence and brawn. Because she too, like myself, is faithful to one ideal, I suppose."

Just then there was a smart rap on the door. Arnold's father did not say a word, but Miss Goering called out in a clear voice: "Who is it?"

"It's me, Arnold's mother," came the answer. "Please let me in right away."

"Just one moment," said Miss Goering, "and I certainly shall."

"No," said Arnold's father. "Don't open the door. She has no right whatsoever to command anyone to open the door."

"You had better open it," said his wife. "Otherwise, I'll call the police, and I mean that very seriously. I have never threatened to call them before, you know."

"Yes, you did threaten to call them once before," said Arnold's father, looking very worried.

"The way I feel about my life," said Arnold's mother, "I'd just as soon open all the doors and let everyone come in the house and witness my disgrace."

"That's the last thing she'd ever do," said Arnold's father. "She talks like a fool when she's angry."

"I'll let her in," said Miss Goering, walking towards the door. She did not feel very frightened because Arnold's mother, judging from her voice, sounded more as though she was sad than angry. But when Miss Goering opened the door she was surprised to see that, on the contrary, her face was blanched with anger and her eyes were little narrow slits.

"Why do you pretend always to sleep so well?" said Arnold's father. This was the only remark he was able to think of, although he realized himself how inadequate it must have sounded to his wife.

"You're a harlot," said his wife to Miss Goering. Miss Goering was gravely shocked by this remark, and very much to her own amazement, for she had always thought that such things meant nothing to her.

"I am afraid you are entirely on the wrong track," said Miss Goering, "and I believe that some day we shall be great friends."

"I'll thank you to let me choose my own friends," Arnold's mother answered her. "I already have my friends, as a matter of fact, and I don't expect to add any more to my list, and least of all, you."

"Still, you can't tell," said Miss Goering rather weakly backing up a bit, and trying to lean in an easy manner against the bureau. Unfortunately, in calling Miss

Goering a harlot Arnold's mother had suggested to her husband the stand that he would take to defend himself.

"How dare you!" he said. "How dare you call anyone that is staying in our house a harlot! You are violating the laws of hospitality to the hundredth degree and I am not going to stand for it."

"Don't bully me," said Arnold's mother. "She's got to go right away this minute or I will make a scandal and you'll be sorry."

"Look, my dear," said Arnold's father to Miss Goering. "Perhaps it would be better if you did go, for your own sake. It is beginning to grow light, so that you needn't be at all frightened."

Arnold's father looked around nervously and then hurried out of the room and down the hall, followed by his wife. Miss Goering heard a door slam and she imagined that they would continue their argument in private.

She herself ran headlong down the hall and out of the house. She found a taxicab after walking a little while and she hadn't been riding more than a few minutes before she fell asleep.

ON THE FOLLOWING DAY the sun was shining and both Miss Gamelon and Miss Goering were sitting on the lawn arguing. Miss Goering was stretched out on the grass. Miss Gamelon seemed the more discontented of the two. She was frowning and looking over her shoulder at the house, which was behind them. Miss

Goering had her eyes shut and there was a faint smile on her face.

"Well," said Miss Gamelon turning around, "you know so little about what you're doing that it's a real crime against society that you have property in your hands. Property should be in the hands of people who like it."

"I think," said Miss Goering, "that I like it more than most people. It gives me a comfortable feeling of safety, as I have explained to you at least a dozen times. However, in order to work out my own little idea of salvation I really believe that it is necessary for me to live in some more tawdry place and particularly in some place where I was not born."

"In my opinion," said Miss Gamelon, "you could perfectly well work out your salvation during certain hours of the day without having to move everything."

"No," said Miss Goering, "that would not be in accordance with the spirit of the age."

Miss Gamelon shifted in her chair.

"The spirit of the age, whatever that is," she said, "I'm sure it can get along beautifully without you—probably would prefer it."

Miss Goering smiled and shook her head.

"The idea," said Miss Goering, "is to change first of our own volition and according to our own inner promptings before they impose completely arbitrary changes on us."

"I have no such promptings," said Miss Gamelon, "and I think you have a colossal nerve to identify yourself with anybody else at all. As a matter of fact, I think that if you leave this house, I shall give you up as a hopeless lunatic. After all, I am not the sort of person that is interested in living with a lunatic, nor is anyone else."

"When I have given you up," said Miss Goering, sitting up and throwing her head back in an exalted manner, "when I have given you up, I shall have given up more than my house, Lucy."

"That's one of your nastinesses," said Miss Gamelon. "It goes in one of my ears and then out the other."

Miss Goering shrugged her shoulders and went inside the house.

She stood for a while in the parlor rearranging some flowers in a bowl and she was just about to go to her room and sleep when Arnold appeared.

"Hello," said Arnold, "I meant to come and see you earlier, but I couldn't quite make it. We had one of those long family lunches. I think flowers look beautiful in this room."

"How is your father?" Miss Goering asked him.

"Oh," said Arnold, "he's all right, I guess. We have very little to do with each other." Miss Goering noticed that he was sweating again. He had evidently been terribly excited about arriving at her house, because he had forgotten to remove his straw hat.

"This is a really beautiful house," he told her. "It has a quality of past splendor about it that thrills me. You must hate to leave it ever. Well, Father seemed to be quite taken with you. Don't let him get too cocky. He thinks the girls are crazy about him."

"I'm devoted to him," said Miss Goering.

"Well, I hope that the fact that you're devoted to him," said Arnold, "won't interfere with our friendship, because I have decided to see quite a bit of you, providing of course that it is agreeable to you that I do."

"Of course," said Miss Goering, "whenever you like."

"I think that I shall like being here in your home, and you needn't feel that it's a strain. I'm quite happy to sit alone and think, because as you know I'm very anxious to establish myself in some other way than I am now established, which is not satisfactory to me. As you can well imagine, it is even impossible for me to give a dinner party for a few friends because neither Father nor Mother ever stirs from the house unless I do."

Arnold seated himself in a chair by a big bay window and stretched his legs out.

"Come here!" he said to Miss Goering, "and watch the wind rippling through the tops of the trees. There is nothing more lovely in the world." He looked up at her very seriously for a little while.

"Do you have some milk and some bread and marmalade?" he asked her. "I hope there is to be no ceremony between us."

Miss Goering was surprised that Arnold should ask for something to eat so shortly after his luncheon, and she decided that this was undoubtedly the reason why he was so fat.

"Certainly we have," she said sweetly, and she went away to give the servant the order.

Meanwhile Miss Gamelon had decided to come inside and if possible pursue Miss Goering with her argument. When Arnold saw her he realized that she was the companion about whom Miss Goering had spoken the night before.

He rose to his feet immediately, having decided that it was very important for him to make friends with Miss Gamelon.

Miss Gamelon herself was very pleased to see him, as they seldom had company and she enjoyed talking to almost anyone better than to Miss Goering.

They introduced themselves and Arnold pulled up a chair for Miss Gamelon near his own.

"You are Miss Goering's companion," he said to Miss Gamelon. "I think that's lovely."

"Do you think it's lovely?" asked Miss Gamelon. "That's very interesting indeed."

Arnold smiled happily at this remark of Miss Gamelon's and sat on without saying anything for a little while.

"This house is done in exquisite taste," he said finally, "and it is filled with rest and peace."

"It all depends on how you look at it," said Miss Gamelon quickly, jerking her head around and looking out of the window.

"There are certain people," she said, "who turn peace from the door as though it were a red dragon breathing fire out of its nostrils and there are certain people who won't leave God alone either."

Arnold leaned forward trying to appear deferential and interested at the same time.

"I think," he said gravely, "I think I understand what you mean to say."

Then they both looked out of the window at the same time and they saw Miss Goering in the distance wearing a cape over her shoulders and talking to a young man whom they were scarcely able to distinguish because he was directly against the sun.

"That's the agent," said Miss Gamelon. "I suppose there is nothing to look forward to from now on."

"What agent?" asked Arnold.

"The agent through whom she's going to sell her house," said Miss Gamelon. "Isn't it all too dreadful for words?"

"Oh, I'm sorry," said Arnold. "I think it's very foolish of her, but I suppose it's not my affair."

"We're going to live," added Miss Gamelon, "in a four-room frame house and do our own cooking. It's to be in the country surrounded by woods."

"That does sound gloomy, doesn't it?" said Arnold. "But why should Miss Goering have decided to do such a thing?"

"She says it is only a beginning in a tremendous scheme."

Arnold seemed to be very sad. He no longer spoke to Miss Gamelon but merely pursed his lips and looked at the ceiling.

"I suppose the most important thing in the world," he said at length, "is friendship and understanding." He looked at Miss Gamelon questioningly. He seemed to have given up something.

"Well, Miss Gamelon," he said again, "do you not agree with me that friendship and understanding are the most important things in the world?"

"Yes," said Miss Gamelon, "and keeping your head is, too." Soon Miss Goering came in with a batch of papers under her arm.

"These," she said, "are the contracts. My, they are lengthy, but I think the agent is a sweet man. He said he thought this house was lovely." She held out the contracts first to Arnold and then to Miss Gamelon.

"I should think," said Miss Gamelon, "that you would be afraid to look in the mirror for fear of seeing something too wild and peculiar. I don't want to have to look at these contracts. Please take them off my lap right away. Jesus God Almighty!"

Miss Goering, as a matter of fact, did look a little wild, and Miss Gamelon with a wary eye had noticed immediately that the hand in which she held the contracts was trembling.

"Where is your little house, Miss Goering?" Arnold asked her, trying to introduce a more natural note into the conversation.

"It's on an island," said Miss Goering, "not far from the city by ferryboat. I remember having visited this island as a child and always having disliked it because one can smell the glue factories from the mainland even when walking through the woods or across the fields. One end of the island is very well populated, although you can only buy third-rate goods in any of the stores. Farther out the island is wilder and more old-fashioned; nevertheless there is a little train that meets the ferry frequently and carries you out to the other end. There you land in a little town that is quite lost and looks very tough, and you feel a bit frightened, I think, to find that the mainland opposite the point is as squalid as the island itself and offers you no protection at all."

"You seem to have looked the situation over very carefully and from every angle," said Miss Gamelon. "My compliments to you!" She waved at Miss Goering from her seat, but one could easily see that she was not feeling frivolous in the least.

Arnold shifted about uneasily in his chair. He coughed and then he spoke very gently to Miss Goering.

"I am sure that the island has certain advantages too, which you know about, but perhaps you prefer to surprise us with them rather than disappoint us."

"I know of none at the moment," said Miss Goering. "Why, are you coming with us?"

"I think that I would like to spend quite a bit of time with you out there; that is, if you will invite me."

Arnold was sad and uneasy, but he felt that he must at any cost remain close to Miss Goering in whatever world she chose to move.

"If you will invite me," he said again, "I will be glad to come out with you for a little while anyway and we will see how it goes. I could continue to keep up my end of the apartment that I share with my parents without having to spend all my time there. But I don't advise you to sell your beautiful house; rather rent it or board it up while you are away. Certainly you might have a change of heart and want to return to it."

Miss Gamelon flushed with pleasure.

"That would be too human a thing for her to consider doing," she said, but she looked a little more hopeful.

Miss Goering seemed to be dreaming and not listening to what either of them was saying.

"Well," said Miss Gamelon, "aren't you going to answer him? He said: why not board your house up or rent it and then if you have a change of heart you can return to it."

"Oh, no," said Miss Goering. "Thank you very much, but I couldn't do that. It wouldn't make much sense to do that."

Arnold coughed to hide his embarrassment at having suggested something so obviously displeasing to Miss Goering.

"I mustn't," he said to himself, "I mustn't align myself too much on the side of Miss Gamelon, or Miss Goering will begin to think that my mind is of the same caliber."

"Perhaps it is better after all," he said aloud, "to sell everything."

2

MR. AND MRS. COPPERFIELD stood on the foredeck of the boat as it sailed into the harbor at Panama. Mrs. Copperfield was very glad to see land at last.

"You must admit now," she said to Mr. Copperfield, "that the land is nicer than the sea." She herself had a great fear of drowning.

"It isn't only being afraid of the sea," she continued, "but it's boring. It's the same thing all the time. The colors are beautiful, of course."

Mr. Copperfield was studying the shore line.

"If you stand still and look between the buildings on the docks," he said, "you'll be able to catch a glimpse of some green trains loaded with bananas. They seem to go by every quarter of an hour."

His wife did not answer him; instead she put on the sun-helmet which she had been carrying in her hand.

"Aren't you beginning to feel the heat already? I am," she said to him at last. As she received no answer she moved along the rail and looked down at the water.

Presently a stout woman whose acquaintance she had made on the boat came up to talk with her. Mrs. Copperfield brightened.

"You've had your hair marcelled!" she said. The woman smiled.

"Now remember," she said to Mrs. Copperfield, "the minute you get to your hotel, stretch yourself out and rest. Don't let them drag you through the streets, no matter what kind of a wild time they promise you. Nothing but monkeys in the streets anyway. There isn't a fine-looking person in the whole town that isn't connected with the American Army, and the Americans stick pretty much in their own quarter. The American quarter is called Cristobal. It's separated from Colon. Colon is full of nothing but half-breeds and monkeys. Cristobal is nice. Everyone in Cristobal has got his own little screened-in porch. They'd never dream of screening themselves in, the monkeys in Colon. They don't know when a mosquito's biting them anyway, and even if they did know they wouldn't lift their arm up to shoo him off. Eat plenty of fruit and be careful of the stores. Most of them are owned by Hindus. They're just like Jews, you know. They'll gyp you right and left."

"I'm not interested in buying anything," said Mrs. Copperfield, "but may I come and visit you while I'm in Colon?"

"I love you, dear," answered the woman, "but I like to spend every minute with my boy while I'm here."

"That's all right," said Mrs. Copperfield.

"Of course it's all right. You've got that beautiful husband of yours."

"That doesn't help," said Mrs. Copperfield, but no sooner had she said this than she was horrified at herself.

"Well now, you've had a tussle?" said the woman.

"No."

"Then I think you're a terrible little woman talking that way about your husband," she said, walking away. Mrs. Copperfield hung her head and went back to stand beside Mr. Copperfield.

"Why do you speak to such dopes?" he asked.

She did not answer.

"Well," he said, "for Heaven's sake, look at the scenery now, will you?"

They got into a taxicab and Mr. Copperfield insisted on going to a hotel right in the center of town. Normally all tourists with even a small amount of money stayed at the Hotel Washington, overlooking the sea, a few miles out of Colon.

"I don't believe," Mr. Copperfield said to his wife, "I don't believe in spending money on a luxury that can only be mine for a week at the most. I think it's more fun to buy objects which will last me perhaps a lifetime.

We can certainly find a hotel in the town that will be comfortable. Then we will be free to spend our money on more exciting things."

"The room in which I sleep is so important to me," Mrs. Copperfield said. She was nearly moaning.

"My dear, a room is really only a place in which to sleep and dress. If it is quiet and the bed is comfortable, nothing more is necessary. Don't you agree with me?"

"You know very well I don't agree with you."

"If you are going to be miserable, we'll go to the Hotel Washington," said Mr. Copperfield. Suddenly he lost his dignity. His eyes clouded over and he pouted. "But I'll be wretched there, I can assure you. It's going to be so God-damned dull." He was like a baby and Mrs. Copperfield was obliged to comfort him. He had a trick way of making her feel responsible.

"After all, it's mostly my money," she said to herself. "I'm footing the bulk of the expenditures for this trip." Nevertheless, she was unable to gain a sense of power by reminding herself of this. She was completely dominated by Mr. Copperfield, as she was by almost anyone with whom she came in contact. Still, certain people who knew her well affirmed that she was capable of suddenly making a very radical and independent move without a soul to back her up.

She looked out the window of the taxicab and she noticed that there was a terrific amount of activity going on around her in the streets. The people, for the most part Negroes and uniformed men from the fleets of all nations, were running in and out and making so much noise that Mrs. Copperfield wondered if it was not a holiday of some kind.

"It's like a city that is being constantly looted," said her husband.

The houses were painted in bright colors and they had wide porches on the upper floors, supported beneath by long wooden posts. Thus they formed a kind of arcade to shade the people walking in the street.

"This architecture is ingenious," remarked Mr. Copperfield. "The streets would be unbearable if one had to walk along them with nothing overhead."

"You could not stand that, mister," said the cab-driver, "to walk along with nothing over your head."

"Anyway," said Mrs. Copperfield, "do let's choose one of these hotels quickly and get into it."

They found one right in the heart of the red-light district and agreed to look at some rooms on the fifth floor. The manager had told them that these were sure to be the least noisy. Mrs. Copperfield, who was afraid of lifts, decided to go up the stairs on foot and wait for her husband to arrive with the luggage. Having climbed to the fifth floor, she was surprised to find that the main hall contained at least a hundred straight-backed dining-room chairs and nothing more. As she looked around, her anger mounted and she could barely wait for Mr. Copperfield to arrive on the lift in order to tell him what she thought of him. "I must get to the Hotel Washington," she said to herself.

Mr. Copperfield finally arrived, walking beside a boy with the luggage. She ran up to him.

"It's the ugliest thing I've ever seen," she said.

"Wait a second, please, and let me count the luggage; I want to make sure it's all here."

"As far as I'm concerned, it could be at the bottom of the sea—all of it."

"Where's my typewriter?" asked Mr. Copperfield.

"Talk to me this minute," said his wife, beside herself with anger.

"Do you care whether or not you have a private bath?" asked Mr. Copperfield.

"No, no. I don't care about that. It's not a question of comfort at all. It's something much more than that."

Mr. Copperfield chuckled. "You're so crazy," he said to her with indulgence. He was delighted to be in the tropics at last and he was more than pleased with himself that he had managed to dissuade his wife from stopping at a ridiculously expensive hotel where they would have been surrounded by tourists. He realized that this hotel was sinister, but that was what he loved.

They followed the bellhop to one of the rooms, and no sooner had they arrived there than Mrs. Copperfield began pushing the door backwards and forwards. It opened both ways and could only be locked by means of a little hook.

"Anyone could break into this room," said Mrs. Copperfield.

"I dare say they could, but I don't think they would be very likely to, do you?" Mr. Copperfield made a point of never reassuring his wife. He gave her fears their just due. However, he did not insist, and they decided upon another room, with a stronger door.

MRS. COPPERFIELD WAS AMAZED at her husband's vivacity. He had washed and gone out to buy a papaya.

She lay on the bed thinking.

"Now," she said to herself, "when people believed in God they carried Him from one place to another. They carried Him through the jungles and across the Arctic Circle. God watched over everybody, and all men were brothers. Now there is nothing to carry with you from one place to another, and as far as I'm concerned, these people might as well be kangaroos; yet somehow there must be someone here who will remind me of something . . . I must try to find a nest in this outlandish place."

Mrs. Copperfield's sole object in life was to be happy, although people who had observed her behavior over a period of years would have been surprised to discover that this was all.

She rose from her bed and pulled Miss Goering's present, a manicuring set, from her grip. "Memory," she whispered. "Memory of the things I have loved since I was a child. My husband is a man without memory." She felt intense pain at the thought of this man whom she liked above all other people, this man for whom each thing he had not yet known was a joy. For her, all that which was not already an old dream was an outrage. She got back on her bed and fell sound asleep.

When she awoke, Mr. Copperfield was standing near the foot of the bed eating a papaya.

"You must try some," he said. "It gives you lots of energy and besides it's delicious. Won't you have some?" He looked at her shyly.

"Where have you been?" she asked him.

"Oh, walking through the streets. As a matter of fact, I've walked for miles. You should come out, really. It's a madhouse. The streets are full of soldiers and sailors and whores. The women are all in long dresses . . . incredibly cheap dresses. They'll all talk to you. Come on out."

THEY WERE WALKING through the streets arm in arm. Mrs. Copperfield's forehead was burning hot and her hands were cold. She felt something trembling in the pit of her stomach. When she looked ahead of her the very end of the street seemed to bend and then straighten out again. She told this to Mr. Copperfield and he explained that it was a result of their having so recently come off the boat. Above their heads the children were jumping up and down on the wooden porches and making the houses shake. Someone bumped against Mrs. Copperfield's shoulder and she was almost knocked over. At the same time she was very much aware of the strong and fragrant odor of rose perfume. The person who had collided with her was a Negress in a pink silk evening dress.

"I can't tell you how sorry I am. I can't tell you," she said to them. Then she looked around her vaguely and began to hum.

"I told you it was a madhouse," Mr. Copperfield said to his wife.

"Listen," said the Negress, "go down the next street and you'll like it better. I've got to meet my beau over at that bar." She pointed it out to them. "That's a beautiful barroom. Everyone goes in there," she said. She moved up closer and addressed herself solely to Mrs. Copperfield. "You come along with me, darling, and you'll have the happiest time you've ever had before. I'll be your type. Come on."

She took Mrs. Copperfield's hand in her own and started to drag her away from Mr. Copperfield. She was bigger than either of them.

"I don't believe that she wants to go to a bar just now," said Mr. Copperfield. "We'd like to explore the town awhile first."

The Negress caressed Mrs. Copperfield's face with the palm of her hand. "Is that what you want to do, darling, or do you want to come along with me?" A policeman stopped and stood a few feet away from them. The Negress released Mrs. Copperfield's hand and bounded across the street laughing.

"Wasn't that the strangest thing you've ever seen?" said Mrs. Copperfield, breathlessly.

"You better mind your own business," said the policeman. "Why don't you go over and look at the stores? Everybody walks along the streets where the stores are. Buy something for your uncle or your cousin."

"No, that's not what I want to do," said Mrs. Copperfield.

"Well, then, go to a movie," said the policeman, walking away.

Mr. Copperfield was hysterical with laughter. He had his handkerchief up to his mouth. "This is the sort of thing I love," he managed to say. They walked along farther and turned down another street. The sun was setting and the air was still and hot. On this street there were no balconies, only little one-storey houses. In front of every door at least one woman was seated. Mrs. Copperfield walked up to the window of one house and looked in. The room inside was almost entirely filled by a large double bed with an extremely bumpy mattress over which was spread a lace throw. An electric bulb under a lavender chiffon lamp shade threw a garish light over the bed, and there was a fan stamped *Panama City* spread open on the pillow.

The woman seated in front of this particular house was rather old. She sat on a stool with her elbows resting on her knees, and it seemed to Mrs. Copperfield, who had now turned to look at her, that she was probably a West Indian type. She was flat-chested and raw-boned, with very muscular arms and shoulders. Her long disgruntled-looking face and part of her neck were carefully covered with a light-colored face powder, but her chest and arms remained dark. Mrs. Copperfield was amused to see that her dress was of lavender theatrical gauze. There was an attractive gray streak in her hair.

The Negress turned around, and when she saw that both Mr. and Mrs. Copperfield were watching her, she stood up and smoothed the folds of her dress. She was almost a giantess.

"Both of you for a dollar," she said.

"A dollar," Mrs. Copperfield repeated after her. Mr. Copperfield, who had been standing nearby at the curb, came closer to them.

"Frieda," he said, "let's walk down some more streets."

"Oh, please!" said Mrs. Copperfield. "Wait a minute."

"A dollar is the best price I can make," said the Negress.

"If you care to stay here," suggested Mr. Copperfield, "I'll walk around a bit and come back for you in a little while. Maybe you'd better have some money with you. Here is a dollar and thirty-five cents, just in case . . ."

"I want to talk to her," said Mrs. Copperfield, looking fixedly into space.

"I'll see you, then, in a few minutes. I'm restless," he announced, and he walked away.

"I love to be free," Mrs. Copperfield said to the woman after he had left. "Shall we go into your little room? I've been admiring it through the window . . ."

Before she had finished her phrase the woman was pushing her through the door with both hands and they were inside the room. There was no rug on the floor, and the walls were bare. The only adornments were those which had been visible from the street. They sat down on the bed.

"I had a little gramophone in that corner over there," said the woman. "Someone who came off a ship lent it to me. His friend came and took it back."

"Te-ta-ta-tee-ta-ta," she said and tapped her heels for a few seconds. She took both Mrs. Copperfield's hands in her own and pulled her off the bed. "Come on now, honey." She hugged Mrs. Copperfield to her. "You're awful little and very sweet. You *are* sweet, and maybe you are lonesome." Mrs. Copperfield put her cheek on the woman's breast. The smell of the theatrical gauze reminded her of her first part in a school play. She smiled up at the Negress, looking as tender and as gentle as she was able.

"What do you do in the afternoons?" she asked the woman. "Play cards. Go to a movie . . ."

Mrs. Copperfield stepped away from her. Her cheeks were flamed-red. They both listened to the people walking by. They could now hear every word that was being said outside the window. The Negress was frowning. She wore a look of deep concern.

"Time is gold, honey," she said to Mrs. Copperfield, "but maybe you're too young to realize that."

Mrs. Copperfield shook her head. She felt sad, looking at the Negress. "I'm thirsty," she said. Suddenly they heard a man's voice saying:

"You didn't expect to see me back so soon, Podie?" Then several girls laughed hysterically. The Negress's eyes came to life.

"Give me one dollar! Give me one dollar!" she screamed excitedly at Mrs. Copperfield. "You have stayed your time here anyway." Mrs. Copperfield hurriedly gave her a dollar and the Negress rushed out into the street. Mrs. Copperfield followed her.

In front of the house several girls were hanging onto a heavy man who was wearing a crushed linen suit. When he saw Mrs. Copperfield's Negress in the lavender dress, he broke away from the others and put his arms around her. The Negress rolled her eyes joyously and led him into the house without so much as nodding good-by to Mrs. Copperfield. Very shortly the others ran down the street and Mrs. Copperfield was left alone. People passed by on either side of her, but none of them interested her yet. On the other hand, she herself was of great interest to everyone, particularly to those women who were seated in front of their doors. She was soon accosted by a girl with fuzzy hair.

"Buy me something, Momma," said the girl.

As Mrs. Copperfield did not answer but simply gave the girl a long sad look, the girl said:

"Momma, you can pick it out yourself. You can buy me even a feather, I don't care." Mrs. Copperfield shuddered. She thought she must be dreaming.

"What do you mean, a feather? What do you mean?" The girl squirmed with delight.

"Oh, Momma," she said in a voice which broke in her throat. "Oh, Momma, you're funny! You're so funny. I don't know what is a feather, but anything you want with your heart, you know."

They walked down the street to a store and came out with a little box of face powder. The girl said good-by and disappeared round the corner with some friends. Once again Mrs. Copperfield was alone. The hacks went past filled with tourists. "Tourists, generally speaking," Mrs. Copperfield had written in her journal, "are human beings so impressed with the importance and immutability of their own manner of living that they are capable of traveling through the most fantastic places without experiencing anything more than a visual reaction. The hardier tourists find that one place resembles another."

Very soon Mr. Copperfield came back and joined her. "Did you have a wonderful time?" he asked her.

She shook her head and looked up at him. Suddenly she felt so tired that she began to cry.

"Cry-baby," said Mr. Copperfield.

Someone came up behind them. A low voice said: "She was lost?" They turned around to see an intelligent-looking girl with sharp features and curly hair standing right behind them. "I wouldn't leave her in the streets here if I were you," she said.

"She wasn't lost; she was just depressed," Mr. Copperfield explained.

"Would you think I was fresh if I asked you to come to a nice restaurant where we can all eat dinner?" asked the girl. She was really quite pretty.

"Let's go," said Mrs. Copperfield vehemently. "By all means." She was now excited; she had a feeling that this girl would be all right. Like most people, she never really believed that one terrible thing would happen after another.

The restaurant wasn't really nice. It was very dark and very long and there was no one in it at all.

"Wouldn't you rather eat somewhere else?" Mrs. Copperfield asked the girl.

"Oh no! I would never go anywhere else. I'll tell you if you are not angry. I can get a little bit of money here when I come and bring some people."

"Well, let me give you the money and we'll go somewhere else. I'll give you whatever he gives you," said Mrs. Copperfield.

"That's silly," said the girl. "That's very silly."

"I have heard there is a place in this city where we can order wonderful lobster. Couldn't we go there?" Mrs. Copperfield was pleading with the girl now.

"No—that's silly." She called a waiter who had just arrived with some newspapers under his arm.

"Adalberto, bring us some meat and some wine. Meat first." This she said in Spanish.

"How well you speak English!" said Mr. Copperfield.

"I always love to be with Americans when I can," said the girl.

"Do you think they're generous?" asked Mr. Copperfield.

"Oh, sure," said the girl. "Sure they're generous. They're generous when they have the money. They're even more generous when they've got their family with them. I once knew a man. He was an American man. A real one, and he was staying at the Hotel Washington. You know that's the most beautiful hotel in the world. In the afternoon every day his wife would take a siesta.

He would come quickly in a taxicab to Colon and he was so excited and frightened that he would not get back to his wife on time that he would never take me into a room and so he would go with me instead to a store and he would say to me: 'Quick, quick—pick something—anything that you want, but be in a hurry about it."

"How terrifying!" said Mrs. Copperfield.

"It was terrible," said the Spanish girl. "I always went so crazy that once I was really crazy and I said to him: 'All right, I will buy this pipe for my uncle.' I don't like my uncle, but I had to give it to him."

Mr. Copperfield roared with laughter.

"Funny, isn't it?" said the girl. "I tell you if he ever comes back I will never buy another pipe for my uncle when he takes me to the store. She's not a bad-looker."

"Who?" asked Mr. Copperfield.

"Your wife."

"I look terrible tonight," said Mrs. Copperfield.

"Anyway it does not matter because you are married. You have nothing to worry about."

"She'll be furious with you if you tell her that," said Mr. Copperfield.

"Why will she be furious? That is the most beautiful thing in the whole world, not to have something to worry about."

"That is not what beauty is made of," interposed Mrs. Copperfield. "What has the absence of worry to do with beauty?"

"That has everything to do with what is beautiful in the world. When you wake up in the morning and the first minute you open your eyes and you don't know who you are or what your life has been—that is beautiful. Then when you know who you are and what day in your life it is and you still think you are sailing in the air like a happy bird—that is beautiful. That is, when you don't have any worries. You can't tell me you like to worry."

Mr. Copperfield simpered. After dinner he suddenly felt very tired and he suggested that they go home, but Mrs. Copperfield was much too nervous, so she asked the Spanish girl if she would not consent to spend a little more time in her company. The girl said that she would if Mrs. Copperfield did not mind returning with her to the hotel where she lived.

They said good-by to Mr. Copperfield and started on their way.

The walls of the Hotel de las Palmas were wooden and painted a bright green. There were a good many bird-cages standing in the halls and hanging from the ceilings. Some of them were empty. The girl's room was on the second floor and had brightly painted wooden walls the same as the corridors.

"Those birds sing all day long," said the girl, motioning to Mrs. Copperfield to sit down on the bed beside her. "Sometimes I say to myself: 'Little fools, what are you singing about in your cages?' And then I think: 'Pacifica, you are just as much a fool as those birds. You are also in a cage because you don't have any money. Last night you were laughing for three hours with a German man because he had given you some drinks. And you thought he was stupid.' I laugh in my cage and they sing in their cage."

"Oh well," said Mrs. Copperfield, "there really is no rapport between ourselves and birds."

"You don't think it is true?" asked Pacifica with feeling. "I tell you it is true."

She pulled her dress over her head and stood before Mrs. Copperfield in her underslip.

"Tell me," she said, "What do you think of those beautiful silk kimonos that the Hindu men sell in their shops? If I were with such a rich husband I would tell him to buy me one of those kimonos. You don't know how lucky you are. I would go with him every day to the stores and make him buy me pretty things instead of standing around and crying like a little baby. Men don't like to see women cry. You think they like to see women cry?"

Mrs. Copperfield shrugged her shoulders. "I can't think," she said.

"You're right. They like to see women laugh. Women have got to laugh all night. You watch some pretty girl one time. When she laughs she is ten years older. That is because she does it so much. You are ten years older when you laugh."

"True," said Mrs. Copperfield.

"Don't feel bad," said Pacifica. "I like women very much. I like women sometimes better than men. I like my grandmother and my mother and my sisters. We always had a good time together, the women in my house. I was always the best one. I was the smartest one and the one who did the most work. Now I wish I was back there in my nice house, contented. But I still want too many things, you know. I am lazy but I have a terrible temper too. I like these men that I meet very much. Sometimes they tell me what they will do in their future life when they get off the boat. I always wish for them that it will happen very soon. The damn boats. When they tell me they just want to go around the world all their life on a boat I tell them: 'You don't know what you're missing. I'm through with you, boy.' I don't like them when they are like that. But now I am in love with this nice man who is here in business. Most of the time he can pay my rent for me. Not always every week. He is very happy to have me. Most of the men are very happy to have me. I don't hold my head too high for that. It's from God that it comes." Pacifica crossed herself.

"I once was in love with an older woman," said Mrs. Copperfield eagerly. "She was no longer beautiful, but in her face I found fragments of beauty which were much more exciting to me than any beauty that I have known at its height. But who hasn't loved an older person? Good Lord!"

"You like things which are not what other people like, don't you? I would like to have this experience of loving an older woman. I think that is sweet, but I really am always in love with some nice man. It is lucky for me, I think. Some of the girls, they can't fall in love any more. They only think of money, money, money. You don't think so much about money, do you?" She asked Mrs. Copperfield.

"No, I don't."

"Now we rest a little while, yes?" The girl lay down on the bed and motioned to Mrs. Copperfield to lie down beside her. She yawned, folded Mrs. Copperfield's hand in her own, and fell asleep almost instantly. Mrs. Copperfield thought that she might as well get some sleep too. At that moment she felt very peaceful.

They were awakened by a terrific knocking at the door. Mrs. Copperfield opened her eyes and in a second she was a prey to the most overwhelming terror. She looked at Pacifica, and her friend's face was not very much more reassuring than her own.

"Callate!" she whispered to Mrs. Copperfield reverting to her native tongue.

"What is it? What is it?" asked Mrs. Copperfield in a harsh voice. "I don't understand Spanish."

"Don't say a word," repeated Pacifica in English.

"I can't lie here without saying a word. I know I can't. What is it?"

"Drunken man. In love with me. I know him well. He hurt me very bad when I sleep with him. His boat has come in again."

The knocking grew more insistent and they heard a man's voice saying:

"I know you are there, Pacifica, so open the bloody door." "Oh, open it, Pacifica!" pleaded Mrs. Copperfield, jumping up from the bed. "Nothing could be worse than this suspense." "Don't be crazy. Maybe he is drunk enough and he will go away."

Mrs. Copperfield's eyes were glazed. She was becoming hysterical.

"No, no—I have always promised myself that I would open the door if someone was trying to break in. He will be less of an enemy then. The longer he stays out there, the angrier he will get. The first thing I will say to him when I open the door is: 'We are your friends,' and then perhaps he will be less angry."

"If you make me even more crazy than I am I don't know what to do," said Pacifica. "Now we just wait here and see if he goes away. We might move this bureau against the door. Will you help me move it against the door?"

"I can't push anything!" Mrs. Copperfield was so weak that she slid along the wall onto the floor.

"Have I got to break the God-damned door in?" the man was saying.

Mrs. Copperfield rose to her feet, staggered over to the door, and opened it.

The man who came in was hatchet-faced and very tall. He had obviously had a great deal to drink.

"Hello, Meyer," said Pacifica. "Can't you let me get some sleep?" She hesitated a minute, and as he did not answer her she said again: "I was trying to get some sleep."

"I was tight asleep," said Mrs. Copperfield. Her voice was higher than usual and her face was very bright. "I am sorry we did not hear you right away. We must have kept you waiting a long time."

"Nobody ever kept me waiting a long time," said Meyer, getting redder in the face. Pacifica's eyes were narrowing. She was beginning to lose her temper.

"Get out of my room," she said to Meyer.

In answer to this, Meyer fell diagonally across the bed,

and the impact of his body was so great that it almost broke the slats.

"Let's get out of here quickly," said Mrs. Copperfield to Pacifica. She was no longer able to show any composure. For one moment she had hoped that the enemy would suddenly burst into tears as they do sometimes in dreams, but now she was convinced that this would not happen. Pacifica was growing more and more furious.

"Listen to me, Meyer," she was saying. "You go back into the street right away. Because I'm not going to do anything with you except hit you in the nose if you don't go away. If you were not such hot stuff we could sit downstairs together and drink a glass of rum. I have hundreds of boy friends who just like to talk to me and drink with me until they are stiffs under the table. But you always try to bother me. You are like an ape-man. I want to be quiet."

"Who the hell cares about your house!" Meyer bellowed at her. "I could put all your houses together in a row and shoot at them like they were ducks. A boat's better than a house any day! Any time! Come rain, come shine! Come the end of the world!"

"No one is talking about houses except you," said Pacifica, stamping her foot, "and I don't want to listen to your foolish talk."

"Why did you lock the door, then, if you weren't living in this house like you were duchesses having tea together, and praying that none of us were ever going to come on shore again. You were afraid I'd spoil the furniture and spill something on the floor. My mother had a house, but I always slept in the house next door to her house. That's how much I care about houses!"

"You misunderstand," said Mrs. Copperfield in a trembling voice. She wanted very much to remind him gently that this was not a house but a room in a hotel. However, she felt not only afraid but ashamed to make this remark.

"Jesus Christ, I'm disgusted," Pacifica said to Mrs. Copperfield without even bothering to lower her voice.

Meyer did not seem to hear this, but instead he leaned over the edge of the bed with a smile on his face and stretched one arm towards Pacifica. He managed to get hold of the hem of her slip and pull her towards him.

"Not as long as I live!" Pacifica screamed at him, but he had already wrapped his arms around her waist and he was kneeling on the bed, pulling her towards him.

"Housekeeper," he said, laughing, "I'll bet if I took you out to sea you'd vomit. You'd mess up the boat. Now lie down here and stop talking."

Pacifica looked darkly at Mrs. Copperfield for a moment. "Well then," she said, "give me first the money, because I don't trust you. I will sleep with you only for my rent."

He dealt her a terrific blow on the mouth and split her lip. The blood started to run down her chin.

Mrs. Copperfield rushed out of the room. "I'll get help, Pacifica," she yelled over her shoulder. She ran down the hall and down the stairs, hoping to find someone to whom she could report Pacifica's plight, but she knew she would not have the courage to approach any men. On the ground floor she caught sight of a middle-aged woman who was knitting in her room with the door ajar. Mrs. Copperfield rushed in to her.

"Do you know Pacifica?" she gasped.

"Certainly I know Pacifica," said the woman. She spoke like an Englishwoman who has lived for many years among Americans. "I know everybody that lives here for more than two nights. I'm the proprietor of this hotel."

"Well then, do something quickly. Mr. Meyer is in there and he's very drunk."

"I don't do anything with Meyer when he's drunk." The woman was silent for a moment and the idea of doing something with Meyer struck her sense of humor and she chuckled. "Just imagine it," she said, " 'Mr. Meyer, will you kindly leave the room? Pacifica is tired of you. Ha-ha-ha—*Pacifica* is tired of you.' Have a seat, lady, and calm down. There's some gin in that cut-glass decanter over there next to the avocados. Would you like some?"

"You know I'm not used to violence," Mrs. Copperfield said. She helped herself to some gin, and repeated that she was not used to violence. "I doubt that I shall ever get over this evening. The stubbornness of that man. He was like an insane person."

"Meyer isn't insane," said the proprietress. "Some of them are much worse. He told me he was very fond of Pacifica. I've always been decent to him and he's never given me any trouble."

They heard screams from the next floor. Mrs. Copperfield recognized Pacifica's voice.

"Oh, please, let's get the police," pleaded Mrs. Copperfield.

"Are you crazy?" said the woman. "Pacifica doesn't want to get mixed up with the police. She would rather have both legs chopped off. I can promise you that is true."

"Well then, let's go up there," said Mrs. Copperfield. "I'm ready to do anything."

"Keep seated, Mrs.—what's your name? My name is Mrs. Quill."

"I'm Mrs. Copperfield."

"Well, you see, Mrs. Copperfield, Pacifica can take care of herself better than we can take care of her. The fewer people that get involved in a thing, the better off everybody is. That's one law I have here in the hotel."

"All right," said Mrs. Copperfield, "but meanwhile she might be murdered."

"People don't murder as easy as that. They do a lot of hitting around but not so much murdering. I've had some murders here, but not many. I've discovered that most things turn out all right. Of course some of them turn out bad."

"I wish I could feel as relaxed as you about everything. I don't understand how you can sit here, and I don't understand how Pacifica can go through things like this without ending up in an insane asylum."

"Well, she's had a lot of experience with these men. I don't think she's scared really. She's much tougher than us. She's just bothered. She likes to be able to have her room and do what she likes. I think sometimes women don't know what they want. Do you think maybe she has a little yen for Meyer?"

"How could she possibly? I don't understand what you mean."

"Well now, that boy she says she's in love with; now, I don't really think she's in love with him at all. She's had one after another of them like that. All nice dopes. They worship the ground she walks on. I think she gets so jealous and nervous while Meyer's away that she likes to pretend to herself that she likes these other little men better. When Meyer comes back she really believes she's mad at him for interfering. Now, maybe I'm right and maybe I'm wrong, but I think it goes a little something like that."

"I think it's impossible. She wouldn't allow him to hurt her, then, before she went to bed with him."

"Sure she would," said Mrs. Quill, "but I don't know anything about such things. Pacifica's a nice girl, though. She comes from a nice family too."

Mrs. Copperfield drank her gin and enjoyed it.

"She'll be coming down here soon to have a talk," said Mrs. Quill. "It's balmy here and they all enjoy themselves. They talk and they drink and they make love; they go on picnics; they go to the movies; they dance, sometimes all night long . . . I need never be lonely unless I want to . . . I can always go and dance with them if I feel like it. I have a fellow who takes me out to the dancing places whenever I want to go and I can always string along. I love it here. Wouldn't go back home for a load of monkeys. It's hot sometimes, but mostly balmy, and nobody's in a hurry. Sex doesn't interest me and I sleep like a baby. I am never bothered with dreams unless I eat something which sits on my stomach. You have to pay a price when you indulge yourself. I have a terrific yen for lobster à la Newburg, you see. I know exactly what I'm doing when I eat it. I go to Bill Grey's restaurant I should say about once every month with this fellow."

"Go on," said Mrs. Copperfield, who was enjoying this.

"Well, we order lobster à la Newburg. I tell you it's the most delicious thing in the world . . ."

"How do you like frogs' legs?" asked Mrs. Copperfield.

"Lobster à la Newburg for me."

"You sound so happy I have a feeling I'm going to nestle right in here, in this hotel. How would you like that?"

"You do what you want to with your own life. That's my motto. For how long would you want to stay?"

"Oh, I don't know," said Mrs. Copperfield. "Do you think I'd have fun here?"

"Oh, no end of fun," said the proprietess. "Dancing, drinking . . . all the things that are pleasant in this world. You don't need much money, you know. The men come off the ships with their pockets bulging. I tell you this place is God's own town, or maybe the Devil's." She laughed heartily.

"No end of fun," she repeated. She got up from her chair with some difficulty and went over to a box-like phonograph which stood in the corner of the room. After winding it up she put on a cowboy song.

"You can always listen to this," she said to Mrs. Copperfield, "whenever your little heart pleases. There are the needles and the records and all you've got to do is wind it up. When I'm not here, you can sit in this rocker and listen. I've got famous people singing on those records like Sophie Tucker and Al Jolson from the United States, and I say that music is the ear's wine."

"And I suppose reading would be very pleasant in this room—at the same time that one listened to the gramophone," said Mrs. Copperfield.

"Reading—you can do all the reading you want."

They sat for some time listening to records and drinking gin. After an hour or so Mrs. Quill saw Pacifica coming down the hall. "Now," she said to Mrs. Copperfield, "here comes your friend."

Pacifica had on a little silk dress and bedroom slippers. She had made up her face very carefully and she had perfumed herself.

"Look what Meyer brought me," she said, coming towards them and showing them a very large wrist watch with a radium dial. She seemed to be in a very pleasant mood.

"You been talking here one to the other," she said, smiling at them kindly. "Now suppose we all three of us go and take a walk through the street and get some beer or whatever we want."

"That would be nice," said Mrs. Copperfield. She was beginning to worry a bit about Mr. Copperfield. He hated her to disappear this way for a long time because it gave him an unbalanced feeling and interfered very much with his sleep. She promised herself to drop by the room and let him know that she was still out, but the very idea of going near the hotel made her shudder.

"Hurry up, girls," said Pacifica.

They went back to the quiet restaurant where Pacifica had taken Mr. and Mrs. Copperfield to dinner. Opposite was a very large saloon all lighted up. There was a ten-piece band playing there, and it was so crowded that the people were dancing in the streets.

Mrs. Quill said: "Oh boy, Pacifica! There's the place where you could have the time of your life tonight. Look at the time *they're* having."

"No, Mrs. Quill," said Pacifica. "We can stay here fine. The light is not so bright and it is more quiet and then we will go to bed."

"Yes," said Mrs. Quill, her face falling. Mrs. Copperfield thought she saw in Mrs. Quill's eyes a terribly pained and thwarted look.

"I'll go there tomorrow night," said Mrs. Quill softly. "It doesn't mean a thing. Every night they have those dances. That's because the boats never stop coming in. The girls are never tired either," she said to Mrs. Copperfield. "That's because they sleep all they want in the daytime. They can sleep as well in the daytime as they do at night. They don't get tired. Why should they? It doesn't make you tired to dance. The music carries you along."

"Don't be a fool," said Pacifica. "They're always tired."

"Well, which is it?" asked Mrs. Copperfield.

"Oh," said Mrs. Quill, "Pacifica is always looking on the darkest side of life. She's the gloomiest thing I ever knew."

"I don't look at the dark side, I look at the truth. You're a little foolish sometimes, Mrs. Quill."

"Don't talk to me that way when you know how much I love you," said Mrs. Quill, her lips beginning to tremble.

"I'm sorry, Mrs. Quill," said Pacifica gravely.

"There is something very lovable about Pacifica," Mrs. Copperfield thought to herself. "I believe she takes everyone quite seriously."

She took Pacifica's hand in her own.

"In a minute we're going to have something nice to drink," she said, smiling up at Pacifica. "Aren't you glad?"

"Yes, it will be nice to have something to drink," said Pacifica politely; but Mrs. Quill understood the gaiety of it. She rubbed her hands together and said: "I'm with you."

Mrs. Copperfield looked out into the street and saw Meyer walking by. He was with two blondes and some sailors.

"There goes Meyer," she said. The other two women looked across the street and they all watched him disappear.

MR. AND MRS. COPPERFIELD had gone over to Panama City for two days. The first day after lunch Mr. Copperfield proposed a walk towards the outskirts of the city. It was the first thing he always did when he arrived in a new place. Mrs. Copperfield hated to know what was around her, because it always turned out to be even stranger than she had feared.

They walked for a long time. The streets began to look all alike. On one side they went gradually uphill, and on the other they descended abruptly to the muddy regions near the sea. The stone houses were completely colorless in the hot sun. All the windows were heavily grilled; there was very little sign of life anywhere. They came to three naked boys struggling with a football, and turned downhill towards the water. A woman dressed in black silk came their way slowly. When they had passed her she turned around and stared at them shamelessly. They looked over their shoulders several times and they could still see her standing there watching them.

The tide was out. They made their way along the muddy beach. Back of them there was a huge stone hotel built in front of a low cliff, so that it was already in the shade. The mud flats and the water were still in the sunlight. They walked along until Mr. Copperfield found a large, flat rock for them to sit on.

"It's so beautiful here," he said.

A crab ran along sideways in the mud at their feet.

"Oh, look!" said Mr. Copperfield. "Don't you love them?"

"Yes, I do love them," she answered, but she could not suppress a rising feeling of dread as she looked around her at the landscape. Someone had painted the words *Cerveza—Beer* in green letters on the façade of the hotel.

Mr. Copperfield rolled up his trousers and asked if she would care to go barefoot to the edge of the water with him.

"I think I've gone far enough," she said.

"Are you tired?" he asked her.

"Oh, no. I'm not tired." There was such a pained expression on her face as she answered him that he asked her what the trouble was.

"I'm unhappy," she said.

"Again?" asked Mr. Copperfield. "What is there to be unhappy about now?"

"I feel so lost and so far away and so frightened."

"What's frighening about this?"

"I don't know. It's all so strange and it has no connection with anything."

"It's connected with Panama," observed Mr. Copperfield acidly. "Won't you ever understand that?" He paused. "I don't think really that I'm going to try to make you understand any more . . . But I'm going to walk to the water's edge. You spoil all my fun. There's absolutely nothing anyone can do with you." He was pouting.

"Yes, I know. I mean go to the water's edge. I guess I am tired after all." She watched him picking his way among the tiny stones, his arms held out for balance like a tight-rope walker's, and wished that she were able to join him because she was so fond of him. She began to feel a little exalted. There was a strong wind, and some lovely sailboats were passing by very swiftly not far from the shore. She threw her head back and closed her eyes, hoping that perhaps she might become exalted enough to run down and join her husband. But the wind did not blow quite hard enough, and behind her closed eyes she saw Pacifica and Mrs. Quill standing in front of the Hotel de las Palmas. She had said good-by to them from the old-fashioned hack that she had hired to drive her to the station. Mr. Copperfield had preferred to walk, and she had been alone with her two friends. Pacifica had been wearing the satin kimono which Mrs. Copperfield had bought her, and a pair of bedroom slippers decorated with pompons. She had stood near the wall of the hotel squinting, and complaining about being out in the street dressed only in a kimono, but Mrs. Copperfield had had only a minute to say good-by to them and she would not descend from the carriage.

"Pacifica and Mrs. Quill," she had said to them, leaning out of the victoria, "you can't imagine how I dread leaving you even for only two days. I honestly don't know how I'll be able to stand it."

"Listen, Copperfield," Mrs. Quill had answered, "you go and have the time of your life in Panama. Don't you think about us for one minute. Do you hear me? My, oh my, if I was young enough to be going to Panama City with my husband, I'd be wearing a different expression on my face than you are wearing now."

"That means nothing to be going to Panama City with your husband," Pacifica had insisted very firmly. "That does not mean that she is happy. Everyone likes to do different things. Maybe Copperfield likes better to go fishing or buy dresses." She had then smiled gratefully at Pacifica.

"Well," Mrs. Quill had retorted somewhat feebly, "I'm sure you would be happy, Pacifica, if you were going to Panama City with your husband . . . It's beautiful over there."

"Anyway, she has been in Paris," Pacifica had answered.

"Well, promise me you will be here when I get back," Mrs. Copperfield had begged them. "I'm so terrified that you might suddenly vanish."

"Don't make up such stories to yourself, my dear; life is difficult enough. Where are we going away?" Pacifica had said to her, yawning and starting to go inside. Then she had blown a kiss to Mrs. Copperfield from the doorway and waved her hand.

"Such fun, to be with them," she said, audibly, opening her eyes. "They are a great comfort."

Mr. Copperfield was on his way back to the flat rock where she was sitting. He had a stone of strange texture and formation in his hand. He was smiling as he came towards her.

"Look," he said, "isn't this an amusing stone? It's really quite beautiful. I thought you would like to see it, so I brought it to you." Mrs. Copperfield examined the stone and said: "Oh, it is beautiful and very strange. Thanks ever so much." She looked at it lying in the palm of her hand. As she examined it Mr. Copperfield pressed her shoulder and said: "Look at the big steamer plowing through the water. Do you see it?" He twisted her neck slightly so that she might look in the right direction.

"Yes, I see it. It's wonderful too . . . I think we had better be walking back home. It's going to be dark soon."

They left the beach and started walking through the streets again. It was getting dark, but there were more people standing around now. They commented openly on Mr. and Mrs. Copperfield as they passed by.

"It's really been the most wonderful day," Mr. Copperfield said. "You must have enjoyed some of it, because we've seen such incredible things." Mrs. Copperfield squeezed his hand harder and harder.

"I don't have winged feet like you," she said to him. "You must forgive me. I can't move about so easily. At thirty-three I have certain habits."

"That's bad," he answered. "Of course, I have certain habits too—habits of eating, habits of sleeping, habits of working—but I don't think that is what you meant, was it?"

"Let's not talk about it. That isn't what I meant, no."

THE NEXT DAY Mrs. Copperfield said that they would go out and see some of the jungle. Mrs. Copperfield said they hadn't the proper equipment and he explained that he hadn't meant that they would go exploring into the jungle but only around the edges where there were paths.

"Don't let the word 'jungle' frighten you," he said. "After all it only means tropical forest."

"If I don't feel like going in I won't. It doesn't matter. Tonight we are going back to Colon, aren't we?"

"Well, maybe we'll be too tired and we'll have to stay here another night."

"But I told Pacifica and Mrs. Quill that we would be back tonight. They'll be so disappointed if we aren't."

"You aren't really considering *them*, are you . . ? After all, Frieda! Anyway, I don't think they'll mind. They'll understand."

"Oh, no, they won't," answered Mrs. Copperfield. "They'll be disappointed. I told them I would be back before midnight and that we would go out and celebrate. I'm positive that Mrs. Quill will be very disappointed. She loves to celebrate."

"Who on earth is Mrs. Quill?"

"Mrs. Quill . . . Mrs. Quill and Pacifica."

"Yes, I know, but it's so ridiculous. It seems to me you wouldn't care to see them for more than one evening. I should think it would be easy to know what they were like in a very short time."

"Oh, I know what they're like, but I do have so much fun with them." Mr. Copperfield did not answer.

They went out and walked through the streets until they came to a place where there were some buses. They inquired about schedules, and boarded a bus called *Shirley Temple*. On the insides of the doors were painted pictures of Mickey Mouse. The driver had pasted postcards of the saints and the holy virgin on the windshield above his head. He was drinking a Coca-Cola when they got in the bus.

"*¿En que barco vinieron?*" asked the driver.

"*Venimos de Colon*," said Mr. Copperfield.

"What was that?" Mrs. Copperfield asked him.

"Just what boat did we come on, and I answered we have just arrived from Colon. You see, most people have just come off a boat. It corresponds to asking people where they live, in other places."

"*J'adore Colon, c'est tellement . . .*" began Mrs. Copperfield. Mr. Copperfield looked embarrassed. "Don't speak in French to him. It doesn't make any sense. Speak to him in English."

"I adore Colon."

The driver made a face. "Dirty wooden city. I am sure you have made a big mistake. You will see. You will like Panama City better. More stores, more hospitals, wonderful cinemas, big clean restaurants, wonderful houses in stone; Panama City is a big place. When we drive through Ancon I will show you how nice the lawns are and the trees and the sidewalks. You can't show me anything like that in Colon. You know who likes Colon?" He leaned way over the back of his seat, and as they were sitting behind him he was breathing right in their faces.

"You know who likes Colon?" He winked at Mr. Copperfield. "They're all over the streets. That is what it is there; nothing else much. We have that here too, but in a separate place. If you like that you can go. We have everything here."

"You mean the whores?" asked Mrs. Copperfield in a clear voice.

"*Las putas*," Mr. Copperfield explained in Spanish to the driver. He was delighted at the turn in the conversation and fearful lest the driver should not get the full savor of it.

The driver covered his mouth with his hand and laughed.

"She loves that," said Mr. Copperfield, giving his wife a push.

"No—no," said the driver, "she could not."

"They've all been very sweet to me."

"*Sweet!*" said the driver, almost screaming. "There is not this much sweet in them." He made a tiny little circle with his thumb and forefinger. "No, not sweet—someone has been fooling you. He knows." He put his hand on Mr. Copperfield's leg.

"I'm afraid I don't know anything about it," said Mr. Copperfield. The driver winked at him again, and then he said, "She thinks she knows *las*—I will not say the word, but she has never met one of them."

"But I have. I have even taken a siesta with one."

"*Siesta!*" the driver roared with laughter. "Don't make fun please, lady. That is not very nice, you know." He suddenly looked very sober. "No, no, no." He shook his head sadly.

By now the bus had filled up and the driver was obliged to start off. Every time they stopped he would turn around and wag a finger at Mrs. Copperfield. They went through Ancon and passed several long low buildings set up on some small hills.

"Hospitals," yelled the driver for the benefit of Mr. and Mrs. Copperfield. "They have doctors here for every kind of thing in the world. The Army can go there for nothing. They eat and they sleep and they get well all for nothing. Some of the old ones live there for the rest of their lives. I dream to be in the American Army and not driving this dirty bus."

"I should hate to be regimented," said Mr. Copperfield with feeling.

"They are always going to dinners and balls, balls and dinners," commented the driver. There was a murmuring from the back of the bus. The women were all eager to know what the driver had said. One of them who spoke English explained rapidly to the others in Spanish. They all giggled about it for fully five mintues afterwards. The driver started to sing *Over There*, and the laughter reached the pitch of hysteria. They were now almost in the country, driving alongside a river. Across the river was a very new road and behind that a tremendous thick forest.

"Oh, look," said Mr. Copperfield, pointing to the forest. "Do you see the difference? Do you see how enormous the trees are and how entangled the undergrowth is? You can tell that even from here. No northern forests ever look so rich."

"That's true, they don't," said Mrs. Copperfield.

The bus finally stopped at a tiny pier. Only three women and the Copperfields remained inside by now. Mrs. Copperfield looked at them hoping that they were going to the jungle, too.

Mr. Copperfield descended from the bus and she followed reluctantly. The driver was already in the street smoking. He was standing beside Mr. Copperfield, hoping that he would start another conversation. But Mr. Copperfield was much too excited at being so near the jungle to think of anything else. The three women did not get out. They remained in their seats talking. Mrs. Copperfield looked back into the bus and stared at them with a perplexed expression on her face. She seemed to be saying: "Please come out, won't you?" They were embarrassed and they started to giggle again.

Mrs. Copperfield went over to the driver and said to him: "Is this the last stop?"

"Yes," he said.

"And they?"

"Who?" he asked, looking dumb.

"Those three ladies in the back."

"They ride. They are very nice ladies. This is not the first time they are riding on my bus."

"Back and forth?"

"Sure," said the driver.

Mr. Copperfield took Mrs. Copperfield's hand and led her onto the pier. A little ferry was coming towards them. There seemed to be no one on the ferry at all.

Suddenly Mrs. Copperfield said to her husband: "I just don't want to go to the jungle. Yesterday was such a strange, terrible day. If I have another day like it I shall be in an awful state. Please let me go back on the bus."

"But," said Mr. Copperfield, "after you've come all the way here, it seems to me so silly and so senseless to go back. I can assure you that the jungle will be of some interest to you. I've been in them before. You see the strangest-shaped leaves and flowers. And I'm sure you would hear wonderful noises. Some of the birds in the tropics have voices like xylophones, others like bells."

"I thought maybe when I arrived here I would feel inspired; that I would feel the urge to set out. But I don't in the least. Please let's not discuss it."

"All right," said Mr. Copperfield. He looked sad and lonely. He enjoyed so much showing other people the things he liked best. He started to walk away towards the edge of the water and stared out across the river at the opposite shore. He was very slight and his head was beautifully shaped.

"Oh, please don't be sad!" said Mrs. Copperfield, hurrying over to him. "I refuse to allow you to be sad. I feel like an ox. Like a murderer. But I would be such a nuisance over on the other side of the river in the jungle. You'll love it once you're over there and you will be able to go much farther in without me."

"But my dear—I don't mind . . . I only hope you will be able to get home all right on the bus. Heaven knows when I'll get home. I might decide to just wander around and around . . . and you don't like to be alone in Panama."

"Well then," said Mrs. Copperfield, "suppose I take the train back to Colon. It's a simple trip, and I have only one grip with me. Then you can follow me tonight if you get back early from the jungle, and if you don't you can come along tomorrow morning. We had planned to go back tomorrow anyway. But you must give me your word of honor that you will come."

"It's all so complicated," said Mr. Copperfield. "I thought we were going to have a nice day in the jungle.

I'll come back tomorrow. The luggage is there, so there is no danger of my not coming back. Good-by." He gave her his hand. The ferry was scraping against the dock.

"Listen," she said, "if you're not back by twelve tonight, I shall sleep at the Hotel de las Palmas. I'll phone our hotel at twelve and see if you're there, in case I'm out."

"I won't be there until tomorrow."

"I'm at the Hotel de las Palmas if I'm not home, then."
"All right, but be good and get some sleep."

"Yes, of course I will."

He got into the boat and it pulled out.

"I hope his day has not been spoiled," she said to herself. The tenderness that she was feeling for him now was almost overwhelming. She got back on the bus and stared fixedly out the window because she did not want anyone to see that she was crying.

MRS. COPPERFIELD WENT straight to the Hotel de las Palmas. As she descended from the carriage she saw Pacifica walking towards her alone. She paid the driver and rushed up to her.

"Pacifica! How glad I am to see you!"

Pacifica's forehead had broken out. She looked tired.

"Ah, Copperfield," she said, "Mrs. Quill and I did not think we would ever see you again and now you are back."

"But, Pacifica, how can you say a thing like that? I'm surprised at both of you. Didn't I promise you I would be back before midnight and that we would celebrate?"

"Yes, but people often say this. After all, nobody gets angry if they don't come back."

"Let's go and say hello to Mrs. Quill."

"All right, but she has been in a terrible humor all the day, crying a lot and not eating anything."

"What on earth is the matter?"

"She had some fight, I think, with her boy friend. He don't like her. I tell her this but she won't listen."

"But the first thing she told me was that sex didn't interest her."

"To go to bed she don't care so much, but she is terribly sentimental, like she was sixteen years old. I feel sorry to see an old woman making such a fool."

Pacifica was still wearing her bedroom slippers. They went past the bar, which was filled with men smoking cigars and drinking.

"My God! how in one minute they make a place stink," said Pacifica. "I wish I could go and have a nice little house with a garden somewhere."

"I'm going to live here, Pacifica, and we'll all have lots of fun."

"The time for fun is over," said Pacifica gloomily.

"You'll feel better after we've all had a drink," said Mrs. Copperfield.

They knocked on Mrs. Quill's door.

They heard her moving about in her room and rattling some papers. Then she came to the door and opened it. Mrs. Copperfield noticed that she looked weaker than usual.

"Do come in," she said to them, "although I have nothing to offer you. You can sit down for a while."

Pacifica nudged Mrs. Copperfield. Mrs. Quill went back to her chair and took up a handful of bills which had been lying on the table near her.

"I must look over these. You will excuse me, but they're terribly important."

Pacifica turned to Mrs. Copperfield and talked softly.

"She can't even see them, because she does not have her glasses on. She is behaving like a child. Now she will be mad at us because her boy friend, like she calls him, has left her alone. I will not be treated like a dog very long."

Mrs. Quill overheard what Pacifica was saying, and reddened. She turned to Mrs. Copperfield.

"Do you still intend to come and live in this hotel?" she asked her.

"Yes," said Mrs. Copperfield buoyantly, "I wouldn't live anywhere else for the world. Even if you do growl at me."

"You probably will not find it comfortable enough."

"Don't growl at Copperfield," put in Pacifica. "First, she's been away for two days, and second, she doesn't know, like I do, what you are like."

"I'll thank you to keep your common little mouth shut," retorted Mrs. Quill, shuffling the bills rapidly.

"I am sorry to have disturbed you, Mrs. Quill," said Pacifica, rising to her feet and going towards the door.

"I wasn't yelling at Copperfield, I just said that I didn't think she would be comfortable here." Mrs. Quill laid down the bills. "Do you think she would be comfortable here, Pacifica?"

"A common little thing does not know anything about these questions," answered Pacifica and she left the room, leaving Mrs. Copperfield behind with Mrs. Quill.

Mrs. Quill took some keys from the top of her dresser and motioned to Mrs. Copperfield to follow her. They walked through some halls and up a flight of stairs and Mrs. Quill opened the door of one of the rooms.

"Is it near Pacifica's?" asked Mrs. Copperfield.

Mrs. Quill without answering led her back through the halls and stopped near Pacifica's room.

"This is dearer," said Mrs. Quill, "but it's near Miss Pacifica's room if that's your pleasure and you can stand the noise."

"What noise?"

"She'll start yammering away and heaving things around the minute she wakes up in the morning. It don't affect her any. She's tough. She hasn't got a nerve in her body."

"Mrs. Quill—"

"Yes."

"Could you have someone bring me a bottle of gin to my room?"

"I think I can do that . . . Well, I hope you are comfortable." Mrs. Quill walked away. "I'll have your bag sent up," she said, looking over her shoulder.

Mrs. Copperfield was appalled at the turn of events.

"I thought," she said to herself, "that they would go on the way they were forever. Now I must be patient and wait until everything is all right again. The longer I live, the less I can foresee anything." She lay down on the bed, put her knees up, and held onto her ankles with her hands.

"Be gay . . . be gay . . . be gay," she sang, rocking back and forth on the bed. There was a knock on the door and a man in a striped sweater entered the room without waiting for an answer to his knock.

"You ask for a bottle of gin?" he said.

"I certainly did—hooray!"

"And here's a suitcase. I'm putting it down here."

Mrs. Copperfield paid him and he left.

"Now," she said, jumping off the bed, "now for a little spot of gin to chase my troubles away. There just isn't any other way that's as good. At a certain point gin takes everything off your hands and you flop around like a little baby. Tonight I want to be a little baby." She took a hookerful, and shortly after that another. The third one she drank more slowly.

The brown shutters of her window were wide open and a small wind was bringing the smell of frying fat into the room. She went over to the window and looked down into the alleyway which separated the Hotel de las Palmas from a group of shacks.

There was an old lady seated in a chair in the alleyway eating her dinner.

"Eat every bit of it!" Mrs. Copperfield said. The old lady looked up dreamily, but she did not answer.

Mrs. Copperfield put her hand over her heart. "*Le bonheur*," she whispered, "*le bonheur* . . . what an angel a happy moment is—and how nice not to have to struggle too much for inner peace! I know that I shall enjoy certain moments of gaiety, willy-nilly. No one among my friends speaks any longer of character—and what interests us most, certainly, is finding out what we are like."

"Copperfield!" Pacifica burst into the room. Her hair was messy and she seemed to be out of breath. "Come on downstairs and have some fun. Maybe they are not the kind of men you like to be with, but if you don't like them you just walk away. Put some rouge on your face. Can I have some of your gin, please?"

"But a moment ago you said the time for fun was over!"

"What the hell!"

"By all means what the hell," said Mrs. Copperfield. "That's music to anyone's ears . . . If you could only stop me from thinking, always, Pacifica."

"You don't want to stop thinking. The more you can think, the more you are better than the other fellow. Thank your God that you can think."

Downstairs in the bar Mrs. Copperfield was introduced to three or four men.

"This man is Lou," said Pacifica, pulling out a stool from under the bar and making her sit next to him.

Lou was small and over forty. He wore a light-weight gray suit that was too tight for him, a blue shirt, and a straw hat. "She wants to stop thinking," said Pacifica to Lou.

"Who wants to stop thinking?" asked Lou.

"Copperfield. The little girl who is sitting on a stool, you big boob."

"Boob yourself. You're gettin' just like one of them New York girls," said Lou.

"Take me to Nueva York, take me to Nueva York," said Pacifica, bouncing up and down on her stool.

Mrs. Copperfield was shocked to see Pacifica behaving in this kittenish manner.

"Remember the belly buttons," said Lou to Pacifica.

"The belly buttons! The belly buttons!" Pacifica threw up her arms and screeched with delight.

"What about the belly buttons?" asked Mrs. Copperfield.

"Don't you think those two are the funniest words in the whole world? Belly and button—belly and button—in Spanish it is only *ombligo*."

"I don't think anything's that funny. But you like to laugh, so go ahead and laugh," said Lou, who made no attempt to talk to Mrs. Copperfield at all.

Mrs. Copperfield pulled at his sleeve. "Where do you come from?" she asked him.

"Pittsburgh."

"I don't know anything about Pittsburgh," said Mrs. Copperfield. But Lou was already turning his eyes in Pacifica's direction.

"Belly button," he said suddenly without changing his expression. This time Pacifica did not laugh. She did not seem to have heard him. She was standing up on the rail of the bar waving her arms in an agitated and officious manner.

"Well, well," she said, "I see that nobody has yet bought for Copperfield a drink. Am I with grown men or little boys? No, no . . . Pacifica will find other friends." She started to climb down from the bar, commanding Mrs. Copperfield to follow her. In the meantime she knocked off the hat of the man who was seated next to her with her elbow.

"Toby," she said to him, "you ought to be ashamed." Toby had a sleepy fat face and a broken nose. He was dressed in a dark brown heavy-weight suit.

"What? Did you want a drink?"

"Of course I wanted a drink." Pacifica's eyes were flashing. Everyone was served and she settled back on her stool.

"Come on now," she said, "what are we going to sing?" "I'm a monotone," said Lou.

"Singing ain't in my line," said Toby.

They were all surprised to see Mrs. Copperfield throw her head back as though filled with a sudden feeling of exaltation and start to sing.

"Who cares if the sky cares to fall into the sea
Who cares what banks fail in Yonkers
As long as you've got the kiss that conquers
Why should I care?
Life is one long jubilee
As long as I care for you
And you care for me."

"Good, fine . . . now another one," said Pacifica in a snappy voice.

"Did you ever sing in a club?" Lou asked Mrs. Copperfield. Her cheeks were very red.

"Actually, I didn't. But when I was in the mood, I used to sing very loudly at a table in a restaurant and attract a good bit of attention."

"You wasn't such good friends with Pacifica the last time I was in Colon."

"My dear man, I wasn't here. I was in Paris, I suppose."

"She didn't tell me you were in Paris. Are you a screwball or were you really in Paris?"

"I was in Paris . . . After all, stranger things have happened."

"Then you're fancy?"

"What do you mean, fancy?"

"Fancy is what fancy does."'

"Well, if you care to be mysterious it's your right, but the word 'fancy' doesn't mean a thing to me."

"Hey," said Lou to Pacifica, "is she tryin' to be highhat with me?"

"No, she's very intelligent. She's not like you."

For the first time Mrs. Copperfield sensed that Pacifica was proud of her. She realized that all this time Pacifica had been waiting to show her to her friends and she was not so sure that she was pleased. Lou turned to Mrs. Copperfield again.

"I'm sorry, Duchess. Pacifica says you got something on the ball and that I shouldn't address myself to you."

Mrs. Copperfield was bored with Lou, so she jumped down and went and stood between Toby and Pacifica. Toby was talking in a thick low voice with Pacifica.

"I'm tellin' you if she gets a singer in here and paints the place up a little she could make a lot of money on the joint. Everybody knows it's a good place to hit the hay in, but there ain't no music. You're here, you got a lot of friends, you got a way with you . . ."

"Toby, I don't want to start with music and a lot of friends. I'm quiet . . ."

"Yeah, you're quiet. This week you're quiet and maybe next week you won't want to be so quiet."

"I don't change my mind like that, Toby. I have a boy friend. I don't want to live in here much longer, you know."

"But you're livin' here now."

"Yes."

"Well, you want to make a little money. I'm tellin' you, with a little money we could fix up the joint."

"But why must I be here?"

"Because you got contacts."

"I never saw such a man. Talking all the time about business."

"You're not such a bad one for business yourself. I saw you hustlin' up a drink for that pal of yours. You get your cut, don't you?"

Pacifica kicked Toby with her heel.

"Listen, Pacifica, I like to have fun. But I can't see somethin' that could be coinin' the money takin' in petty cash."

"Stop being so busy." Pacifica pushed his hat off his head. He realized there was nothing to be done and sighed.

"How's Emma?" he asked her listlessly.

"Emma? I have not seen her since that night on the boat. She looked so gorgeous dressed up like a sailor."

"Women look fantastic dressed up in men's clothes," put in Mrs. Copperfield with enthusiasm.

"That's what you think," said Toby. "They look better to me in ruffles."

"She was only talking for a *minute* they look nice," said Pacifica.

"Not for me," said Toby.

"All right, Toby, maybe not for you, but for her they look nice that way."

"I still think I'm right. It ain't only a matter of opinion."

"Well, you can't prove it mathematically," said Mrs. Copperfield. Toby looked at her with no interest in his face.

"What about Emma?" said Pacifica. "You are really not interested finally in somebody?"

"You asked me to talk about somethin' besides business, so I asked you about Emma, just to show how sociable I am. We both know her. We were on a party together. Ain't that the right thing to do? How's Emma, how's your momma and poppa. That's the kind of talk you like. Next I tell you how my family is gettin' along and maybe I bring in another friend who we both forgot we knew, and then we say prices are goin' up and comes the revolution and we all eat strawberries. Prices are goin' up fast and that's why I wanted you to cash in on this joint."

"My God!" said Pacifica, "my life is hard enough and I am all alone, but I can still enjoy myself like a young girl. *You*, you are an old man."

"Your life don't have to be hard, Pacifica."

"Well, your life is still very hard and you are always trying to make it easy. That's the hardest part even of your life."

"I'm just waitin' to get a break. With my ideas and a break my life can be easy overnight."

"And then what will you do?"

"Keep it that way or maybe make it even easier. I'll be plenty busy."

"You will never have any time for anything."

"What's a guy like me want time for—plantin' tulips?"

"You don't enjoy to talk to me, Toby."

"Sure. You're friendly and cute and you got a good brain aside from a few phony ideas."

"And what about me? Am I friendly and cute too?" asked Mrs. Copperfield.

"Sure. You're all friendly and cute."

"Copperfield, I think we have just been insulted," said Pacifica, drawing herself up.

Mrs. Copperfield started to march out of the room in mock anger, but Pacifica was already thinking of something else and Mrs. Copperfield found herself to be in the ridiculous position of the performer who is suddenly without an audience. She came back to the bar.

"Listen," said Pacifica, "go upstairs and knock on Mrs. Quill's door. Tell her that Mr. Toby wants to meet her very much. Don't say Pacifica sent you. She will know this anyway and it will be easier for her if you don't say it. She will love to come down. That I know like if she was my mother."

"Oh, I'd love to, Pacifica," said Mrs. Copperfield, running out of the room.

When Mrs. Copperfield arrived in Mrs. Quill's room, Mrs. Quill was busy cleaning the top drawer of her dresser. It was very quiet in her room and very hot.

"I never have the heart to throw these things away," said Mrs. Quill, turning around and patting her hair. "I suppose you've met half of Colon," she said sadly, studying Mrs. Copperfield's flushed face.

"No, I haven't, but would you care to come down and meet Mr. Toby?"

"Who is Mr. Toby, dear?"

"Oh, please come, please come just for me."

"I will, dear, if you'll sit down and wait while I change into something better."

Mrs. Copperfield sat down. Her head was spinning. Mrs. Quill pulled out a long black silk dress from her closet. She drew it over her head and then selected some strings of black beads from her jewel-box, and a cameo pin. She powdered her face carefully and stuck several more hairpins into her hair.

"I'm not going to bother to take a bath," she said when she had finished. "Now, do you really think that I should meet this Mr. Toby, or do you think perhaps another night would be better?"

Mrs. Copperfield took Mrs. Quill's hand and pulled her out of the room. Mrs. Quill's entrance into the barroom was gracious and extremely formal. She was already using the hurt that her beau had caused her to good advantage.

"Now, dear," she said quietly to Mrs. Copperfield, "tell me which one is Mr. Toby."

"That one over there, sitting next to Pacifica," Mrs. Copperfield said hesitantly. She was fearful lest Mrs. Quill should find him completely unattractive and leave the room.

"I see. The stout gentleman."

"Do you hate fat people?"

"I don't judge people by their bodies. Even when I was a young girl I liked men for their minds. Now that I'm middle-aged I see how right I was."

"I've always been a body-worshipper," said Mrs. Copperfield, "but that doesn't mean that I fall in love with people who have beautiful bodies. Some of the bodies I've liked have been awful. Come, let's go over to Mr. Toby."

Toby stood up for Mrs. Quill and took off his hat.

"Come sit down with us and have a drink."

"Let me get my bearings, young man. Let me get my bearings."

"This bar belongs to you, don't it?" said Toby, looking worried.

"Yes, yes," said Mrs. Quill blandly. She was staring at the top of Pacifica's head. "Pacifica," she said, "don't you drink too much. I have to watch out for you."

"Don't you worry, Mrs. Quill. I have been taking care of myself for a long time." She turned to Lou and said solemnly: "Fifteen years." Pacifica was completely natural. She behaved as though nothing had occurred between her and Mrs. Quill. Mrs. Copperfield was enchanted. She put her arms around Mrs. Quill's waist and hugged her very tight.

"Oh," she said, "oh, you make me so happy!"

Toby smiled. "The girl's feelin' good, Mrs. Quill. Now don't you want a drink?"

"Yes, I'll have a glass of gin. It pains me the way these girls come away from their homes so young. I had my home and my mother and my sisters and my brothers until the age of twenty-six. Even so, when I got married I felt like a scared rabbit. As if I was going out into the world. Mr. Quill was like a family to me, though, and it wasn't until he died that I really got out into the world. I was in my thirties then, and more of a scared rabbit than ever. Pacifica's really been out in the world much longer than I have. You know, she is like an old sea captain. Sometimes I feel very silly when she tells me of some of her experiences. My eyes almost pop right out of my head. It isn't so much a question of age as it is a question of experience. The Lord has spared me more than he has spared Pacifica. She hasn't been spared a single thing. Still, she's not as nervous as I am."

"Well, she certainly don't know how to look out for herself for someone who's had so much experience," said Toby. "She don't know a good thing when she sees it."

"Yes, I expect you're right," said Mrs. Quill, warming up to Toby.

"Sure I'm right. But she's got lots of friends here in Panama, ain't she?"

"I dare say Pacifica has a great many friends," said Mrs. Quill.

"Come on, you know she's got lots of friends, don't you?"

As Mrs. Quill looked as though she had been somewhat startled by the pressing tone in his voice, Toby decided he was hurrying things too much.

"Who the hell cares, anyway?" he said, looking at her out of the corner of his eye. This seemed to have the right effect on Mrs. Quill, and Toby breathed a sigh of relief.

Mrs. Copperfield went over to a bench in the corner and lay down. She shut her eyes and smiled.

"That's the best thing for her," said Mrs. Quill to Toby. "She's a nice woman, a dear sweet woman, and she'd had a little too much to drink. Pacifica, she can really take care of herself like she says. I've seen her drink as much as a man, but with her it's different. As I said, she's had all the experience in the world. Now, Mrs. Copperfield and me, we have to watch ourselves more carefully or else have some nice man watching out for us."

"Yeah," said Toby, twisting around on his stool. "Bartender, another gin. You want one, don't you?" he asked Mrs. Quill.

"Yes, if you'll watch out for me."

"Sure I will. I'll even take you home in my arms if you fall down."

"Oh, no." Mrs. Quill giggled and flushed. "You wouldn't try that, young man. I'm heavy, you know."

"Yeah . . . Say—"

"Yes?"

"Would you mind telling me something?"

"I'd be delighted to tell you anything you'd like to hear."

"How is it you ain't never bothered to fix this place up?"

"Oh, dear, isn't it awful? I've always promised myself I would and I never get around to it."

"No dough?" asked Toby. Mrs. Quill looked vague. "Haven't you got no money to fix it up with?" he repeated.

"Oh yes, certainly I have." Mrs. Quill looked around at the bar. "I even have some things upstairs that I always promised myself to hang up on the walls here. Everything is so dirty, isn't it? I feel ashamed."

"No, no," said Toby impatiently. He was now very animated. "That ain't what I mean at all."

Mrs. Quill smiled at him sweetly.

"Listen," said Toby, "I been handlin' restaurants and bars and clubs all my life, and I can make them go."

"I'm certain that you can."

"I'm tellin' you that I can. Listen, let's get out of here; let's go some place else where we can really talk. Any place in town you name I'll take you to. It's worth it to me and it'll be worth it to you even more. You'll see. We can have more to drink or maybe a little bite to eat. Listen"—he grabbed hold of Mrs. Quill's upper arm—"would you like to go to the Hotel Washington?"

At first Mrs. Quill did not react, but when she realized what he had said, she answered that she would enjoy it very much, in a voice trembling with emotion. Toby jumped off the stool, pulled his hat down over his face, and started walking out of the bar, saying: "Come on, then," over his shoulder to Mrs. Quill. He looked annoyed but resolute.

Mrs. Quill took Pacifica's hand in her own and told her that she was going to the Hotel Washington.

"If there was any possible way I would take you with us, I would, Pacifica. I feel very badly to be going there without you, but I don't see how you can come, do you?"

"Now, don't you worry about that, Mrs. Quill. I'm having a very good time here," said Pacifica in a sincerely world-weary tone of voice.

"That's a hocus-pocus joint," said Lou.

"Oh no," said Pacifica, "it is very nice there, very beautiful. She will have a lovely time." Pacifica pinched Lou. "You don't know," she said to him.

Mrs. Quill walked out of the bar slowly and joined Toby on the sidewalk. They got into a hack and started for the hotel.

Toby was silent. He sprawled way back in his seat and lighted a cigar.

"I regret that automobiles were ever invented," said Mrs. Quill.

"You'd go crazy tryin' to get from one place to another if they wasn't."

"Oh, no. I always take my time. There isn't anything that can't wait."

"That's what you think," said Toby in a surly tone of voice, sensing that this was just the thing that he would have to combat in Mrs. Quill. "It's just that extra second that makes Man O'War or any other horse come in first," he said.

"Well, life isn't a horse race."

"Nowadays that's just what life is."

"Well, not for me," said Mrs. Quill.

Toby was disgusted.

The walk which led up to the veranda of the Hotel Washington was lined with African date-palms. The hotel itself was very impressive. They descended from the carriage. Toby stood in the middle of the walk between the scraping palms and looked towards the hotel. It was all lighted up. Mrs. Quill stood beside Toby.

"I'll bet they soak you for drinks in there," said Toby. "I'll bet they make two hundred per cent profit."

"Oh, please," said Mrs. Quill, "if you don't feel you can afford it let's take a carriage and go back. The ride is so pleasant anyway." Her heart was beating very quickly.

"Don't be a God-damn fool!" Toby said to her, and they headed for the hotel.

The floor in the lobby was of imitation yellow marble. There was a magazine stand in one corner where the guests were able to buy chewing gum and picture postcards, maps, and souvenirs. Mrs. Quill felt as though she had just come off a ship. She wandered about in circles, but Toby went straight up to the man behind the magazine stand and asked him where he could get a drink. He suggested to Toby that they go out on the terrace.

"It's generally where everyone goes," he said.

They were seated at a table on the edge of the terrace, and they had a very nice view of a stretch of beach and the sea.

Between them on the table there was a little lamp with a rose-colored shade. Toby began at once to twirl the lamp shade. His cigar by now was very short and very wet.

Here and there on the terrace small groups of people were talking together in low voices.

"Dead!" said Toby.

"Oh, I think it's lovely," said Mrs. Quill. She was shivering a little, as the wind kept blowing over her shoulder, and it was a good deal cooler than in Colon.

A waiter was standing beside them with his pencil poised in the air waiting for an order.

"What do you want?" asked Toby.

"What would you suggest, young man, that's really delicious?" said Mrs. Quill, turning to the waiter.

"Fruit punch à la Washington Hotel," said the waiter abruptly.

"That *does* sound good."

"O.K.," said Toby, "bring one, and a straight rye for me."

When Mrs. Quill had sipped quite a bit of her drink Toby spoke to her. "So you got the dough, but you never bothered to fix it up."

"Mmmmmm!" said Mrs. Quill. "They've got every kind of fruit in the world in this drink. I'm afraid I'm behaving just like a baby, but there's no one who likes the good things in this world better than me. Of course, I've never had to do without them, you know."

"You don't call livin' the way you're livin' havin' the good things in life, do you?" said Toby.

"I live much better than you think. How do you know how I live?"

"Well, you could have more style," said Toby, "and you could have that easy. I mean the place could be better very easy."

"It probably would be easy, wouldn't it?"

"Yeah." Toby waited to see if she would say anything more by herself before he addressed her again.

"Take all these people here," said Mrs. Quill. "There aren't many of them, but you'd think they'd all get together instead of staying in twos and threes. As long as they're all living here in this gorgeous hotel, you'd think they'd have on their ball dresses and be having a wonderful time every minute, instead of looking out over the terrace or reading. You'd think they'd always be dressed up to the hilt and flirting together instead of wearing those plain clothes."

"They got on sport clothes," said Toby. "They don't want to be bothered dressin'. They probably come here for a rest. They're probably business people. Maybe some of them belong to society. They got to rest too. They got so many places they got to show up at when they're home."

"Well, I wouldn't pay out all that money just to rest. I'd stay in my own house."

"It don't make no difference. They got plenty."

"That's true enough. Isn't it sad?"

"I don't see nothin' sad about it. What looks sad to me," said Toby, leaning way over and crushing his cigar out in the ash-tray, "what looks sad to me is that you've got that bar and hotel set-up and you ain't makin' enough money on it."

"Yes, isn't it terrible?"

"I like you and I don't like to see you not gettin' what you could." He took hold of her hand with a certain amount of gentleness. "Now, I know what to do with your place. Like I told you before. Do you remember what I told you before?"

"Well, you've told me so many things."

"I'll tell you again. I've been working with restaurants and bars and hotels all my life and makin' them go. I said makin' them go. If I had the dough right now, if it wasn't that I'm short because I had to help my brother and his family out of a jam, I'd take my own dough before you could say Jack Robinson and sink it into your joint and fix it up. I know that I'd get it right back anyway, so it wouldn't be no act of charity."

"Certainly it wouldn't," said Mrs. Quill. Her head was swaying gently from side to side. She looked at Toby with luminous eyes.

"Well, I got to go easy now until next October, when I got a big contract comin'. A contract with a chain. I could use a little money now, but that ain't the point."

"Don't bother to explain, Toby," said Mrs. Quill.

"What do you mean, don't bother to explain? Ain't you interested in what I've got to tell you?"

"Toby, I'm interested in every word you have to say. But you must not worry about the drinks. Your friend Flora Quill tells you that you needn't worry. We're out to enjoy ourselves and Heaven knows we're going to, aren't we, Toby?"

"Yeah, but just let me explain this to you. I think the

reason you ain't done nothin' about the place is because you didn't know where to begin, maybe. Understand? You don't know the ropes. Now, I know all about gettin' orchestras and carpenters and waiters, cheap. I know how to do all that. You got a name, and lots of people like to come there even now because they can go right from the bar upstairs. Pacifica is a big item because she knows every bloke in town and they like her and they trust her. The trouble is, you ain't got no atmosphere, no bright lights, no dancin'. It ain't pretty or big enough. People go to the other places and then they come to your place late. Just before they go to bed. If I was you, I'd turn over in my grave. It's the other guys that are gettin' the meat. You only get a little bit. What's left near the bone, see?"

"The meat nearest the bone is the sweetest," said Mrs. Quill.

"Hey, is there any use my talkin' to you or are you gonna be silly? I'm serious. Now, you got some money in the bank. You got money in the bank, ain't you?"

"Yes, I've got money in the bank," said Mrs. Quill.

"O.K. Well, you let me help you fix up the joint. I'll take everything off your hands. All you got to do is lie back and enjoy the haul."

"Nonsense," said Mrs. Quill.

"Now come on," said Toby, beginning to get angry. "I'm not askin' you for nothin' except maybe a little percentage in the place and a little cash to pay expenses for a while. I can do it all for you cheap and quick and I can manage the joint for you so that it won't cost you much more than it's costin' you now."

"But I think that's wonderful, Toby. I think it's so wonderful."

"You don't have to tell me it's wonderful. I know it's wonderful. It ain't wonderful, it's swell. It's marvelous. We ain't got no time to lose. Have another drink."

"Yes, yes."

"I'm spendin' my last cent on you," he said recklessly.

Mrs. Quill was drunk by now and she just nodded her head.

"It's worth it." He sat back in his chair and studied the horizon. He was very busy calculating in his head. "What percentage in the place do you think I ought to get? Don't forget I'm gonna manage the whole thing for you for a year."

"Oh, dear," said Mrs. Quill, "I'm sure I haven't got any idea." She smiled at him blissfully.

"O.K. How much advance will you give me just so I can stay on here until I get the place goin'?"

"I don't know."

"Well, we'll figure it this way," said Toby cautiously. He was not sure yet that he had taken the right move. "We'll figure it this way. I don't want you to do more than you can. I want to go in this deal with you. You tell me how much money you got in the bank. Then I'll figure out how much fixin' the place up will cost you and then how much I think is a minimum for me. If you ain't got much I'm not gonna let you go busted. You be honest with me and I'll be honest with you."

"Toby," said Mrs. Quill seriously, "don't you think I'm an honest woman?"

"What the hell," said Toby, "do you think I'd put a proposition like that to you if I didn't think you were?"

"No, I guess you wouldn't," said Mrs. Quill sadly.

"How much you got?" asked Toby, looking at her intently. "What?" asked Mrs. Quill.

"How much money you got in the bank?"

"I'll show you, Toby. I'll show you right away." She started to fumble in her big black leather pocketbook.

Toby had his jaw locked and his eyes averted from the face of Mrs. Quill.

"Messy—messy—messy," Mrs. Quill was saying. "I have everything in this pocketbook but the kitchen stove."

There was a very still look in Toby's eyes as he stared first at the water and then at the palm trees. He considered that he had already won, and he was beginning to wonder whether or not it was really a good thing.

"Dear me," said Mrs. Quill, "I live just like a gypsy. Twenty-two fifty in the bank and I don't even care."

Toby snatched the book from her hands. When he saw that the balance was marked twenty-two dollars and fifty cents, he rose to his feet and, clutching his napkin in one hand and his hat in the other, he walked off the terrace.

After Toby had left the table so abruptly, Mrs. Quill felt deeply ashamed of herself.

"He's just so disgusted," she decided, "that he can't even look me in the face without feeling like throwing up. It's because he thinks I'm barmy to go around gay as a lark with only twenty-two fifty in the bank. Well, well,

I expect I'd better start worrying a little more. When he comes back I'll tell him I'll turn over a new leaf."

Everyone had left the terrace by now with the exception of the waiter who had served Mrs. Quill. He stood with his hands behind his back and stared straight ahead of him.

"Sit down for a bit and talk to me," said Mrs. Quill to him. "I'm lonesome on this dark old terrace. It's really a beautiful terrace. You might tell me something about yourself. How much money have you got in the bank? I know you think I'm fresh to ask you, but I'd really like to know."

"Why not?" answered the waiter. "I've got about three hundred and fifty dollars in the bank." He did not sit down. "Where did you get it?" asked Mrs. Quill.

"From my uncle."

"I guess you feel pretty secure."

"No."

Mrs. Quill began to wonder whether or not Toby would come back at all. She pressed her hands together and asked the young waiter if he knew where the gentleman who had been sitting next to her had gone.

"Home, I guess," said the waiter.

"Well, let's just have one look in the lobby," said Mrs. Quill nervously. She beckoned to the waiter to follow her.

They went into the lobby and together they searched the faces of the guests, who were either standing around in groups or sitting along the wall in armchairs. The hotel was much livelier now than it had been when Mrs. Quill first arrived with Toby. She was deeply troubled and hurt at not seeing Toby anywhere.

"I guess I'd better go home and let you get some sleep," she said absentmindedly to the waiter, "but not before I've bought something for Pacifica . . ." She had been trembling a little, but the thought of Pacifica filled her with assurance.

"Such an awful, dreadful, mean thing to be alone in the world even for a minute," she said to the waiter. "Come with me and help me choose something, nothing important, just some remembrance of the hotel."

"They're all the same," said the waiter, following her reluctantly. "Just a lot of junk. I don't know what your friend wants. You might get her a little pocketbook with *Panama* painted on it."

"No, I want it to be specially marked with the name of the hotel."

"Well," said the waiter, "most people don't go in for that."

"Oh my—oh my," said Mrs. Quill emphatically, "must I always be told what other people do? I've had just about enough of it." She marched up to the magazine stand and said to the young man behind the counter: "Now, I want something with *Hotel Washington* written on it. For a woman."

The man looked through his stock and pulled out a handkerchief on the corner of which were painted two palm trees and the words: *Souvenir of Panama.*

"Most people prefer this, though," he said, drawing a tremendous straw hat from under the counter and placing it on his own head.

"You see, it gives you as much shadow as an umbrella and it is very becoming." There was nothing written on the hat at all.

"That handkerchief," continued the young man, "most people consider it kind of, you know . . ."

"My dear young man," said Mrs. Quill, "I expressly told you that I wanted this gift to bear the words *Hotel Washington* and if possible also a picture of the hotel."

"But, lady, nobody wants that. People don't want pictures of hotels on their souvenirs. Palm trees, sunsets, sometimes even bridges, but not hotels."

"Do you or do you not have anything that bears the words *Hotel Washington?*" said Mrs. Quill, raising her voice.

The salesman was beginning to get angry. "I *do* have," he said, his eyes flashing, "if you will wait one minute please, madam." He opened a little gate and went out into the lobby. He was back in a short time carrying a heavy black ash-tray which he set on the counter in front of Mrs. Quill. The name of the hotel was stamped in the center of the ash-tray in yellow lettering.

"Is this the type of thing you wanted?" asked the salesman. "Why, yes," said Mrs. Quill, "it is."

"All right, madam, that'll be fifty cents."

"That's not worth fifty cents." whispered the waiter to Mrs. Quill.

Mrs. Quill looked through her purse; she was able to find no more than a quarter in change and no bills at all.

"Look," she said to the young man, "I'm the proprietress of the Hotel de las Palmas. I will show you my bank book with my address written in the front of it. Are you going to trust me with this ash-tray just this once? You see, I came with a gentleman friend and we had a falling out and he went home ahead of me."

"I can't help that, madam," said the salesman.

Meanwhile one of the assistant managers who had been watching the group at the magazine stand from another corner of the lobby thought it time to intervene. He was exceedingly suspicious of Mrs. Quill, who did not appear to him to measure up to the standard of the other guests in any way, not even from a distance. He also wondered what could possibly be keeping the waiter standing in front of the magazine stand for such a long while. He walked over to them looking as serious and as thoughtful as he was able.

"Here's my bank book," Mrs. Quill was saying to the salesman.

The waiter, seeing the assistant manager approaching, was frightened and immediately presented Mrs. Quill with the check for the drinks she and Toby had consumed together.

"You owe six dollars on the terrace," he said to Mrs. Quill. "Didn't he pay for them?" she said. "I guess he must have been in an awful state."

"Can I help you?" the assistant manager asked of Mrs. Quill. "I'm sure you can," she said. "I'm the owner of the Hotel de las Palmas."

"I'm sorry," the manager said, "but I'm not familiar with the Hotel de las Palmas."

"Well," said Mrs. Quill, "I have no money with me. I came here with a gentleman, we had a falling out, but I have my bank book here with me which will prove to you that I will have the money as soon as I can run over to the bank tomorrow. I can't sign a check because it's in the savings bank."

"I'm sorry," said the assistant manager, "but we extend credit only to guests residing in the hotel."

"I do that too, in my hotel," said Mrs. Quill, "unless it is something out of the ordinary."

"We make a rule of never extending credit . . ."

"I wanted to take this ash-tray home to my girl friend. She admires your hotel."

"That ash-tray is the property of the Hotel Washington," said the assistant manager, frowning sternly at the salesman, who said quickly: "She wanted something with *Hotel Washington* written on it. I didn't have anything so I thought I'd sell her one of these—for fifty cents," he added, winking at the assistant manager, who was standing farther and farther back on his heels.

"These ash-trays," he repeated, "are the property of the Hotel Washington. We have only a limited number of them in stock and every available tray is in constant use."

The salesman, not caring to have anything more to do with the ash-tray lest he lose his job, carried it back to the table from which he had originally removed it and took up his position again behind the counter.

"Do you want either the handkerchief or the hat?" he asked of Mrs. Quill as though nothing had happened.

"She's got all the hats and the hankies she needs," said Mrs. Quill. "I suppose I'd better go home."

"Would you care to come to the desk with me and settle the bill?" asked the assistant manager.

"Well, if you'll just wait until tomorrow—"

"I'm afraid it is definitely against the rules of the hotel, madam. If you'll just step this way with me." He turned to the waiter, who was following the conversation intently. "*Te necesitan afuera*," he said to him, "go on."

The waiter was about to say something, but he decided against it and walked slowly away towards the terrace. Mrs. Quill began to cry.

"Wait a minute," she said, taking a handkerchief from her bag. "Wait a minute—I would like to telephone to my friend Pacifica."

The assistant manager pointed in the direction of the telephone booths, and she hurried away, her face buried in her handkerchief. Fifteen minutes later she returned, crying more pitifully than before.

"Mrs. Copperfield is coming to get me—I told her all about it. I think I'll sit down somewhere and wait."

"Does Mrs. Copperfield have the necessary funds with which to cover your bill?"

"I don't know," said Mrs. Quill, walking away from him.

"You mean you don't know whether or not she will be able to pay your bill?"

"Yes, yes, she'll pay my bill. Please let me sit down over there."

The manager nodded. Mrs. Quill fell into an armchair that stood beside a tall palm tree. She covered her face with her hands and continued to cry.

Twenty minutes later Mrs. Copperfield arrived. In spite of the heat she was wearing a silver-fox cape which she had brought with her for use only in higher altitudes.

Although she was perspiring and badly made up, she felt assured of being treated with a certain amount of deference by the hotel employees because of the silver-fox cape.

She had awakened quite some time before and was again a little drunk. She rushed up to Mrs. Quill and kissed her on the top of her head.

"Where's the man who made you cry?" she asked.

Mrs. Quill looked around through her tear-veiled eyes and pointed to the assistant manager. Mrs. Copperfield beckoned to him with her index finger.

He came over to them and she asked him where she could get some flowers for Mrs. Quill.

"There's nothing like flowers when you're either sick at heart or physically ill," she said to him. "She's been under a terrible strain. Would you get some flowers?" she asked, taking a twenty-dollar bill from her purse.

"There is no florist in the hotel," said the assistant manager. "That's not very luxurious," said Mrs. Copperfield.

He did not reply.

"Well then," she continued, "the next best thing to do is to buy her something nice to drink. I suggest that we all go to the bar."

The assistant manager declined.

"But," said Mrs. Copperfield, "I insist that you come along. I want to talk things over with you. I think you've been horrid."

The assistant manager stared at her.

"The most horrid thing about you," continued Mrs. Copperfield, "is that you're just as grouchy now that you know your bill will be paid as you were before. You were mean and worried then and you're mean and worried now. The expression on your face hasn't changed one bit. It's a dangerous man who reacts more or less in the same way to good news or bad news."

Since he still made no effort to speak, she continued: "You've not only made Mrs. Quill completely miserable for no reason at all, but you've spoiled my fun too. You don't even know how to please the rich." The assistant manager raised his eyebrows.

"You won't understand this but I shall tell it to you anyway. I came here for two reasons. The first reason, naturally, was in order to get my friend Mrs. Quill out of trouble; the second reason was in order to see your face when you realized that a bill which you never expected to be paid was to be paid after all. I expected to be able to watch the transition. You understand—enemy into friend—that's always terribly exciting. That's why in a good movie the hero often hates the heroine until the very end. But you, of course, wouldn't dream of lowering your standards. You think it would be cheap to turn into an affable human being because you discovered there was money where you had been sure there was no money to be forthcoming. Do you think the rich mind? They never get enough of it. They want to be liked for their money too, and not only for themselves. You're not even a good hotel manager. You're definitely a boor in every way."

The assistant manager looked down with loathing at Mrs. Copperfield's upturned face. He hated her sharp features and her high voice. He found her even more disgusting than Mrs. Quill. He was not fond of women anyway.

"You have no imagination," she said, "none whatever! You are missing everything. Where do I pay my bill?"

All the way home Mrs. Copperfield felt sad because Mrs. Quill was dignified and remote and did not give her the lavish thanks which she had been expecting.

EARLY THE NEXT MORNING Mrs. Copperfield and Pacifica were together in Pacifica's bedroom. The sky was beginning to grow light. Mrs. Copperfield had never seen Pacifica this drunk. Her hair was pushed up on her head. It looked now somewhat like a wig which is a little too small for the wearer. Her pupils were very large and slightly filmed. There was a large dark spot on the front of her checked skirt, and her breath smelled very strongly of whisky. She stumbled over to the window and looked out. It was quite dark in the room. Mrs. Copperfield could barely discern the red and purple squares in Pacifica's skirt. She could not see her legs at all, the shadows were so deep, but she knew the heavy yellow silk stockings and the white sneakers well.

"It's so lovely," said Mrs. Copperfield.

"Beautiful," said Pacifica, turning around, "beautiful." She moved unsteadily around the room. "Listen," she said, "the most wonderful thing to do now is to go to the beach and swim in the water. If you have enough money we can take a taxicab and go. Come on. Will you?"

Mrs. Copperfield was very startled indeed, but Pacifica was already pulling a blanket from the bed. "Please," she said. "You cannot know how much pleasure this would give me. You must take that towel over there."

The beach was not very far away. When they arrived, Pacifica told the cab-driver to come back in two hours.

The shore was strewn with rocks; this was a disappointment to Mrs. Copperfield. Although the wind was not very strong, she noticed that the top branches of the palm trees were shaking.

Pacifica took her clothes off and immediately walked into the water. She stood for a time with her legs wide apart, the water scarcely reaching to her shins, while Mrs. Copperfield sat on a rock trying to decide whether or not to remove her own clothes. There was a sudden splash and Pacifica started to swim. She swam first on her back and then on her stomach, and Mrs. Copperfield was certain that she could hear her singing. When at last Pacifica grew tired of splashing about in the water, she stood up and walked towards the beach. She took tremendous strides and her pubic hair hung between her legs sopping wet. Mrs. Copperfield looked a little embarrassed, but Pacifica plopped down beside her and asked her why she did not come in the water.

"I can't swim," said Mrs. Copperfield.

Pacifica looked up at the sky. She could see now that it was not going to be a completely fair day.

"Why do you sit on that terrible rock?" said Pacifica. "Come, take your clothes off and we go in the water. I will teach you to swim."

"I was never able to learn."

"I will teach you. If you cannot learn I will let you sink. No, this is only a joke. Don't take it serious."

Mrs. Copperfield undressed. She was very white and thin, and her spine was visible all the way along her back. Pacifica looked at her body without saying a word.

"I know I have an awful figure," said Mrs. Copperfield. Pacifica did not answer. "Come," she said, getting up and putting her arm around Mrs. Copperfield's waist.

They stood with the water up to their thighs, facing the beach and the palm trees. The trees appeared to be moving behind a mist. The beach was colorless. Behind them the sky was growing lighter very rapidly, but the sea was still almost black. Mrs. Copperfield noticed a red fever sore on Pacifica's lip. Water was dripping from her hair onto her shoulders.

She turned away from the beach and pulled Mrs. Copperfield farther out into the water.

Mrs. Copperfield held onto Pacifica's hand very hard. Soon the water was up to her chin.

"Now lie on your back. I will hold you under your head," said Pacifica.

Mrs. Copperfield looked around wildly, but she obeyed, and floated on her back with only the support of Pacifica's open hand under her head to keep her from sinking. She could see her own narrow feet floating on top of the water. Pacifica started to swim, dragging Mrs. Copperfield along with her. As she had only the use of one arm, her task was an arduous one and she was soon breathing like a bull. The touch of her hand underneath the head of Mrs. Copperfield was very light—in fact, so light that Mrs. Copperfield feared that she would be left alone from one minute to the next. She looked up. The sky was packed with gray clouds. She wanted to say something to Pacifica, but she did not dare to turn her head.

Pacifica swam a little farther inland. Suddenly she stood up and placed both her hands firmly in the small of Mrs. Copperfield's back. Mrs. Copperfield felt happy and sick at once. She turned her face and in so doing she brushed Pacifica's heavy stomach with her cheek. She held on hard to Pacifica's thigh with the strength of years of sorrow and frustration in her hand.

"Don't leave me," she called out.

At this moment Mrs. Copperfield was strongly reminded of a dream that had recurred often during her life. She was being chased up a short hill by a dog. At the top of the hill there stood a few pine trees and a mannequin about eight feet high. She approached the mannequin and discovered her to be fashioned out of flesh, but without life. Her dress was of black velvet, and tapered to a very narrow width at the hem. Mrs. Copperfield wrapped one of the mannequin's arms tightly around her own waist. She was startled by the thickness of the arm and very pleased. The mannequin's other arm she bent upward from the elbow with her free hand. Then the mannequin began to sway backwards and forwards. Mrs. Copperfield clung all the more tightly to the mannequin and together they fell off the top of the hill and continued rolling for quite a distance until they landed on a little walk, where they remained locked in each other's arms. Mrs. Copperfield loved this part of the dream best; and the fact that all the way down the hill the mannequin acted as a buffer between herself and the broken bottles and little stones over which they fell gave her particular satisfaction.

Pacifica had resurrected the emotional content of her dream for a moment, which Mrs. Copperfield thought was certainly the reason for her own peculiar elation.

"Now," said Pacifica, "if you don't mind I will take one more swim by myself." But first she helped Mrs. Copperfield to her feet and led her back to the beach, where Mrs. Copperfield collapsed on the sand and hung her head like a wilted flower. She was trembling and exhausted as one is after a love experience. She looked up at Pacifica, who noticed that her eyes were more luminous and softer than she had ever seen them before.

"You should go in the water more," said Pacifica; "you stay in the house too much."

She ran back into the water and swam back and forth many times. The sea was now blue and much rougher than it had been earlier. Once during the course of her swimming Pacifica rested on a large flat rock which the outgoing tide had uncovered. She was directly in the line of the hazy sun's pale rays. Mrs. Copperfield had a difficult time being able to see her at all and soon she fell asleep.

UPON ARRIVING BACK at the hotel, Pacifica announced to Mrs. Copperfield that she was going to sleep like a dead person. "I hope I don't wake up for ten days," she said.

Mrs. Copperfield watched her stumble down the bright green corridor, yawning and tossing her head.

"Two weeks I'll sleep," she said again, and then she went into her room and shut the door behind her. In her own room Mrs. Copperfield decided that she had better call on Mr. Copperfield. She went downstairs and walked out into the street, which seemed to be moving as it had on the first day of her arrival. There were a few people already seated on their balconies who were looking down at her. A very thin girl, wearing a red silk dress which hung down to her ankles, was crossing the street towards her. She looked surprisingly young and fresh. When Mrs. Copperfield was nearer to her she decided that she was a Malayan. She was rather startled when the girl stopped directly in front of her and addressed her in perfect English.

"Where have you been that you got your hair all wet?" she said.

"I've been taking a swim with a friend of mine. We—we went early to the beach." Mrs. Copperfield didn't feel much like talking.

"What beach?" asked the girl.

"I don't know," said Mrs. Copperfield.

"Well, did you walk there or did you ride?"

"We rode."

"There isn't any beach really near enough to walk to, I guess," said the girl.

"No, I guess there isn't," said Mrs. Copperfield, sighing and looking around her. The girl was walking along with her.

"Was the water cold?" asked the girl.

"Yes and no," said Mrs. Copperfield.

"Did you swim in the water naked with your friend?"

"Yes."

"Then there weren't any people around, I suppose."

"No, there wasn't a soul there. Do you swim?" Mrs. Copperfield asked the girl.

"No," she said, "I never go near the water." The girl had a shrill voice. She had light hair and brows. She could easily have been partly English. Mrs. Copperfield decided not to ask her. She turned to the girl.

"I'm going to make a telephone call. Where is the nearest place with a phone?"

"Come to Bill Grey's restaurant. They keep it very cool. I generally spend my mornings there drinking like a fish. By the time it's noon I'm cockeyed drunk. I shock the tourists. I'm half Irish and half Javanese. They make bets about what I am. Whoever wins has to buy me a drink. Guess how old I am."

"God knows," said Mrs. Copperfield.

"Well, I'm sixteen."

"Very possible," said Mrs. Copperfield. The girl seemed peeved. They walked in silence to Bill Grey's restaurant, where the girl pushed Mrs. Copperfield through the door and along the floor towards a table in the middle of the restaurant.

"Sit down and order whatever you like. It's on me," said the girl.

There was an electric fan whirling above their heads.

"Isn't it delicious in here?" she said to Mrs. Copperfield.

"Let me make my phone call," said Mrs. Copperfield, who was terrified lest Mr. Copperfield should have come in a few hours ago and be waiting impatiently for her call even at this very moment.

"Make all the phone calls you like," said the girl.

Mrs. Copperfield went into the booth and phoned her husband. He said that he had arrived a short time ago, and that he would have breakfast and join her afterwards at Bill Grey's. He sounded cold and tired.

The girl, while waiting anxiously for her return, had ordered two old-fashioneds. Mrs. Copperfield came back to the table and flopped into her seat.

"I never can sleep late in the mornings," said the girl. "I don't even like to sleep at night if I have anything better to do. My mother told me that I was as nervous as a cat, but very healthy. I went to dancing school but I was too lazy to learn the steps."

"Where do you live?" asked Mrs. Copperfield.

"I live alone in a hotel. I've got plenty of money. A man in the Army is in love with me. He's married but I never go with anyone else. He gives me plenty of money.

He's even got more money at home. I'll buy you what you want. Don't tell anyone around here, though, that I've got money to spend on other people. I never buy them anything. They give me a pain. They live such terrible lives. So cheap; so stupid; so very stupid! They don't have any privacy. I have two rooms. You can use one of them if you like."

Mrs. Copperfield said she wouldn't need to, very firmly. She wasn't fond of this girl in the least.

"What is your name?" the girl asked her.

"Frieda Copperfield."

"My name is Peggy—Peggy Gladys. You looked kind of adorable to me with your hair all wet and your little nose as shiny as it was. That's why I asked you to drink with me."

Mrs. Copperfield jumped. "Please don't embarrass me," she said.

"Oh, let me embarrass you, adorable. Now finish your drink and I'll get you some more. Maybe you're hungry and would like some steak."

The girl had the bright eyes of an insatiable nymphomaniac. She wore a ridiculous little watch on a black ribbon around her wrist.

"I live at the Hotel de las Palmas," said Mrs. Copperfield. "I am a friend of the manager there, Mrs. Quill, and one of her guests, Pacifica."

"That's no good, that hotel," said Peggy. "I went in there with some fellows for drinks one night and I said to them: 'If you don't turn right around and leave this hotel, I'll never allow you to take me out again.' It's a cheap place; awful place; it's filthy dirty besides. I'm surprised at you living there. My hotel is much nicer. Some Americans stay there when they come off the boat if they don't go to the Hotel Washington. It's the Hotel Granada."

"Yes, that is where we were staying originally," said Mrs. Copperfield. "My husband is there now. I think it is the most depressing place I have ever set foot in. I think the Hotel de las Palmas is a hundred million times nicer."

"But," said the girl, opening her mouth wide in dismay, "I think you have not looked very carefully. I've put all my own things around in my room of course, and that makes a lot of difference."

"How long have you been living there?" asked Mrs. Copperfield. She was completely puzzled by this girl and a little bit sorry for her.

"I have been living there for a year and a half. It seems like a lifetime. I moved in a little while after I met the man in the Army. He's very nice to me. I think I'm smarter than he is. That's because I'm a girl. Mother told me that girls were never dumb like men, so I just go ahead and do whatever I think is right."

The girl's face was elfin and sweet. She had a cleft chin and a small snub-nose.

"Honestly," she said, "I've got lots of money. I can always get more. I'd love to get you anything you like, because I love the way you talk and look and the way you move; you're elegant." She giggled and put her own dry rough hand in Mrs. Copperfield's.

"Please," she said, "be friendly to me. I don't often see people I like. I never do the same thing twice, really I don't. I haven't asked anyone up to my rooms in the longest while because I'm not interested and because they get everything so dirty. I know you wouldn't get everything dirty because I can tell that you come from a nice class of people. I love people with a good education. I think it's wonderful."

"I have so much on my mind," said Mrs. Copperfield. "Generally I haven't."

"Well, forget it," said the young girl imperiously. "You're with Peggy Gladys and she's paying for your drinks. Because she wants to pay for your drinks with all her heart. It's such a beautiful morning. Cheer up!" She took Mrs. Copperfield by the sleeve and shook her.

Mrs. Copperfield was still deep in the magic of her dream and in thoughts of Pacifica. She was uneasy and the electric fan seemed to blow directly on her heart. She sat staring ahead of her, not listening to a word the girl was saying.

She could not tell how Iong she had been dreaming when she looked down and saw a lobster lying on a plate in front of her.

"Oh," she said, "I can't eat this. I can't possibly eat this."

"But I ordered it for you," said Peggy, "and there is some beer coming along. I had your old-fashioned taken away because you weren't touching it." She leaned across the table and tucked Mrs. Copperfield's napkin under her chin.

"Please eat, dearest," said Peggy, "you'll give me such great pleasure if you do."

"What do you think you're doing?" said Mrs. Copperfield fretfully. "Playing house?"

Peggy laughed.

"You know," said Mrs. Copperfield, "my husband is coming here to join us. He'll think we're both stark raving mad to be eating lobster in the morning. He doesn't understand such things."

"Well, let's eat it up quickly, then," said Peggy. She looked wistfully at Mrs. Copperfield. "I wish he wasn't coming," she said. "Couldn't you telephone him and tell him not to come?"

"No, my dear, that would be impossible. Besides, I don't have any reason to tell him not to come. I am very anxious to see him." Mrs. Copperfield could not resist being just a little bit sadistic with Peggy Gladys.

"Of course you want to see him," said Peggy, looking very shy and demure. "I'll be quiet while he's here, I'll promise you."

"That's just what I don't want you to do. Please continue to prattle when he's here."

"Of course, darling. Don't be so nervous."

Mr. Copperfield arrived as they were eating their lobster. He was wearing a dark green suit and looking extremely well. He came over to them smiling pleasantly.

"Hello," said Mrs. Copperfield. "I'm very glad to see you. You look very well. This is Peggy Gladys; we've just met."

He shook hands with her and seemed very pleased. "What on earth are you eating?" he asked them.

"Lobster," they answered. He frowned. "But," he said, "you'll have indigestion, and you're drinking beer too! Good God!" He sat down.

"I don't mean to interfere, of course," said Mr. Copperfield, "but it's very bad. Have you had breakfast?"

"I don't know," said Mrs. Copperfield purposely. Peggy Gladys laughed. Mr. Copperfield raised his brows.

"You must know," he murmured. "Don't be ridiculous." He asked Peggy Gladys where she was from.

"I'm from Panama," she told him, "but I'm half Irish and half Javanese."

"I see," said Mr. Copperfield. He kept smiling at her. "Pacifica's asleep," said Mrs. Copperfield suddenly.

Mr. Copperfield frowned. "Really," he said, "are you going back there?"

"What do you think I'm going to do?"

"There isn't any point in staying here much longer. I thought we'd pack. I've made arrangements in Panama. We can sail tomorrow. I have to phone them tonight. I've found out a lot about the various countries in Central America. It might be possible for us to stay on a kind of cattle ranch in Costa Rica. A man told me about it. It's completely isolated. You have to get there on a river boat."

Peggy Gladys looked bored.

Mrs. Copperfield put her head in her hands.

"Imagine red and blue guacamayos flying over the cattle," Mr. Copperfield laughed. "Latin Texas. It must be completely crazy."

"Red and blue guacamayos flying over the cattle,"

Peggy Gladys repeated after him. "What are guacamayos?" she asked.

"They're tremendous red and blue birds, more or less like parrots," said Mr. Copperfield. "As long as you are eating lobster I think I shall have ice cream with whipped cream on top."

"He's nice," said Peggy Gladys.

"Listen," said Mrs. Copperfield, "I feel sick. I don't think I can sit through the ice cream."

"I won't take long," said Mr. Copperfield. He looked at her. "It must be the lobster."

"Maybe I'd better take her to my Hotel Granada," said Peggy Gladys, jumping to her feet with alacrity. "She'll be very comfortable there. Then you can come after you've eaten your ice cream."

"That seems sensible, don't you think so, Frieda?"

"No," said Mrs. Copperfield vehemently, clutching at the chain she wore around her neck. "I think I'd better go right straight back to the Hotel de las Palmas. I *must* go. I must go immediately . . ." She was so distraught that she rose from the table, forgetting her pocketbook and her scarf, and started to leave the restaurant.

"But you've left everything behind you," Mr. Copperfield called out after her.

"I'll take them," exclaimed Peggy Gladys. "You eat your ice cream and come later." She rushed after Mrs. Copperfield and together they ran down the suffocatingly hot street towards the Hotel de las Palmas.

Mrs. Quill was standing in the doorway drinking something out of a bottle.

"I'm on the cherry-pop wagon until dinner time," she said.

"Oh, Mrs. Quill, come up to my room with me!" said Mrs. Copperfield, putting her arms around Mrs. Quill and sighing deeply. "Mr. Copperfield is back."

"Why don't you come upstairs with me?" said Peggy Gladys. "I promised your husband I'd take care of you."

Mrs. Copperfield wheeled round. "Please be quiet," she shouted, looking fixedly at Peggy Gladys.

"Now, now," said Mrs. Quill, "don't upset the little girl. We'll have to be giving her a honey bun to quiet her. Of course it took more than a honey bun to quiet me at her age."

"I'm all right," said Peggy Gladys. "Will you kindly take us to her room? She's supposed to be flat on her back."

The young girl sat on the edge of Mrs. Copperfield's bed with her hand on Mrs. Copperfield's forehead.

"I'm sorry," she said. "You look very badly. I wish you wouldn't be so unhappy. Couldn't you possibly not think about it now and think about it some other day? Sometimes if you let things rest . . . I'm not sixteen, I'm seventeen. I feel like a child. I can't seem to say anything unless people think I'm very young. Maybe you don't like the fact that I'm so fresh. You're white and green. You don't look pretty. You looked much prettier before. After your husband has been here I'll take you for a ride in a carriage if you like. My mother's dead," she said softly.

"Listen," said Mrs. Copperfield. "If you don't mind going away now . . . I'd like to be by myself. You can come back later."

"What time can I come back?"

"I don't know; come back later; can't you see? I don't know."

"All right," said Peggy Gladys. "Maybe I should just go downstairs and talk to that fat woman, or drink. Then when you're ready you can come down. I have nothing to do for three days. You really want me to go?"

Mrs. Copperfield nodded.

The girl left the room reluctantly.

Mrs. Copperfield started to tremble after the girl had closed the door behind her. She trembled so violently that she shook the bed. She was suffering as much as she had ever suffered before, because she was going to do what she wanted to do. But it would not make her happy. She did not have the courage to stop from doing what she wanted to do. She knew that it would not make her happy, because only the dreams of crazy people come true. She thought that she was only interested in duplicating a dream, but in doing so she necessarily became the complete victim of a nightmare.

Mr. Copperfield came very quietly into her room. "How do you feel now?" he asked.

"I'm all right," she said.

"Who was that young girl? She was very pretty—from a sculptural point of view."

"Her name is Peggy Gladys."

"She spoke very well, didn't she? Or am I wrong?"

"She spoke beautifully."

"Have you been having a nice time?"

"I've had the most wonderful time in my whole life," said Mrs. Copperfield, almost weeping.

"I had a nice time too, exploring Panama City. But my room was so uncomfortable. There was too much noise. I couldn't sleep."

"Why didn't you take a nicer room in a better hotel?"

"You know me. I hate to spend money. I never think it's worth it. I guess I should have. I should have been drinking too. I'd have had a better time. But I didn't."

They were silent. Mr. Copperfield drummed on the bureau. "I guess we should be leaving tonight," he said, "instead of staying on here. It's terribly expensive here. There won't be another boat for quite a few days."

Mrs. Copperfield did not answer.

"Don't you think I'm correct?"

"I don't want to go," she said, twisting on the bed.

"I don't understand," said Mr. Copperfield.

"I can't go. I want to stay here."

"For how long?"

"I don't know."

"But you can't plan a trip that way. Perhaps you don't intend to plan a trip."

"Oh, I'll plan a trip," said Mrs. Copperfield vaguely.

"You will?"

"No, I won't."

"It's up to you," said Mr. Copperfield. "I just think you'll be missing a great deal by not seeing Central America. You're certain to get bored here unless you start to drink. You probably will start to drink."

"Why don't you go, and then come back when you've seen enough?" she suggested.

"I won't come back because I can't look at you," said Mr. Copperfield. "You're a horror." So saying, he took an empty pitcher from the bureau, threw it out of the window into the alley, and left the room.

An hour later Mrs. Copperfield went downstairs into the bar. She was surprised and glad to see Pacifica there. Although Pacifica had powdered her face very heavily, she looked tired. She was sitting at a little table holding her pocketbook in her hands.

"Pacifica," said Mrs. Copperfield, "I didn't know that you were awake. I was certain that you were asleep in your room. I'm so glad to see you."

"I could not close my eyes. I was sleeping for fifteen minutes and then after that I could not close my eyes. Someone came to see me."

Peggy Gladys walked over to Mrs. Copperfield. "Hello," she said, running her fingers through Mrs. Copperfield's hair. "Are you ready to take that ride yet?"

"What ride?" asked Mrs. Copperfield.

"The ride in the carriage with me."

"No, I'm not ready," said Mrs. Copperfield.

"When will you be?" asked Peggy Gladys.

"I'm going to buy some stockings," said Pacifica. "You want to come with me, Copperfield?"

"Yes. Let's go."

"Your husband looked upset when he left the hotel," said Peggy Gladys. "I hope you didn't have a fight."

Mrs. Copperfield was walking out of the door with Pacifica. "Excuse us," she called over her shoulder to Peggy Gladys. She was standing still and looking after them like a hurt animal!

It was so hot out that even the most conservative women tourists, their faces and chests flame-red, were pulling off their hats and drying their foreheads with their handkerchiefs. Most of them, to escape the heat, were dropping into the little Hindu stores where, if the shop wasn't too crowded, the salesman offered them a little chair so that they might view twenty or thirty kimonos without getting tired.

"*Qué calor!*" said Pacifica.

"To hell with stockings," said Mrs. Copperfield, who thought she was about to faint. "Let's get some beer."

"If you want, go and get yourself some beer. I must have stockings. I think bare legs on a woman is something terrible."

"No, I'll come with you." Mrs. Copperfield put her hand in Pacifica's.

"Ay!" cried Pacifica, releasing her hand. "We are both too wet, darling. *Qué barbaridad!*"

The store into which Pacifica took Mrs. Copperfield was very tiny. It was even hotter in there than on the street.

"You see you can buy many things here," said Pacifica. "I come here because he knows me and I can get my stockings for very little money."

While Pacifica was buying her stockings Mrs. Copperfield looked at all the other little articles in the store. Pacifica took such a long time that Mrs. Copperfield grew more and more bored. She stood first on one foot and then on the other. Pacifica argued and argued. There were dark perspiration stains under her arms, and the wings of her nose were streaming.

When it was all over and Mrs. Copperfield saw that the salesman was wrapping the package, she went over and paid the bill. The salesman wished her good luck and they left the store.

There was a letter for her at home. Mrs. Quill gave it to her.

"Mr. Copperfield left this for you," she said. "I tried to urge him to stay and have a cup of tea or some beer, but he was in a hurry. He's one handsome fellow."

Mrs. Copperfield took the letter and started towards the bar. "Hello, sweet," said Peggy Gladys softly.

Mrs. Copperfield could see that Peggy was very drunk. Her hair was hanging over her face and her eyes were dead.

"Maybe you're not ready yet . . . but I can wait a long time. I love to wait. I don't mind being by myself."

"You'll excuse me a minute if I read a letter which I just received from my husband," said Mrs. Copperfield.

She sat down and tore open the envelope.

Dear Frieda [she read],

I do not mean to be cruel but I shall write to you exactly what I consider to be your faults and I hope sincerely that what I have written will influence you. Like most people, you are not able to face more than one fear during your lifetime. You also spend your life fleeing from your first fear towards your first hope. Be careful that you do not, through your own wiliness, end up always in the same position in which you began. I do not advise you to spend your life surrounding yourself with those things which you term necessary to your existence, regardless of whether or not they are objectively interesting in themselves or even to your own particular intellect. I believe sincerely that only those men who reach the stage where it is possible for them to combat a second tragedy within themselves, and not the first over again, are worthy of being called mature. When you think someone is going ahead, make sure that he is not really standing still. In order to go ahead, you must leave things behind which most people are unwilling to do. Your first pain, you carry it with you like a lodestone in your breast because all tenderness will come from there. You must carry it with you through your whole life but you must not circle around it. You must give up the search for those symbols which only serve to hide its face from you. You will have the illusion that they are disparate and manifold but they are always the same. If you are only interested in a bearable life, perhaps this letter does not concern you. For God's sake, a ship leaving port is still a wonderful thing to see.

J.C.

Mrs. Copperfield's heart was beating very quickly. She crushed the letter in her hand and shook her head two or three times.

"I'll never bother you unless you ask me to bother you," Peggy Gladys was saying. She did not seem to be addressing anyone in particular. Her eyes wandered from the ceiling to the walls. She was smiling to herself.

"She is reading a letter from her husband," she said, letting her arm fall down heavily on the bar. "I myself don't want a husband—never—never—never . . ."

Mrs. Copperfield rose to her feet.

"*Pacifica*," she shouted, "*Pacifica!*"

"Who is Pacifica?" asked Peggy Gladys. "I want to meet her. Is she as beautiful as you are? Tell her to come here . . ."

"Beautiful?" the bartender laughed. "Beautiful? Neither of them is beautiful. They're both old hens. You're beautiful even if you are blind drunk."

"Bring her in here, darling," said Peggy Gladys, letting her head fall down on the bar.

"Listen, your pal's been out of the room two whole minutes already. She's gone to look for Pacifica."

3

IT WAS SEVERAL MONTHS LATER, and Miss Goering, Miss Gamelon, and Arnold had been living for nearly four weeks in the house which Miss Goering had chosen.

This was gloomier even than Miss Gamelon had expected it would be, since she hadn't much imagination, and reality was often more frightening to her than her wildest dreams. She was now more incensed against Miss Goering than she had been before they had changed houses, and her disposition was so bad that scarcely an hour went by that she did not complain bitterly about her life, or threaten to leave altogether. Behind the house was a dirt bank and some bushes, and if one walked over the bank and followed a narrow path through some more bushes, one soon came to the woods. To the right of the house was a field that was filled with daisies in the summertime. This field might have been quite pleasant to look at had there not been lying right in the middle of it the rusted engine of an old car. There was very little place to sit out of doors, since the front porch had rotted away, so they had, all three of them, got into the habit of sitting close by the kitchen door, where the house protected them from the wind. Miss Gamelon had been suffering from the cold ever since she had arrived. In fact, there was no central heating in the house: only a few little oil stoves, and although it was still only early fall, on certain days it was already quite chilly.

Arnold returned to his own home less and less frequently, and more and more often he took the little train and the ferry boat into the city from Miss Goering's house and then returned again after his work was done to have his dinner and sleep on the island.

Miss Goering never questioned his presence. He became more careless about his clothing, and three times in the last week he had neglected to go in to his office at all. Miss Gamelon had made a terrible fuss over this.

One day Arnold was resting upstairs in one of the little bedrooms directly under the roof and she and Miss Goering were seated in front of the kitchen door warming themselves in the afternoon sun.

"That slob upstairs," said Miss Gamelon, "is eventually going to give up going to the office at all. He's going to move in here completely and do nothing but eat and sleep. In another year he's going to be as big as an elephant and you won't be able to rid yourself of him. Thank the Lord I don't expect to be here then."

"Do you really think that he will be so very, very fat in one year?" said Miss Goering.

"I know it!" said Miss Gamelon. There was a sudden blast of wind which blew the kitchen door open. "Oh, I hate this," said Miss Gamelon vehemently, getting up from her seat to fix the door.

"Besides," she continued, "who ever heard of a man living together with two ladies in a house which does not even contain one extra bedroom, so that he is obliged to sleep fully clothed on the couch! It is enough to take one's appetite away, just to walk through the parlor and see him there at all hours of the day, eyes open or shut, with not a care in the world. Only a man who is a slob could be willing to live in such a way. He is even too lazy to court either of us, which is a most unnatural thing you must admit—if you have any conception at all of the male physical make-up. Of course he is not a man. He is an elephant."

"I don't think," said Miss Goering, "that he is as big as all that."

"Well, I told him to rest in my room because I couldn't stand seeing him on the couch any more. And as for you," she said to Miss Goering, "I think you are the most insensitive person that I have ever met in my life."

At the same time Miss Gamelon was really worried—although she scarcely admitted this to herself—that Miss Goering was losing her mind. Miss Goering seemed thinner and more nervous and she insisted on doing most of the housework all by herself. She was constantly cleaning the house and polishing the doorknobs and the silver; she tried in many small ways to make the house livable without buying any of the things which were needed to make it so; she had in these last few weeks suddenly developed an extreme avarice and drew only enough money from the bank to enable them to live in the simplest manner possible. At the same time she seemed to think nothing of paying for Arnold's food, as he scarcely ever offered to contribute anything to the upkeep of the house. It was true that he went on paying his own share in his family's apartment, which perhaps left him very little to pay for anything else. This made Miss Gamelon furious, because although she did not understand why it was necessary for Miss Goering to live on less than one tenth of her income, she had nevertheless adjusted herself to this tiny scale of living and was trying desperately to make the money stretch as far as possible.

They sat in silence for a few minutes. Miss Gamelon was thinking seriously about all these things when suddenly a bottle broke against her head, inundating her with perfume and making quite a deep cut just above her forehead. She started to bleed profusely and sat for a moment with her hands over her eyes.

"I didn't actually mean to draw blood," said Arnold leaning out of the window. "I just meant to give her a start."

Miss Goering, although she was beginning to regard Miss Gamelon more and more as the embodiment of evil, made a swift and compassionate gesture towards her friend.

"Oh, my dear, let me get you something to disinfect the cut with." She went into the house and passed Arnold in the hall. He was standing with his hand on the front door, unable to decide whether to stay in or go out. When Miss Goering came down again with the medicine, Arnold had disappeared.

It was near evening, and Miss Gamelon, with a bandaged head, was standing in front of the house. She could see the road between the trees, from where she was standing. Her face was very white and her eyes were swollen because she had been weeping bitterly. She was weeping because it was the first time in her life that anyone had ever struck her physically. The more she thought about it, the more serious it became in her mind, and while she stood in front of the house she was suddenly frightened for the first time in her life. How far she had traveled from her home! Twice she had begun to pack her bags and twice she had decided not to do so, only because she could not bring herself to leave Miss Goering, since in her own way, though she scarcely knew it herself, she was deeply attached to her. It was dark before Miss Gamelon went into the house.

Miss Goering was terribly upset because Arnold had not yet returned, although she did not care for him very much more than she had in the beginning. She, too, stood outside in the dark for nearly an hour because her anxiety was so great that she was unable to remain in the house.

While she was still outside, Miss Gamelon, seated in the parlor before an empty fireplace, felt that all of God's wrath had descended upon her own head. The world and the people in it had suddenly slipped beyond her comprehension and she felt in great danger of losing the whole world once and for all—a feeling that is difficult to explain.

Each time that she looked over her shoulder into the kitchen and saw Miss Goering's dark shape still standing in front of the door, her heart failed her a little more. Finally Miss Goering came in.

"Lucy!" she called. Her voice was very clear and a little higher than usual. "Lucy, let's go and find Arnold." She sat opposite Miss Gamelon, and her face looked extraordinarily bright.

Miss Gamelon said: "Certainly not."

"Well, after all," said Miss Goering, "he lives in my house." "Yes, that he does," said Miss Gamelon.

"And it is only right," said Miss Goering, "that people in the same house should look after each other. They always do, I think, don't they?"

"They're more careful about who gets under the same roof with them," said Miss Gamelon, coming to life again.

"I don't think so, really," said Miss Goering. Miss Gamelon breathed a deep sigh and got up. "Never mind," she said, "soon I'll be in the midst of real human beings again."

They started through the woods along a path which was a short cut to the nearest town, about twenty minutes from their house on foot. Miss Goering screeched at every strange noise and clutched at Miss Gamelon's sweater all the way. Miss Gamelon was sullen and suggested that they take the long way around on their way back.

At last they came out of the woods and walked a short stretch along the highway. On either side of the road were restaurants which catered mainly to automobilists. In one of these Miss Goering saw Arnold seated at a table near the window, eating a sandwich.

"There's Arnold," said Miss Goering. "Come along!" She took hold of Miss Gamelon's hand and almost skipped in the direction of the restaurant.

"It is really almost too good to be true," said Miss Gamelon; "he is eating again."

It was terribly hot inside. They removed their sweaters and went to sit with Arnold at his table.

"Good evening," said Arnold. "I didn't expect to see you here." This he said to Miss Goering. He avoided looking in the direction of Miss Gamelon.

"Well," said Miss Gamelon, "are you going to explain yourself?"

Arnold had just taken quite a large bite of his sandwich so that he was unable to answer her. But he did roll his eyes in her direction. It was impossible to tell with his cheeks so full whether or not he looked angry. Miss Gamelon was terribly annoyed at this, but Miss Goering sat smiling at them because she was glad to have them both with her again.

Finally Arnold swallowed his food.

"I don't have to explain myself," he said to Miss Gamelon, looking very grouchy indeed now that he had swallowed his food. "You owe a profound apology to me for hating me and telling Miss Goering about it."

"I have a perfect right to hate whom I please," said Miss Gamelon, "and also, since we live in a free country, I can talk about it on the street corner if I want to."

"You don't know me well enough to hate me. You've misjudged me anyway, which is enough to make any man furious, and I *am* furious."

"Well then, get out of the house. Nobody wants you there anyway."

"That's incorrect; Miss Goering, I am sure, wants me there, don't you?"

"Yes, Arnold, of course," said Miss Goering.

"There is no justice," said Miss Gamelon; "you are both outrageous." She sat up very straight, and both Arnold and Miss Goering stared at her bandage.

"Well," said Arnold, wiping his mouth and pushing his plate away, "I am sure there is some way whereby we can arrange it so we can both live in the house together."

"Why are you so attached to the house?" screamed Miss Gamelon. "All you ever do when you're in it is to stretch out in the parlor and go to sleep."

"The house gives me a certain feeling of freedom."

Miss Gamelon looked at him.

"You mean an opportunity to indulge your laziness."

"Now look," said Arnold, "suppose that I am allowed to use the parlor after dinner and in the morning. Then you can use it the rest of the time."

"All right," said Miss Gamelon, "I agree, but see that you don't set your foot in it during the entire afternoon."

On the way home both Miss Gamelon and Arnold seemed quite contented because they had evolved a plan. Each one thought he had got the better of the bargain and Miss Gamelon was already outlining to herself several pleasant ways of spending an afternoon in the parlor.

When they arrived home she went upstairs to bed almost immediately. Arnold lay on the couch, fully dressed, and pulled a knitted coverlet over him. Miss Goering was sitting in the kitchen. After a little while she heard someone sobbing in the parlor. She went inside and found Arnold crying into his sleeve.

"What's the matter, Arnold?"

"I don't know," said Arnold, "it's so disagreeable to have someone hate you. I really think I had perhaps better leave and go back to my house. But I dislike doing that more than anything in the world and I hate the real-estate business and I hate for her to be angry with me. Can't you tell her it's just a period of adjustment for me—to please wait a little bit?"

"Certainly, Arnold, I shall tell her that the very first thing in the morning. Maybe if you went to business tomorrow, she might feel better about you."

"Do you think so?" asked Arnold, sitting bolt upright in his eagerness. "Then I will." He got up and stood by the window with his feet wide apart. "I just can't stand to have anyone hate me during this period of adjustment," he said, "and then of course I'm devoted to you both."

The next evening, when Arnold came home with a box of chocolates apiece for Miss Goering and Miss Gamelon, he was surprised to find his father there. He was sitting in a straight-backed chair next to the fireplace, drinking a cup of tea, and he had on a motoring cap.

"I came out to see, Arnold, how well you were providing for these young ladies. They seem to be living in a dung-heap here."

"I don't see where you have any right to say such a thing as a guest, Father," said Arnold, gravely handing a box of candy to each of the women.

"Certainly, because of age, my dear son, I am allowed to say a great many things. Remember you are all my children to me, including Princess over here." He hooked Miss Goering's waist with the top of his cane and drew her over to him. She had never imagined she would see him in such a rollicking good humor. He looked to her smaller and thinner than on the night they had met.

"Well, where do you crazy bugs eat?" he asked them.

"We have a square table," said Miss Gamelon, "in the kitchen. Sometimes we put it in front of the fireplace, but it's never very adequate."

Arnold's father cleared his throat and said nothing. He seemed to be annoyed that Miss Gamelon had spoken.

"Well, you're all crazy," he said, looking at his son and at Miss Goering, and purposely excluding Miss Gamelon, "but I'm rooting for you."

"Where is your wife?" Miss Goering asked him.

"She's at home, I gather," said Arnold's father, "and as sour as a pickle and just as bitter to taste."

Miss Gamelon giggled at his remark. It was the kind of thing that she found amusing. Arnold was delighted to see that she was brightening up a bit.

"Come out with me," said Arnold's father to Miss Goering, "into the wind and the sunshine, my love, or shall I say into the wind and the moonlight, never forgetting to add 'my love.' "

They left the room together and Arnold's father led Miss Goering a little way into the field.

"You see," he said, "I've decided to go back to a number of my boyish tastes. For instance, I took a certain delight in nature when I was young. I can frankly say that I have decided to throw away some of my conventions and ideals and again get a kick out of nature—that is, of course if you are willing to be by my side. It all depends on that."

"Certainly," said Miss Goering, "but what does this involve?"

"It involves," said Arnold's father, "your being a true woman. Sympathetic and willing to defend all that I say and do. At the same time prone to scolding me just a little." He put his ice-cold hand in hers.

"Let's go in," said Miss Goering. "I want to go inside." She began tugging at his arm, but he would not move. She realized that although he looked terribly old-fashioned and a little ridiculous in his motoring cap, he was still very strong. She wondered why he had seemed so much more distinguished the first night that they had met.

She tugged at his arm even harder, half in play, half in earnest, and in so doing she quite unwittingly scratched the inside of his wrist with her nail. She drew a little blood, which seemed to upset Arnold's father quite a lot, because he began stumbling through the field as quickly as he could towards the house.

Later he announced to everyone his intention of staying the night in Miss Goering's house. They had lighted a fire and they were all seated around it together. Twice Arnold had fallen asleep.

"Mother would be terribly worried," said Arnold.

"Worried?" said Arnold's father. "She will probably die of a heart attack before morning, but then, what is life but a puff of smoke or a leaf or a candle soon burned out anyway?"

"Don't pretend you don't take life seriously," said Arnold, "and don't pretend, just because there are women around, that you are light-hearted. You're the grim, worrying type and you know it."

Arnold's father coughed. He looked a little upset.

"I don't agree with you," he said.

Miss Goering took him upstairs to her own bedroom.

"I hope you will sleep in peace," she said to him. "You know that I'm delighted to have you in my house any time."

Arnold's father pointed to the trees outside the window.

"Oh, night!" he said. "Soft as a maiden's cheek, and as mysterious as the brooding owl, the Orient, the turbaned sultan's head. How long have I ignored thee underneath my reading lamp, occupied with various and sundry occupations which I have now decided to disregard in favor of thee. Accept my apology and let me be numbered among thy sons and daughters. You see," he said to Miss Goering, "you see what a new leaf I have really turned over; I think we understand each other now. You mustn't ever think people have only one nature. Everything I said to you the other night was wrong."

"Oh," said Miss Goering, a little dismayed.

"Yes, I am now interested in being an entirely new personality as different from my former self as A is from Z. This has been a very lovely beginning. It augurs well, as they say."

He stretched out on the bed, and while Miss Goering was looking at him he fell asleep. Soon he began to snore. She threw a cover over him and left the room, deeply perplexed.

Downstairs she joined the others in front of the fire. They were drinking hot tea into which they had poured a bit of rum.

Miss Gamelon was relaxing. "This is the best thing in the world for your nerves," she said, "and also for softening the sharp angles of your life. Arnold has been telling me about his progress in his uncle's office. How he started as a messenger and has now worked his way up to being one of the chief agents in the office. We've had an extremely pleasant time just sitting here. I think Arnold has been hiding from us a very excellent business sense."

Arnold looked a little distressed. He was still fearful of displeasing Miss Goering.

"Miss Gamelon and I are going to inquire tomorrow whether or not there is a golf course on the island. We have discovered a mutual interest in golf," he said.

Miss Goering could not understand Arnold's sudden change of attitude. It was as though he had just arrived at a summer hotel and was anxious to plan a nice vacation. Miss Gamelon also surprised her somewhat, but she said nothing.

"Golf would be wonderful for you," said Miss Gamelon to Miss Goering; "probably would straighten you out in a week."

"Well," said Arnold apologetically, "she might not like it."

"I don't like sports," said Miss Goering; "more than anything else, they give me a terrific feeling of sinning."

"On the contrary," said Miss Gamelon, "that's exactly what they never do."

"Don't be rude, Lucy dear," said Miss Goering. "After all, I have paid sufficient attention to what happens inside of me and I know better than you about my own feelings."

"Sports," said Miss Gamelon, "can never give you a feeling of sinning, but what is more interesting is that you can never sit down for more than five minutes without introducing something weird into the conversation. I certainly think you have made a study of it."

THE NEXT MORNING Arnold's father came downstairs with his shirt collar open and without a vest. He had rumpled his hair up a bit so that now he looked like an old artist.

"What on earth is Mother going to do?" Arnold asked him at breakfast.

"Fiddlesticks!" said Arnold's father. "You call yourself an artist and you don't even know how to be irresponsible. The beauty of the artist lies in the childlike soul." He touched Miss Goering's hand with his own. She could not help thinking of the speech he had made the night he had come into her bedroom and how opposed it had been to everything he was now saying.

"If your mother has a desire to live, she will live, providing she is willing to leave everything behind her as I have done," he added.

Miss Gamelon was slightly embarrassed by this elderly man who seemed to have just recently made some momentous change in his life. But she was not really curious about him.

"Well," said Arnold, "I imagine you are still providing her with money to pay the rent. I am continuing to contribute my share."

"Certainly," said his father. "I am always a gentleman, although I must say the responsibility weighs heavy on me, like an anchor around my neck. Now," he continued, "let me go out and do the marketing for the day. I feel able to run a hundred-yard dash."

Miss Gamelon sat with furrowed brow, wondering if Miss Goering would permit this crazy old man to live on in the already crowded house. He set out towards town a little while later. They called after him from the window, entreating him to return and put on his coat, but he waved his hand at the sky and refused.

In the afternoon Miss Goering did some serious thinking. She walked back and forth in front of the kitchen door. Already the house, to her, had become a friendly and familiar place and one which she readily thought of as her home. She decided that it was now necessary for her to take little trips to the tip of the island, where she could board the ferry and cross back over to the mainland. She hated to do this as she knew how upsetting it would be, and the more she considered it, the more attractive the life in the little house seemed to her, until she even thought of it as humming with gaiety. In order to assure herself that she would make her excursion that night, she went into her bedroom and put fifty cents on the bureau.

After dinner, when she announced that she was taking a train ride alone, Miss Gamelon nearly wept with indignation. Arnold's father said he thought it was a wonderful idea to take "a train ride into the blue," as he termed it. When Miss Gamelon heard him encouraging Miss Goering, she could no longer contain herself and rushed up into her bedroom. Arnold hastily left the table and lumbered up the steps after her.

Arnold's father begged Miss Goering to allow him to go with her.

"Not this time," she said, "I must go alone"; and Arnold's father, although he said he was very much disappointed, still remained elated. There seemed to be no end to his good humor.

"Well," he said, "setting out into the night like this is just in the spirit of what I'd like to do, and I think that you are cheating me prettily by not allowing me to accompany you."

"It is not for fun that I am going," said Miss Goering, "but because it is necessary to do so."

"Still, I beg you once more," said Arnold's father ignoring the implications of this remark and getting down on his knees with difficulty, "I beg you, take me with you."

"Oh, please, my dear," said Miss Goering, "please don't make it hard for me. I have a weakish personality."

Arnold's father jumped to his feet. "Certainly," he said, "I would not make anything hard for you." He kissed her wrist and wished her good luck. "Do you think the two turtle doves will talk to me?" he asked her, "or do you think they will remain cooped up together all night? I rather hate to be alone."

"So do I," said Miss Goering. "Bang on their door; they'll talk to you. Good-by . . ."

Miss Goering decided to walk along the highway, as it was really too dark to walk through the woods at this hour. She had proposed this to herself as a stint, earlier in the afternoon, but had later decided that it was pure folly even to consider it. It was cold and windy out and she pulled her shawl closer around her. She continued to affect woolen shawls, although they had not been stylish for a good many years. Miss Goering looked up at the sky; she was looking for the stars and hoping very hard to see some. She stood still for a long time, but she could not decide whether it was a starlit night or not because even though she fixed her attention on the sky without once lowering her eyes, the stars seemed to appear and disappear so quickly that they were like visions of stars rather than like actual stars. She decided that this was only because the clouds were racing across the sky so quickly that the stars were obliterated one minute and visible the next. She continued on her way to the station.

When she arrived she was surprised to find that there were eight or nine children who had got there ahead of her. Each one carried a large blue and gold school banner. The children weren't saying much, but they were engaged in hopping heavily first on one foot and then on the other. Since they were doing this in unison, the little wooden platform shook abominably and Miss Goering wondered whether she had not better draw the attention of the children to this fact. Very shortly, however, the train pulled into the station and they all boarded it together. Miss Goering sat in a seat across the aisle from a middle-aged stout woman. She and Miss Goering were the only occupants of the car besides the children. Miss Goering looked at her with interest.

She was wearing gloves and a hat and she sat up very straight. In her right hand she held a long thin package which looked like a fly-swatter. The woman stared ahead of her and not a muscle in her face moved. There were some more packages that she had piled neatly on the seat next to her. Miss Goering looked at her and hoped that she, too, was going to the tip of the island. The train started to move and the woman put her free hand on top of the packages next to her so that they would not slide off the seat.

The children had mostly crowded into two seats and those who would have had to sit elsewhere preferred to stand around the already occupied seats. Soon they began to sing songs, which were all in praise of the school from which they had come. They did this so badly that it was almost too much for Miss Goering to bear. She got out of her seat and was so intent upon getting to the children quickly that she paid no attention to the lurching of the car and consequently in her hurry she tripped and fell headlong on the floor right next to where the children were singing.

She managed to get on her feet again although her chin was bleeding. She first asked the children to please stop their singing. They all stared at her. Then she pulled out a little lace handkerchief and started to mop the blood from her chin. Soon the train stopped and the children got off. Miss Goering went to the end of the car and filled a paper cup with water. She wondered nervously, as she mopped her chin in the dark passage, whether or not the lady with the fly-swatter would still be in the car. When she got back to her seat she saw with great relief that the lady was still there. She still held the fly-swatter, but she had turned her head to the left and was looking out at the little station platform.

"I don't think," said Miss Goering to herself, "that it would do any harm if I changed my seat and sat opposite her. After all, I suppose it's quite a natural thing for ladies to approach each other on a suburban train like this, particularly on such a small island."

She slid quietly into the seat opposite the woman and continued to occupy herself with her chin. The train had started again and the woman stared harder and harder out of the window in order to avoid Miss Goering's eye, for Miss Goering was a little disturbing to certain people. Perhaps because of her red and exalted face and her outlandish clothes.

"I'm delighted that the children have left," said Miss Goering; "now it is really pleasant on this train."

It began to rain and the woman pressed her forehead to the glass in order to stare more closely at the slanting drops on the window-pane. She did not answer Miss Goering. Miss Goering began again, for she was used to forcing people into conversation, her fears never having been of a social nature.

"Where are you going?" Miss Goering asked, first because she was really interested in knowing whether or not the woman was traveling to the tip of the island, and also because she thought it a rather disarming question. The woman studied her carefully.

"Home," she said in a flat voice.

"And do you live on this island?" Miss Goering asked her. "It's really enchanting," she added.

The woman did not answer, but instead she started to gather all her packages up in her arms.

"Where exactly do you live?" asked Miss Goering. The woman's eyes shifted about.

"Glensdale," she said hesitatingly, and Miss Goering, although she was not sensitive to slights, realized that the woman was lying to her. This pained her very much.

"Why do you lie to me?" she asked. "I assure you that I am a lady like yourself."

The woman by then had mustered her strength and seemed more sure of herself. She looked straight into Miss Goering's eyes.

"I live in Glensdale," she said, "and I have lived there all my life. I am on my way to visit a friend who lives in a town a little farther along."

"Why do I terrify you so?" Miss Goering asked her. "I would like to have talked to you."

"I won't stand for this another moment," the woman said, more to herself than to Miss Goering. "I have enough real grief in my life without having to encounter lunatics."

Suddenly she grabbed her umbrella and gave Miss Goering a smart rap on the ankles. She was quite red in the face and Miss Goering decided that in spite of her solid bourgeois appearance she was really hysterical, but since she had met many women like this before, she decided not to be surprised from now on at anything that the woman might do. The woman left her seat with all of her packages and her umbrella and walked down the aisle with difficulty. Soon she returned, followed by the conductor.

They stopped beside Miss Goering. The woman stood behind the conductor. The conductor, who was an old man, leaned way over Miss Goering so that he was nearly breathing in her face.

"You can't talk to anyone on these here trains," he said, "unless you know them." His voice sounded very mild to Miss Goering.

Then he looked over his shoulder at the woman, who still seemed annoyed but more calm.

"The next time," said the conductor, who really was at a loss for what to say, "the next time you're on this train, stay in your seat and don't molest anybody. If you want to know the time you can ask them without any to-do about it or you can just make a little signal with your hand and I'll be willing to answer all your questions." He straightened up and stood for a moment trying to think of something more to say. "Remember also," he added, "and tell this to your relatives and to your friends. Remember also that there are no dogs allowed on this train or people in masquerade costume unless they're all covered up with a big heavy coat; and no more hubbubs," he added, shaking a finger at her. He tipped his hat to the woman and went on his way.

A minute or two later the train stopped and the woman got off. Miss Goering looked anxiously out of the window for her, but she could see only the empty platform and some dark bushes. She held her hand over her heart and smiled to herself.

When she arrived at the tip of the island the rain had stopped and the stars were shining again intermittently. She had to walk down a long narrow boardwalk which served as a passage between the train and the landing pier of the ferry. Many of the boards were loose and Miss Goering had to be very careful where she was stepping. She sighed with impatience, because it seemed to her that as long as she was still on this boardwalk it was not certain that she would actually board the ferry. Now that she was approaching her destination she felt that the whole excursion could be made very quickly and that she would soon be back with Arnold and his father and Miss Gamelon.

The boardwalk was only lighted at intervals and there were long stretches which she had to cross in the dark. However, Miss Goering, usually so timorous, was not frightened in the least. She even felt a kind of elation, which is common in certain unbalanced but sanguine persons when they begin to approach the thing they fear. She became more agile in avoiding the loose boards, and even made little leaps around them. She could now see the landing dock at the end of the boardwalk. It was very brightly lighted and the municipality had erected a good-sized flagpole in the center of the platform. The flag was now wrapped around the pole in great folds, but Miss Goering could distinguish easily the red and white stripes and the stars. She was delighted to see the flag in this far-off place, for she hadn't imagined that there would be any organization at all on the tip of the island.

"Why, people have been living here for years," she said to herself. "It is strange that I hadn't thought of this before. They're here naturally, with their family ties, their neighborhood stores, their sense of decency and morality, and they have certainly their organizations for fighting the criminals of the community." She felt almost happy now that she had remembered all this.

She was the only person waiting for the ferry. Once she had got on, she went straight to the prow of the boat and stood watching the mainland until they reached the opposite shore. The ferry dock was at the foot of a road which joined the main street at the summit of a short steep hill. Trucks were still obliged to stop short at the top of the hill and unload their freight into wheelbarrows, which were then rolled cautiously down to the dock. Looking up from the dock, it was possible to see the side walls of the two stores at the end of the main street but not very much more. The road was so brightly lighted on either side that it was possible for Miss Goering to distinguish most of the details on the clothing of the persons who were coming down the hill to board the ferry.

She saw coming towards her three young women holding onto one another's arms and giggling. They were very fancily dressed and were trying to hold onto their hats as well as one another. This made their progress very slow, but half-way down the hill they called to someone on the dock who was standing near the post to which the ferry had been moored.

"Don't you leave without us, George," they yelled to him, and he waved his hand back in a friendly manner.

There were many young men coming down the hill and they too seemed to be dressed for something special. Their shoes were well shined, and many of them wore flowers in their buttonholes. Even those who had started long after the three young women quickly trotted past them. Each time this happened the girls would go into gales of laughter, which Miss Goering could hear only faintly from where she stood. More and more people kept appearing over the top of the hill and most of them, it seemed to Miss Goering, did not exceed the age of thirty.

She stepped to the side and soon they were talking and laughing together all over the foredeck and the bridge of the ferry. She was very curious to know where they were going, but her spirits had been considerably dampened by witnessing the exodus, which she took as a bad omen. She finally decided that she would question a young man who was still on the dock and standing not very far away from her.

"Young man," she said to him, "would you mind telling me if you are all actually going on some lark together in a group or if it's a coincidence?"

"We're all going to the same place," said the boy, "as far as I know."

"Well, could you tell me where that is?" asked Miss Goering.

"Pig Snout's Hook," he answered. Just then the ferry whistle blew. He hastily took leave of Miss Goering and ran to join his friends on the foredeck.

Miss Goering struggled up the hill entirely alone. She kept her eye on the wall of the last store on the main street. An advertising artist had painted in vivid pinks a baby's face of giant dimensions on half the surface of the wall, and in the remaining space a tremendous rubber nipple. Miss Goering wondered what Pig Snout's Hook was. She was rather disappointed when she arrived at the top of the hill to find that the main street was rather empty and dimly lighted. She had perhaps been misled by the brilliant colors of the advertisement of the baby's nipple and had half hoped that the entire town would be similarly garish.

Before proceeding down the main street she decided to examine the painted sign more closely. In order to do this she had to step across an empty lot. Very near to the advertisement she noticed that an old man was bending over some crates and trying to wrench the nails loose from the boards. She decided that she would ask him whether or not he knew where Pig Snout's Hook was.

She approached him and stood watching for a little while before asking her question. He was wearing a green plaid jacket and a little cap of the same material. He was terribly busy trying to pry a nail from the crate with only a thin stick as a tool.

"I beg your pardon," said Miss Goering to him finally, "but I would like to know where Pig Snout's Hook is and also why anyone would go there, if you know."

The man continued to bother with the nail, but Miss Goering could tell that he was really interested in her question.

"Pig Snout's Hook?" said the man. "That's easy. It's a new place, a cabaret."

"Does everyone go there?" Miss Goering asked him.

"If they are the kind who are fools, they go."

"Why do you say that?"

"Why do I say that?" said the man, getting up finally and putting his stick in his pocket. "Why do I say that? Because they go there for the pleasure of being cheated out of their last penny. The meat is just horsemeat, you know. This size and it ain't red. It's a kind of gray, without a sign of a potato near it, and it costs plenty too. They're all as poor as church mice besides, without a single ounce of knowledge about life in the whole crowd of them. Like a lot of dogs straining at the leash."

"And then they all go together to Pig Snout's Hook every single night?"

"I don't know when they go to Pig Snout's Hook," said the man, "any more than I know what cockroaches are doing every night."

"Well, what's so wrong about Pig Snout's Hook?" Miss Goering asked him.

"There's one thing wrong," said the man growing more and more interested, "and that's that they've got a nigger there that jumps up and down in front of a mirror in his room all day long until he sweats and then he does the same thing in front of these lads and lassies and they think he's playing them music. He's got an expensive instrument all right, because I know where he bought it and I'm not saying whether or not he paid for it, but I know he sticks it in his mouth and then starts moving around with his long arms like the arms of a spider and they just won't listen to nothin' else but him."

"Well," said Miss Goering, "certain people do like that type of music."

"Yes," said the man, "certain people do like that type of music and there are people who live together and eat at table together stark naked all the year long and there are others who we both know about"—he looked very mysterious—"but," he continued, "in my day money was worth a pound of sugar or butter or lard any time. When we went out we got what we paid for plus a dog jumpin' through burning hoops, and steaks you could rest your chin on."

"What do you mean?" asked Miss Goering—"a dog jumping through burning hoops?"

"Well," said the man, "you can train them to do anything with years of real patience and perseverance and lots of headaches too. You get a hoop and you light it all around and these poodles, if they're the real thing, will leap through them like birds flying in the air. Of course it's a rare thing to see them doing this, but they've been right here in this town flying right through the centers of burning hoops. Of course people were older then and they cared for their money better and they didn't want to see a black jumping up and down. They would rather prefer to put a new roof on their house." He laughed.

"Well," said Miss Goering, "did this go on in a cabaret that was situated where the Pig Snout's Hook place is now situated? You understand what I mean."

"It surely didn't!" said the man vehemently. "The place was situated right on this side of the river in a real theater with three different prices for the seats and a show every night and three times a week in the afternoon."

"Well, then," said Miss Goering, "that's quite a different thing isn't it? Because, after all, Pig Snout's Hook is a cabaret, as you said yourself a little while ago, and this place where the poodles jumped through the burning hoops was a theater, so in actuality there is really no point of comparison."

The old man knelt down again and continued to pry the nails from the boards by placing his little stick between the head of the nail and the wood.

Miss Goering did not know what to say to him, but she felt that it was pleasanter to go on talking than to start off down the main street alone. She could tell that he was a little annoyed, so that she was prepared to ask her next question in a considerably softer voice.

"Tell me," she said to him, "is that place at all dangerous, or is it merely a waste of time."

"Surely, it's as dangerous as you want," said the old man immediately, and his ill humor seemed to have passed. "Certainly it's dangerous. There are some Italians running it and the place is surrounded by fields and woods." He looked at her as if to say: "That is all you need to know, isn't it?"

Miss Goering for an instant felt that he was an authority and she in turn looked into his eyes very seriously. "But can't you," she asked, "can't you tell very easily whether or not they have all returned safely? After all, you have only if necessary to stand at the top of the hill and watch them disembark from the ferry." The old man picked up his stick once more and took Miss Goering by the arm.

"Come with me," he said, "and be convinced once and for all." He took her to the edge of the hill and they looked down the brightly lighted street that led to the dock. The ferry was not there, but the man who sold the tickets was clearly visible in his booth, and the rope with which they moored the ferry to the post, and even the opposite shore. Miss Goering took in the entire scene with a clear eye and waited anxiously for what the old man was about to say.

"Well," said the old man, lifting his arm and making a vague gesture which included the river and the sky, "you can see where it is impossible to know anything." Miss Goering looked around her and it seemed to her that there could be nothing hidden from their eyes, but at the same time she believed what the old man said to her. She felt both ashamed and uneasy.

"Come along," said Miss Goering, "I'll invite you to a beer."

"Thank you very much, ma'am," said the old man. His tone had changed to that of a servant, and Miss Goering felt even more ashamed of having believed what he had told her.

"Is there any particular place that you would like to go?" she asked him.

"No, ma'am," he said, shuffling along beside her. He no longer seemed in the least inclined to talk.

There was no one walking along the main street except Miss Goering and the old man. They did pass a car parked in front of a dark store. Two people were smoking on the front seat.

The old man stopped in front of the window of a bar and grill and stood looking at some turkey and some old sausages which were on display.

"Shall we go in here and have something to eat with our little drink?" Miss Goering asked him.

"I'm not hungry," the man said, "but I'll go in with you and sit down."

Miss Goering was disappointed because he didn't seem to have any sense of how to give even the slightest festive air to the evening. The bar was dark, but festooned here and there with crepe paper. "In honor of some recent holiday, no doubt," thought Miss Goering. There was a particularly nice garland of bright green paper flowers strung up along the entire length of the mirror behind the bar. The room was furnished with eight or nine tables, each one enclosed in a dark brown booth.

Miss Goering and the old man seated themselves at the bar.

"By the way," said the old man to her, "wouldn't you like better to seat yourself at a table where you ain't so much in view?"

"No," said Miss Goering, "I think this is very, very pleasant indeed. Now order what you want, will you?"

"I will have," said the man, "a sandwich of turkey and a sandwich of pork, a cup of coffee, and a drink of rye whisky."

"What a curious psychology!" thought Miss Goering. "I should think he would be embarrassed after just having finished saying that he wasn't hungry."

She looked over her shoulder out of curiosity and noticed that behind her in a booth were seated a boy and a girl. The boy was reading a newspaper. He was drinking nothing. The girl was sipping at a very nice cherry-colored drink through a straw. Miss Goering ordered herself two gins in succession, and when she had finished these she turned around and looked at the girl again. The girl seemed to have been expecting this because she already had her face turned in Miss Goering's direction. She smiled softly at Miss Goering and opened her eyes wide. They were very dark. The whites of her eyes, Miss Goering noticed, were shot with yellow. Her hair was black and wiry and stood way out all over her head.

"Jewish, Rumanian, or Italian," Miss Goering said to herself. The boy did not lift his eyes from his newspaper, which he held in such a way that his profile was hidden.

"Having a nice time?" the girl asked Miss Goering in a husky voice.

"Well," said Miss Goering, "it wasn't exactly in order to have a good time that I came out. I have more or less forced myself to, simply because I despise going out in the night-time alone and prefer not to leave my own house. However, it has come to such a point that I am forcing myself to make these little excursions—"

Miss Goering stopped because she actually did not know how she could go on and explain to this girl what she meant without talking a very long time indeed, and she realized that this would be impossible right at that moment, since the waiter was constantly walking back and forth between the bar and the young people's booth.

"Anyway," said Miss Goering, "I certainly think it does no harm to relax a bit and have a lovely time."

"Everyone must have a wonderfully marvelous time," said the girl, and Miss Goering noticed that there was a trace of an accent in her speech. "Isn't that true, my angel Pussycat?" she said to the boy.

The boy put his newspaper down; he looked rather annoyed. "Isn't what true?" he asked her. "I didn't hear a word that you said." Miss Goering knew perfectly well that this was a lie and that he was only pretending not to have noticed that his girl friend had been speaking with her.

"Nothing very important, really," she said, looking tenderly into his eyes. "This lady here was saying that after all it did nobody any harm to relax and have a lovely time."

"Perhaps," said the boy, "it does more harm than anything else to date to have a lovely time." He said this straight to the girl and completely ignored the fact that Miss Goering had been mentioned at all. The girl leaned way over and whispered into his ear.

"Darling," she said, "something terrible has happened to that woman. I feel it in my heart. Please don't be bad-tempered with her."

"With whom?" the boy asked her.

She laughed because she knew there was nothing else much that she could do. The boy was subject to bad moods, but she loved him and was able to put up with almost anything.

The old man who had come with Miss Goering had excused himself and had taken his drinks and sandwiches over to a radio, where he was now standing with his ear close to the box.

Away in the back of the room a man was bowling up a small alley all by himself; Miss Goering listened to the rumble of the balls as they rolled along the wooden runway, and she wished that she were able to see him so that she could be at peace for the evening with the certainty that there was no one who could be considered a menace present in the room. Certainly there was a possibility that more clients would enter through the door, but this had entirely slipped her mind. Hard though she tried, it was impossible for her to get a look at the man who was rolling the balls.

The young boy and the girl were having a fight. Miss Goering could tell by the sound of their voices. She listened to them carefully without turning her head.

"I don't see why," said the girl, "that you must be furious immediately just because I have mentioned that I always like to come in here and sit for a little while."

"There is absolutely no reason," said the boy, "why you should want to come in here and sit more than in any other place."

"Then why—then why do you come in?" the girl asked hesitantly.

"I don't know," said the boy; "maybe because it's the first thing we hit after we leave our room."

"No," said the girl, "there are other places. I wish you would just say that you liked it here; I don't know why, but it would make me so happy; we've been coming here for a long time."

"I'll be God-damned if I'll say it, and I'll be God-damned if I'll come here any more if you're going to invest this place with witches' powers."

"Oh, Pussycat," said the girl, and there was real anguish in her tone, "Pussycat, I am not talking about witches and their powers; not even thinking about them.

Only when I was a little girl. I should never have told you the story."

The boy shook his head back and forth; he was disgusted with her.

"For God's sake," he said, "that isn't anything near what I mean, Bernice."

"I do not understand *what* you mean," said Bernice. "Many people come into this place or some other place every night for years and years and without doing much but having a drink and talking to each other; it is only because it is like home to them. And we come here only because it is little by little becoming a home to us; a second home if you can call our little room a home; it is to me; I love it very much."

The boy groaned with discontent.

"And," she added, feeling that her words and her tone of voice could not help working a spell over the boy, "the tables and the chairs and the walls here have now become like the familiar faces of old friends."

"What old friends?" said the boy, scowling more and more furiously. "What old friends? To me this is just another shit-house where poor people imbibe spirits in order to forget the state of their income, which is non-existent."

He sat up very straight and glared at Bernice.

"I guess that is true, in a way," she said vaguely, "but I feel that there is something more."

"That's just the trouble."

Meanwhile Frank, the bartender, had been listening to Bernice's conversation with Dick. It was a dull night and the more he thought about what the boy had said, the angrier he felt. He decided to go over to the table and start a row.

"Come on, Dick," he said, grabbing him by the collar of his shirt. "If that's the way you feel about this place, get the hell out of here." He yanked him out of his seat and gave him a terrific shove so that Dick staggered a few steps and fell headlong over the bar.

"You big fat-head," Dick yelled at the bartender, lunging out at him. "You hunk of retrogressive lard. I'll push your white face in for you."

The two were now fighting very hard. Bernice was standing on the table and pulling at the shirts of the fighters in an attempt to separate them. She was able to reach them even when they were quite a distance from the table because the benches terminated in posts at either end, and by grabbing hold of one of them she could swing out over the heads of the fighters.

Miss Goering, from where she was now standing, could see the flesh above Bernice's stocking whenever she leaned particularly far out of her booth. This would not have troubled her so much had she not noticed that the man who had been rolling the wooden balls had now moved away from his post and was staring quite fixedly at Bernice's bare flesh wherever the occasion presented itself. The man had a narrow red face, a pinched and somewhat inflamed nose, and very thin lips. His hair was almost orange in color. Miss Goering could not decide whether he was of an exceedingly upright character or of a criminal nature, but the intensity of his attitude almost scared her to death. Nor was it even possible for Miss Goering to decide whether he was looking at Bernice with interest or with scorn.

Although he was getting in some good punches and his face was streaming with sweat, Frank the bartender appeared to be very calm and it seemed to Miss Goering that he was losing interest in the fight and that actually the only really tense person in the room was the man who was standing behind her.

Soon Frank had a split lip and Dick a bloody nose. Very shortly after this they both stopped fighting and walked unsteadily towards the washroom. Bernice jumped off the table and ran after them.

They returned in a few minutes, all washed and combed and holding dirty handkerchiefs to their mouths. Miss Goering walked up to them and took hold of each man by the arm.

"I'm glad that it's all over now, and I want each of you to have a drink as my guest."

Dick looked very sad now and very subdued. He nodded his head solemnly and they sat down together and waited for Frank to fix them their drinks. He returned with their drinks, and after he had served them, he too seated himself at the table. They all drank in silence for a little while. Frank was dreamy and seemed to be thinking of very personal things that had nothing to do with the events of the evening. Once he took out an address book and looked through its pages several times. It was Miss Goering who first broke the silence.

"Now tell me," she said to Bernice and Dick," "tell me what you are interested in."

"I'm interested in the political struggle," said Dick, "which is of course the only thing that any self-respecting human being could be interested in. I am also on the winning side and on the right side. The side that believes in the redistribution of capital." He chuckled to himself and it was very easy to tell that he thought he was conversing with a complete fool.

"I've heard all about that," said Miss Goering. "And what are you interested in?" she asked the girl.

"Anything he is interested in, but it is true that I had believed the political struggle was very important before I met him. You see, I have a different nature than he has. What makes me happy I seem to catch out of the sky with both hands; I only hold whatever it is that I love because that is all I can really see. The world interferes with me and my happiness, but I never interfere with the world except now since I am with Dick." Bernice put her hand out on the table for Dick to take hold of it. She was already a little drunk.

"It makes me sad to hear you talk like this," said Dick. "You, as a leftist, know perfectly well that before we fight for our own happiness we must fight for something else. We are living in a period when personal happiness means very little because the individual has very few moments left. It is wise to destroy yourself first; at least to keep only that part of you which can be of use to a big group of people. If you don't do this you lose sight of objective reality and so forth, and you fall plunk into the middle of a mysticism which right now would be a waste of time."

"You are right, darling Dickie," said Bernice, "but sometimes I would love to be waited on in a beautiful room. Sometimes I think it would be nice to be a bourgeois." (She said the word "bourgeois," Miss Goering noticed, as though she had just learned it.) Bernice continued: "I am such a human person. Even though I am poor I will miss the same things that they do, because sometimes at night the fact that they are sleeping in their houses with security, instead of making me angry, fills me with peace like a child who is scared at night likes to hear grown people talking down in the street. Don't you think there is some sense in what I say, Dickie?"

"None whatsoever!" said the boy. "We know perfectly well that it is this security of theirs that makes us cry out at night."

Miss Goering by now was very anxious to get into the conversation.

"You," she said to Dick, "are interested in winning a very correct and intelligent fight. I am far more interested in what is making this fight so hard to win."

"They have the power in their hands; they have the press and the means of production."

Miss Goering put her hand over the boy's mouth. He jumped. "This is very true," she said, "but isn't it very obvious that there is something else too that you are fighting? You are fighting their present position on this earth, to which they are all grimly attached. Our race, as you know, is not torpid. They are grim because they still believe the earth is flat and that they are likely to fall off it at any minute. That is why they hold on so hard to the middle. That is, to all the ideals by which they have always lived. You cannot confront men who are still fighting the dark and all the dragons, with a new future."

"Well, well," said Dick, "what should I do then?"

"Just remember," said Miss Goering, "that a revolution won is an adult who must kill his childhood once and for all."

"I'll remember," said Dick, sneering a bit at Miss Goering.

The man who had been rolling the balls was now standing at the bar.

"I better go see what Andy wants," said Frank. He had been whistling softly all through Miss Goering's conversation with Dick, but he seemed to have been listening nevertheless, because as he was leaving the table he turned to Miss Goering.

"I think that the earth is a very nice place to be living on," he said to her, "and I never felt that by going one step too far I was going to fall off it either. You can always do things two or three times on the earth and everybody's plenty patient till you get something right. First time wrong doesn't mean you're sunk."

"Well, I wasn't talking about anything like that," said Miss Goering.

"That's what you're talking about all right. Don't try to pussyfoot it out now. But I tell you it's perfectly all right as far as I'm concerned." He was looking with feeling into Miss Goering's eyes. "My life," he said, "is my own, whether it's a mongrel or a prince."

"What on earth is he talking about?" Miss Goering asked Bernice and Dick. "He seems to think I've insulted him."

"God knows!" said Dick. "At any rate I am sleepy. Bernice, let's go home."

While Dick was paying Frank at the bar, Bernice leaned over Miss Goering and whispered in her ear.

"You know, darling," she said, "he's not really like this when we are home together alone. He makes me really happy. He is a sweet boy and you should see the simple things that delight him when he is in his own room and not with strangers. Well"—she straightened up and seemed to be a little embarrassed at her own burst of confidence—"well, I am very glad indeed that I met you and I hope we did not give you too much of a rough time. I promise you that it has never happened before, because underneath, Dick is really like you and me, but he is in a very nervous state of mind. So you must forgive him."

"Certainly," said Miss Goering, "but I do not see what for."

"Well, good-by," said Bernice.

Miss Goering was far too embarrassed and shocked by what Bernice had said behind Dick's back to notice at first that she was now the only person in the barroom besides the man who had been rolling the wooden balls and the old man, who had by now fallen asleep with his head on the bar. When she did notice, however, she felt for one desolate moment that the whole thing had been prearranged and that although she had forced herself to take this little trip to the mainland, she had somehow at the same time been tricked into taking it by the powers above. She felt that she could not leave and that even if she tried, something would happen to interfere with her departure.

She noticed with a faint heart that the man had lifted his drink from the bar and was coming towards her. He stopped about a foot away from her table and stood holding his glass in mid-air.

"You will have a drink with me, won't you?" he asked her without looking particularly cordial.

"I'm sorry," said Frank from behind the bar, "but we're going to close up now. No more drinks served, I'm afraid."

Andy said nothing, but he went out the door and slammed it behind him. They could hear him walking up and down outside of the saloon.

"He's going to have his own way again," said Frank, "damn it all."

"Oh, dear," said Miss Goering, "are you afraid of him?"

"Sure I'm not," said Frank, "but he's disagreeable—that's the only word I can think up for him—disagreeable; and after it's all said and done, life is too short."

"Well," said Miss Goering, "is he dangerous?"

Frank shrugged his shoulders. Soon Andy came back.

"The moon and the stars are out now," he said, "and I could almost see clear to the edge of the town. There are no policemen in sight, so I think we can have our drink."

He slid in, onto the bench opposite Miss Goering.

"It's cold and lifeless without a living thing on the street," he began, "but that's the way I like it nowadays;

you'll forgive me if I sound morose to a gay woman like yourself, but I have a habit of never paying attention to whoever I am talking to. I think people would say, about me: 'Lacking in respect for other human beings.' *You* have great respect for your friends, I'm sure, but that is only because you respect yourself, which is always the starting-off point for everything: yourself."

Miss Goering did not feel very much more at ease now that he was talking to her than she had before he had sat down. He seemed to grow more intense and almost angry as he talked, and his way of attributing qualities to her which were not in any way true to her nature gave his conversation an eerie quality and at the same time made Miss Goering feel inconsequential.

"Do you live in this town" Miss Goering asked him.

"I do, indeed," said Andy. "I have three furnished rooms in a new apartment house. It is the only apartment house in this town. I pay rent every month and I live there all alone. In the afternoon the sun shines into my apartment, which is one of the finest ironies, in my opinion, because of all the apartments in the building, mine is the sunniest and I sleep there all day with my shades drawn down. I didn't always live there. I lived before in the city with my mother. But this is the nearest thing I could find to a penal island, so it suits me; it suits me fine." He fumbled with some cigarettes for a few minutes and kept his eyes purposely averted from Miss Goering's face. He reminded her of certain comedians who are at last given a secondary tragic role and execute it rather well. She also had a very definite impression that one thing was cleaving his simple mind in two, causing him to twist between his sheets instead of sleeping, and to lead an altogether wretched existence. She had no doubt that she would soon find out what it was.

"You have a very special type of beauty," he said to her; "a bad nose, but beautiful eyes and hair. It would please me in the midst of all this horror to go to bed with you. But in order to do this we'll have to leave this bar and go to my apartment."

"Well, I can't promise you anything, but I will be glad to go to your apartment," said Miss Goering.

Andy told Frank to call the hackstand and tell a certain man who was on duty all night to come over and get them.

The taxi drove down the main street very slowly. It was very old and consequently it rattled a good deal. Andy stuck his head out of the window.

"How do you do, ladies and gentlemen?" he shouted at the empty street, trying to approximate an English accent. "I hope, I certainly hope that each and every one of you is having a fine time in this great town of ours." He leaned back against his seat again and smiled in such a horrid manner that Miss Goering felt frightened again.

"You could roll a hoop down this street, naked, at midnight and no one would ever know it," he said to her.

"Well, if you think it is such a dismal place," said Miss Goering, "why don't you move somewhere else, bag and baggage?"

"Oh, no," he said gloomily, "I'll never do that. There's no use in my doing that."

"Is it that your business ties you down here?" Miss Goering asked him, although she knew perfectly well he was speaking of something spiritual and far more important.

"Don't call me a business man," he said to her.

"Then you are an artist?"

He shook his head vaguely as though not quite sure what an artist was.

"Well, all right," said Miss Goering, "I've had two guesses; now won't you tell me what you are?"

"A buml" he said stentoriously, sliding lower in his seat. "You knew that all the time, didn't you, being an intelligent woman?"

The taxicab drew up in front of the apartment house, which stood between an empty lot and a string of stores only one story high.

"You see, I get the afternoon sun all day long," he said, "because I have no obstructions. I look out over this empty lot."

"There is a tree growing in the empty lot," said Miss Goering. "I suppose that you are able to see it from your window?"

"Yes," said Andy. "Weird, isn't it?"

The apartment house was very new and very small. They stood together in the lobby while Andy searched his pockets for the keys. The floor was of imitation marble, yellow in color except in the center where the architect had set in a blue peacock in mosaic, surrounded by various long-stemmed flowers. It was hard to distinguish the peacock in the dim light, but Miss Goering crouched down on her heels to examine it better.

"I think those are water lilies around that peacock," said Andy, "But a peacock is supposed to have thousands of colors in him, isn't he? Multicolored, isn't that the point of a peacock? This one's all blue."

"Well," said Miss Goering, "perhaps it is nicer this way."

They left the lobby and went up some ugly iron steps. Andy lived on the first floor. There was a terrible odor in the hall, which he told her never went away.

"They're cooking in there for ten people," he said, "all day long. They all work at different hours of the day; half of them don't see the other half at all, except on Sundays and holidays."

Andy's apartment was very hot and stuffy. The furniture was brown and none of the cushions appeared to fit the chairs properly.

"Here's journey's end," said Andy. "Make yourself at home. I'm going to take off some of my clothes." He returned in a minute wearing a bathrobe made of some very cheap material. Both ends of his bathrobe cords had been partially chewed away.

"What happened to your bathrobe cords?" Miss Goering asked him.

"My dog chewed them away."

"Oh, have you a dog?" she asked him.

"Once upon a time I had a dog and a future, and a girl," he said, "but that is no longer so."

"Well, what happened?" Miss Goering asked, throwing her shawl off her shoulders and mopping her forehead with her handkerchief. The steam heat had already begun to make her sweat, particularly as she had not been used to central heating for some time.

"Let's not talk about my life," said Andy, putting his hand up like a traffic officer. "Let's have some drinks instead."

"All right, but I certainly think we should talk about your life sooner or later," said Miss Goering. All the while she was thinking that she would allow herself to go home within an hour. "I consider," she said to herself, "that I have done quite well for my first night." Andy was standing up and pulling his bathrobe cord tighter around the waist.

"I was," he said, "engaged to be married to a very nice girl who worked. I loved her as much as a man can love a woman. She had a smooth forehead, beautiful blue eyes, and not so good teeth. Her legs were something to take pictures of. Her name was Mary and she got along with my mother. She was a plain girl with an ordinary mind and she used to get a tremendous kick out of life. Sometimes we used to have dinner at midnight just for the hell of it and she used to say to me: 'Imagine us, walking down the street at midnight to have our dinner. Just two ordinary people. Maybe there isn't any sanity.' Naturally, I didn't tell her that there were plenty of people like the people who live down the hall in 5D who eat dinner at midnight, not because they are crazy, but because they've got jobs that cause them to do so, because then maybe she wouldn't have got so much fun out of it. I wasn't going to spoil it and tell her that the world wasn't crazy, that the world was medium fair; and I didn't know either that a couple of months later her sweetheart was going to become one of the craziest people in it."

The veins in Andy's forehead were beginning to bulge, his face was redder, and the wings of his nostrils were sweaty.

"All this must really mean something to him," thought Miss Goering.

"Often I used to go into an Italian restaurant for dinner; it was right around the corner from my house; I knew mostly all the people that ate there, and the atmosphere was very convivial. There were a few of us who always ate together. I always bought the wine because I was better fixed than most of them. Then there were a couple of old men who ate there, but we never bothered with them. There was one man too who wasn't so old, but he was solitary and didn't mix in with the others. We knew he used to be in the circus, but we never found out what kind of a job he had there or anything. Then one night, the night before he brought her in, I happened to be gazing at him for no reason on earth and I saw him stand up and fold his newspaper into his pocket, which was peculiar-looking because he hadn't finished his dinner yet. Then he turned towards us and coughed like he was clearing his throat.

"'Gentlemen,' he said, 'I have an announcement to make.' I had to quiet the boys because he had such a thin little voice you could hardly hear what he was saying.

"'I am not going to take much of your time,' he continued, like someone talking at a big banquet, 'but I just want to tell you and you'll understand why in a minute. I just want to tell you that I'm bringing a young lady here tomorrow night and without any reservations I want you all to love her: This lady, gentleman, is like a broken doll. She has neither arms nor legs.' Then he sat down very quietly and started right in eating again."

"How terribly embarrassing!" said Miss Goering. "Dear me, what did you answer to that?"

"I don't remember," said Andy, "I just remember that it was embarrassing like you say and we didn't feel that he had to make the announcement anyway.

"She was already in her chair the next night when we got there; nicely made up and wearing a very pretty, clean blouse pinned in front with a brooch shaped like a butterfly. Her hair was marcelled too and she was a natural blonde. I kept my ear cocked and I heard her telling the little man that her appetite got better all the time and that she could sleep fourteen hours a day. After that I began to notice her mouth. It was like a rose petal or a heart or some kind of a little shell. It was really beautiful. Then right away I started to wonder what she would be like; the rest of her, you understand—without any legs." He stopped talking and walked around the room once, looking up at his walls.

"It came into my mind like an ugly snake, this idea, and curled there to stay. I looked at her head so little and so delicate against the dark grimy wall and it was the apple of sin that I was eating for the first time."

"Really for the first time?" said Miss Goering. She looked bewildered and was lost in thought for a moment.

"From then on I thought of nothing else but finding out; every other thought left my head."

"And before what were your thoughts like?" Miss Goering asked him a little maliciously. He didn't seem to hear her.

"Well, this went on for some time—the way I felt about her. I was seeing Belle, who came to the restaurant often, after that first night, and I was seeing Mary too. I got friendly with Belle. There was nothing special about her. She loved wine and I actually used to pour it down her throat for her. She talked a little bit too much about her family and was a little good. Not exactly religious, but a little too full of the milk of human kindness sort of thing. It grew and grew, this terrible curiosity or desire of mine until finally my mind started to wander when I was with Mary and I couldn't sleep with her any more. She was swell all the way through it, though, patient as a lamb. She was much too young to have such a thing happen to her. I was like a horrible old man or one of those impotent kings with a history of syphilis behind him."

"Did you tell your sweetheart what was getting on your nerves?" asked Miss Goering, trying to hurry him up a bit.

"I didn't tell her because I wanted the buildings to stay in place for her and I wanted the stars to be over her head and not cockeyed—I wanted her to be able to walk in the park and feed the birdies in years to come with some other fine human being hanging onto her arm. I didn't want her to have to lock something up inside of her and look out at the world through a nailed window.

It was not long before I went to bed with Belle and got myself a beautiful case of syphilis, which I spent the next two years curing. I took to bowling along about then and I finally left my mother's house and my work and came out to No-man's Land. I can live in this apartment all right on a little money that I get from a building I own down in the slums of the city."

He sat down in a chair opposite Miss Goering and put his face in his hands. Miss Goering judged that he had finished and she was just about to thank him for his hospitality and wish him good-night when he uncovered his face and began again.

"The worst of all I remember clearly; more and more I couldn't face my mother. I'd stay out bowling all day long and half the night. Then on the fourth day of July I decided that I would make a very special effort to spend the day with her. There was a big parade supposed to go by our window at three in the afternoon. Very near to that time I was standing in the parlor with a pressed suit on, and Mother was sitting as close to the window as she could get. It was a sunny day out and just right for a parade. The parade was punctual because about a quarter to three we began to hear some faint music in the distance. Then soon after that my country's red, white, and blue flag went by, held up by some fine-looking boys. The band was playing *Yankee Doodle*. All of a sudden I hid my face in my hands; I couldn't look at my country's flag. Then I knew, once and for all, that I hated myself. Since then I have accepted my status as a skunk. 'Citizen Skunk' happens to be a little private name I have for myself. You can have some fun in the mud, though, you know, if you just accept a seat in it instead of trying to squirm around."

"Well," said Miss Goering, "I certainly think you could pull yourself together with a bit of an effort. I wouldn't put much stock in that flag episode either."

He looked at her vaguely. "You talk like a society lady," he said to her.

"I am a society lady," said Miss Goering. "I am also rich, but I have purposely reduced my living standards. I have left my lovely home and I have moved out to a little house on the island. The house is in very bad shape and costs me practically nothing. What do you think of that?"

"I think you're cuckoo," said Andy, and not at all in a friendly tone. He was frowning darkly. "People like you shouldn't be allowed to have money."

Miss Goering was surprised to hear him making such a show of righteous indignation.

"Please," she said, "could you possibly open the window?"

"There will be an awfully cold wind blowing through here if I do," said Andy.

"Nevertheless," said Miss Goering, "I think I would prefer it."

"I'll tell you," said Andy, moving uncomfortably around his chair. "I just put in a bad spell of grippe and I'm dead afraid of getting into a draft." He bit his lip and looked terribly worried. "I could go and stand in the next room if you want while you get your breath of fresh air," he added, brightening up a bit.

"That's a jolly good idea," said Miss Goering.

He left and closed the bedroom door softly behind him. She was delighted with the chance to get some cool air, and after she had opened the window she placed her two hands on the sill far apart from each other and leaned out. She would have enjoyed this far more had she not been certain that Andy was standing still in his room consumed with boredom and impatience. He still frightened her a little and at the same time she felt that he was a terrible burden. There was a gas station opposite the apartment house. Although the office was deserted at the moment, it was brightly lighted and a radio on the desk had been left on. There was a folksong coming over the air. Soon there was a short rap at the bedroom door, which was just what she had been expecting to hear. She closed the window regretfully before the tune had finished.

"Come in," she called to him, "come in." She was dismayed to see when Andy opened the door that he had removed all of his clothing with the exception of his socks and his underdrawers. He did not seem to be embarrassed, but behaved as though they had both tacitly understood that he was to appear dressed in this fashion.

He walked with her to the couch and made her sit down beside him. Then he flung his arm around her and crossed his legs. His legs were terribly thin, and on the whole he looked inconsequential now that he had removed his clothing. He pressed his cheek to Miss Goering's.

"Do you think you could make me a little happy?" he asked her.

"For Heaven's sake," said Miss Goering, sitting bolt upright, "I thought you were beyond that."

"Well, no man can really look into the future, you know." He narrowed his eyes and attempted to kiss her.

"Now, about that woman," she said, "Belle, who had neither arms nor legs?"

"Please, darling, let's not discuss her now. Will you do me that favor?" His tone was a little sneering, but there was an undercurrent of excitement in his voice. He said: "Now tell me whatever it is that you like. You know . . . I haven't lost all my time these two years. There are a few little things I pride myself on."

Miss Goering looked very solemn. She was thinking of this very seriously, because she suspected that were she to accept Andy's offer it would be far more difficult for her to put a stop to her excursions, should she feel so disposed. Until recently she had never followed too dangerously far in action any course which she had decided upon as being the morally correct one. She scarcely approved of this weakness in herself, but she was to a certain extent sensible and happy enough to protect herself automatically. She was feeling a little tipsy, however, and Andy's suggestion rather appealed to her. "One must allow that a certain amount of carelessness in one's nature often accomplishes what the will is incapable of doing," she said to herself.

Andy looked towards the bedroom door. His mood seemed to have changed very suddenly and he seemed confused. "This does not mean that he is not lecherous," thought Miss Goering. He got up and wandered around the room. Finally he pulled an old gramophone out from behind the couch. He took up a good deal of time dusting it off and collecting some needles that were scattered around and underneath the turntable. As he knelt over the instrument he became quite absorbed in what he was doing and his face took on an almost sympathetic aspect.

"It's a very old machine," he mumbled. "I got it a long, long time ago."

The machine was very small and terribly out of date, and had Miss Goering been sentimental, she would have felt a little sad watching him; however, she was growing impatient.

"I can't hear a word that you are saying," she shouted at him in an unnecessarily loud voice.

He got up without answering her and went into his room. When he returned he was again wearing his bathrobe and holding a record in his hand.

"You'll think I'm silly," he said, "bothering with that machine so long, when all I've got to play for you is this one record. It's a march; here." He handed it to her in order that she might read the title of the piece and the name of the band that was executing it.

"Maybe," he said, "you'd rather not hear it. A lot of people don't like march music."

"No, do play it," said Miss Goering. "I'll be delighted, really."

He put the record on and sat on the edge of a very uncomfortable chair at quite a distance from Miss Goering.

The needle was too loud and the march was the *Washington Post.* Miss Goering felt as uneasy as one can feel listening to parade music in a quiet room. Andy seemed to be enjoying it and he kept time with his feet during the entire length of the record. But when it was over he seemed to be in an even worse state of confusion than before.

"Would you like to see the apartment?" he asked her.

Miss Goering leaped up from the couch quickly lest he should change his mind.

"A woman who made dresses had this apartment before me, so my bedroom is kind of sissyish for a man."

She followed him into the bedroom. He had turned the bed down rather badly and the slips of the two pillows were gray and wrinkled. On his dresser were pictures of several girls, all of them terribly unattractive and plain. They looked more to Miss Goering like the church-going type of young woman than like the mistresses of a bachelor.

"They're nice-looking girls, aren't they?" said Andy to Miss Goering.

"Lovely-looking," she said, "lovely."

"None of these girls live in this town," he said. "They live in different towns in the vicinity. The girls here are guarded and they don't like bachelors my age. I don't blame them. I go take one of these girls in the pictures out now and then when I feel like it. I even sit in their living-rooms of an evening with them, with their parents right in the house. But they don't see much of me, I can tell you that."

Miss Goering was growing more and more puzzled, but she didn't ask him any more questions because she was suddenly feeling weary.

"I think I'll be on my way now," she said, swaying a little on her feet. She realized immediately how rude and unkind she was being and she saw Andy tightening up. He put his fists into his pockets.

"Well, you can't go now," he said to her. "Stay a little longer and I'll make you some coffee."

"No, no, I don't want any coffee. Anyway, they'll be worrying about me at home."

"Who's they?" Andy asked her.

"Arnold and Arnold's father and Miss Gamelon."

"It sounds like a terrible mob to me," he said. "I couldn't stand living with a crowd like that."

"I love it," said Miss Goering.

He put his arms around her and tried to kiss her, but she pulled away, "No, honestly, I'm much too tired."

"All right," he said, "all right!" His brow was deeply furrowed and he looked completely miserable. He took his bathrobe off and got into his bed. He lay there with the sheet up to his neck, threshing his feet about and looking up at the ceiling like someone with a fever. There was a small light burning on the table beside the bed which shone directly into his face, so that Miss Goering was able to distinguish many lines which she had not noticed before. She went over to his bed and leaned over him.

"What *is* the matter?" she asked him. "Now it's been a very pleasant evening and we all need some sleep."

He laughed in her face. "You're some lunatic," he said to her, "and you sure don't know anything about people. I'm all right here, though." He pulled the sheet up farther and lay there breathing heavily. "There's a five o'clock ferry that leaves in about a half hour. Will you come back tomorrow evening? I'll be where I was tonight at that bar."

She promised him that she would return on the following evening, and after he had explained to her how to get to the dock, she opened his window for him and left.

Stupidly enough, Miss Goering had forgotten to take her key with her and she was obliged to knock on the door in order to get into her house. She pounded twice, and almost immediately she heard someone running down the steps. She could tell that it was Arnold even before he had opened the door. He was wearing a rose-colored pajama jacket and a pair of trousers. His suspenders were hanging down over his hips. His beard had grown quite a bit for such a short time and he looked sloppier than ever.

"What's the matter with you, Arnold?" said Miss Goering. "You look dreadful."

"Well, I've had a bad night, Christina. I just put Bubbles to sleep a little while ago; she's terribly worried about you. As a matter of fact, I don't think you've shown us much consideration."

"Who is Bubbles?" Miss Goering asked him.

"Bubbles," he said, "is the name I have for Miss Gamelon."

"Well," said Miss Goering, going into the house and seating herself in front of the fireplace, "I took the ferry back across to the mainland and I became very much involved. I might return tomorrow night," she added, "although I don't really want to very much."

"I don't know why you find it so interesting and intellectual to seek out a new city," said Arnold, cupping his chin in his hand and looking at her fixedly.

"Because I believe the hardest thing for me to do is really move from one thing to another, partly," said Miss Goering.

"Spiritually," said Arnold, trying to speak in a more sociable tone, "spiritually I'm constantly making little journeys and changing my entire nature every six months."

"I don't believe it for a minute," said Miss Goering.

"No, no, it is true. Also I can tell you that I think it is absolute nonsense to move physically from one place to another. All places are more or less alike."

Miss Goering did not answer this. She pulled her shawl closer around her shoulders and of a sudden looked quite old and very sad indeed.

Arnold began to doubt the validity of what he had just said, and immediately resolved to make exactly the same excursion from which Miss Goering had just returned, on the following night. He squared his jaw and pulled out a notebook from his pocket.

"Now, will you give me the particulars on how to reach the mainland?" said Arnold. "The hours when the train leaves, and so forth."

"Why do you ask?" said Miss Goering.

"Because I'm going to go there myself tomorrow night. I should have thought you would have guessed that by this time."

"No, judging by what you just finished saying to me, I would not have guessed it."

"Well, I talk one way," said Arnold, "but I'm really, underneath, the same kind of maniac that you are."

"I would like to see your father," Miss Goering said to him.

"I think he's asleep. I hope he will come to his senses and go home," said Arnold.

"Well, I am hoping the contrary," said Miss Goering. "I'm terribly attached to him. Let's go upstairs and just look into his room."

They went up the stairs together and Miss Gamelon came out to meet them on the landing. Her eyes were all swollen and she was wrapped in a heavy wool bathrobe.

She began speaking to Miss Goering in a voice that was thick with sleep. "Once more, and it will be the last you will see of Lucy Gamelon."

"Now, Bubbles," said Arnold, "remember this is not an ordinary household and you must expect certain eccentricities on the part of the inmates. You see, I have dubbed us all inmates."

"Arnold," said Miss Gamelon, "now don't you begin. You know what I told you this afternoon about talking drivel."

"Please, Lucy," said Arnold.

"Come, come, let's all go and take a peek at Arnold's father," suggested Miss Goering.

Miss Gamelon followed them only in order to continue admonishing Arnold, which she did in a low voice. Miss Goering pulled the door open. The room was very cold and she realized for the first time that it was already bright outdoors. It had all happened very quickly while she was talking to Arnold in the parlor, but there it was nearly always dark because of the thick bushes outside.

Arnold's father was sleeping on his back. His face was still and he breathed regularly without snoring. Miss Goering shook him a few times by the shoulder.

"The procedures in this house," said Miss Gamelon, "are what amount to criminal. Now you're waking up an old man who needs his sleep, at the crack of dawn. It makes me shudder to stand here and see what you've become, Christina."

At last Arnold's father awakened. It took him a little while to realize what had happened, but when he had, he leaned on his elbows and said in a very chipper manner to Miss Goering:

"Good morning, Mrs. Marco Polo. What beautiful treasures have you brought back from the East? I'm glad to see you, and if there's anywhere you want me to go with you, I'm ready." He fell back on his pillow with a thump.

Miss Goering said that she would see him later, that at the moment she was badly in need of some rest. They left the room, and before they had closed the door behind them, Arnold's father was already asleep. On the landing

Miss Gamelon began to cry and she buried her face for a moment in Miss Goering's shoulder. Miss Goering held her very tightly and begged her not to cry. Then she kissed both Arnold and Miss Gamelon good-night. When she arrived in her room she was overcome with fright for a few moments, but shortly she fell into a deep sleep.

AT ABOUT FIVE-THIRTY on the following afternoon Miss Goering announced her intention of returning again that evening to the mainland. Miss Gamelon was standing up, sewing one of Arnold's socks. She was dressed more coquettishly than was her habit, with a ruffle around the neck of her dress and a liberal coating of rouge on her cheeks. The old man was in a big chair in the corner reading the poetry of Longfellow, sometimes aloud, sometimes to himself. Arnold was still dressed in the same fashion as the night before, with the exception of a sweater which he had pulled on over his pajama top. There was a big coffee stain on the front of his sweater, and the ashes of his cigarette had spilled over his chest. He was lying on the couch half asleep.

"You will go back there again over my dead body," said Miss Gamelon. "Now, please, Christina, be sane and do let us all have a pleasant evening together."

Miss Goering sighed. "Well, you and Arnold can have a perfectly pleasant evening together without me. I am sorry. I'd love to stay, but I really feel that I must go."

"You drive me wild with your mysterious talk," said Miss Gamelon. "If only some member of your family were here! Why don't we phone for a taxi," she said hopefully, "and go to the city? We might eat some Chinese food and go to the theater afterwards, or a picture show, if you are still in your pinch-penny mood."

"Why don't you and Arnold go to the city and eat some Chinese food and then go to the theater? I will be very glad to have you go as my guests, but I'm afraid I can't accompany you."

Arnold was growing annoyed at the ease with which Miss Goering disposed of him. Her manner also gave him a very bad sense of being inferior to her.

"I'm sorry, Christina," he said from his couch, "but I have no intention of eating Chinese food. I have been planning all along to take a little jaunt to the mainland opposite this end of the island too, and nothing will stop me. I wish you'd come along with me, Lucy; as a matter of fact, I don't see why we can't all go along together. It is quite senseless that Christina should make such a morbid affair out of this little saunter to the mainland. Actually there is nothing to it."

"Arnold!" Miss Gamelon screamed at him. "You're losing your mind too, and if you think I am going on a wild-goose chase aboard a train and a ferry just to wind up in some little rat-trap, you're doubly crazy. Anyway, I've heard that it is a very tough little town, besides being dreary and without any interest whatsoever."

"Nevertheless," said Arnold, sitting up and planting his two feet on the floor, "I'm going this evening."

"In that case," said Arnold's father, "I'm going too."

Secretly Miss Goering was delighted that they were coming and she did not have the courage to deter them, although she felt that it would have been the correct thing for her to do. Her excursions would be more or less devoid of any moral value in her own eyes if they accompanied her, but she was so delighted that she convinced herself that perhaps she might allow it just this time.

"You had better come along, Lucy," said Arnold; "otherwise you are going to be here all alone."

"That's perfectly all right, my dear," said Lucy. "I'll be the only one that comes out whole, in the end. And it might be very delightful to be here without any of you."

Arnold's father made an insulting noise with his mouth, and Miss Gamelon left the room.

This time the little train was filled with people and there were quite a few boys going up and down the aisle selling candy and fruit. It had been a curiously warm day and there had been a shower of short duration, one of those showers that are so frequent in summer but so seldom occur in the fall.

The sun was just setting and the shower had left in its wake quite a beautiful rainbow, which was only visible to those people who were seated on the left side of the train. However, most of the passengers who had been seated on the right side were now leaning over the more fortunate ones and getting quite a fair view of the rainbow too.

Many of the women were naming aloud to their friends the colors that they were able to distinguish. Everyone on the train seemed to love it except Arnold, who, now that he had asserted himself, felt terribly depressed, partly as a result of having had to move from his couch and consider the prospect of a dull evening and partly also because he doubted very much whether he would be able to make it up with Lucy Gamelon. She was, he felt certain, the type of person who could remain angry for weeks.

"Oh, I think this is terribly, terribly gay," said Miss Goering. "This rainbow and this sunset and all these people jabbering away like magpies. Don't you think it's gay?" Miss Goering was addressing Arnold's father.

"Oh, yes," he said. "It's a real magic carpet."

Miss Goering searched his face because his voice sounded a little sad to her. He did, as a matter of fact, appear to be slightly uneasy. He kept looking around at the passengers and pulling his tie.

They finally left the train and boarded the ferry. They all stood at the prow together as Miss Goering had done on the previous night. This time when the ferry landed, Miss Goering looked up and saw no one coming down the hill.

"Usually," she said to them, forgetting that she herself had only made the trip once before, "this hill is swarming with people. I cannot imagine what has happened to them tonight."

"It's a steep hill," said Arnold's father. "Is there no way of getting into the town without climbing that hill?"

"I don't know," said Miss Goering. She looked at him and noticed that his sleeves were too long for him. As a matter of fact, his overcoat was about a half-size too large.

If there had been no one on the hill going to or from the ferry, the main street was swarming with people.

The cinema was all lighted up and there was a long line forming in front of the box office. There had obviously been a fire, because there were three red engines parked on one side of the street, a few blocks up from the cinema. Miss Goering judged that it had been of no consequence since she could see neither traces of smoke nor charred buildings. However, the engines added to the gaiety of the street as there were many young people crowded around them making jokes with the firemen who remained in the trucks. Arnold walked along at a brisk pace, carefully examining everything on the street and pretending to be very much lost in his own impressions of the town.

"I see what you mean," he said to Miss Goering, "it's glorious."

"What is glorious?" Miss Goering asked him.

"All this." Suddenly Arnold stopped dead. "Oh look, Christina, what a beautiful sight!" He had made them stop in front of a large empty lot between two buildings. The empty lot had been converted into a brand-new basketball court. The court was very elegantly paved with gray asphalt and brightly lighted by four giant lamps that were focused on the players and on the basket. There was a ticket office at one side of the court where the participants bought their right to play in the game for one hour. Most of the people playing were little boys. There were several men in uniform and Arnold judged that they worked for the court and filled in when an insufficient number of people bought tickets to form two complete teams. Arnold flushed with pleasure.

"Look, Christina," he said, "you run along while I try my hand at this; I'll come and get Pop and you later."

She pointed the bar out to him, but she had the feeling that Arnold was not paying much attention to what she was saying. She stood for a moment with Arnold's father and they watched him rush up to the ticket office and hurriedly push his change through the wicket. He was on the court in no time, running around in his overcoat and jumping up in the air with his arms apart. One of the uniformed men had stepped quickly out of the game in order to cede his place to Arnold. But he was now trying desperately to attract his attention because Arnold had been in such a hurry at the ticket office that the agent had not had time to give him the colored arm-band by which the players were able to distinguish the members of their own team.

"I suppose," said Miss Goering, "that we had better go along. Arnold, I imagine, will follow us shortly."

They walked down the street. Arnold's father hesitated a moment before the saloon door.

"What kind of men come in here?" he asked her.

"Oh," said Goering, "all sorts of men, I guess. Rich and poor, workers and bankers, criminals and dwarfs."

"Dwarfs," Arnold's father repeated uneasily.

The minute they were inside, Miss Goering spotted Andy. He was drinking at the farther end of the bar with his hat pulled down over one eye. Miss Goering hastily installed Arnold's father in a booth.

"Take your coat off," she said, "and order yourself a drink from that man over there behind the bar."

She went over to Andy and stretched her hand out to him. He was looking very mean and haughty.

"Hello," he said. "Did you decide to come over to the mainland again?"

"Why, certainly," said Miss Goering. "I told you I would."

"Well," said Andy, "I've learned in the course of years that it doesn't mean a thing."

Miss Goering felt a little embarrassed. They stood side by side for a little while without saying a word.

"I'm sorry," said Andy, "but I have no suggestions to make to you for the evening. There is only one picture show in town and they are showing a very bad movie tonight." He ordered himself another drink and gulped it down straight. Then he turned the dial of the radio very slowly until he found a tango.

"Well, may I have this dance?" he asked, appearing to brighten up a bit.

Miss Goering nodded her head.

He held her very straight and so tightly that she was in an extremely awkward and uncomfortable position. He danced with her into a far corner of the room.

"Well," he said, "are you going to try and make me happy? Because I have no time to waste." He pushed her away from him and stood up very straight facing her, with his arms hanging down along his sides.

"Step back a little farther, please," he said. "Look carefully at your man and then say whether or not you want him."

Miss Goering did not see how she could possibly answer anything but yes. He was standing now with his head cocked to one side, looking very much as though he were trying to refrain from blinking his eyes, the way people do when they are having snapshots taken.

"Very well," said Miss Goering, "I do want you to be my man." She smiled at him sweetly, but she was not thinking very hard of what she was saying.

He held his arms out to her and they continued to dance. He was looking over her head very proudly and smiling just a little. When they had finished their dance, Miss Goering remembered with a pang that Arnold's father had been sitting in his booth alone all this time. She felt doubly sorry because he seemed to have saddened and aged so much since they had boarded the train that he scarcely resembled at all the chipper, eccentric man he had been for a few days at the island house, or even the fanatical gentleman he had appeared to Miss Goering on the first night that they had met.

"Dear me, I must introduce you to Arnold's father," she said to Andy. "Come over this way with me."

She felt even more remorse when she arrived at the booth because Arnold's father had been sitting there all the while without having ordered himself a drink.

"What's the matter?" asked Miss Goering, her voice rising way up in the air like the voice of an excited mother. "Why on earth didn't you order yourself something to drink?"

Arnold's father looked around him furtively. "I don't know," he said, "I didn't feel any desire to."

She introduced the two men to each other and they all sat down together. Arnold's father asked Andy very politely whether or not he lived in this town and what his business was. During the course of their conversation they both discovered that not only had they been born in the same town, but they had, in spite of difference in age, also lived there once at the same time without ever having met. Andy, unlike most people, did not seem to become more lively when they both happened upon this fact.

"Yes," he answered wearily to the questions of Arnold's father, "I did live there in 1920."

"Then certainly," said Arnold's father sitting up straighter, "then certainly you were well acquainted with the McLean family. They lived up on the hill. They had seven children, five girls and two boys. All of them, as you must remember, were the possessors of a terrific shock of bright red hair."

"I did not know them," said Andy quietly, beginning to get red in the face.

"That's very strange," said Arnold's father. "Then you must have known Vincent Connelly, Peter Jacketson, and Robert Bull."

"No," said Andy, "no, I didn't." His good spirits seemed to have vanished entirely.

"They," said Arnold's father, "controlled the main business interests of the town." He studied Andy's face carefully.

Andy shook his head once more and looked off into space.

"Riddleton?" Arnold's father asked him abruptly.

"What?" said Andy.

"Riddleton, president of the bank."

"Well, not exactly," said Andy.

Arnold's father leaned back against the bench and sighed. "Where did you live?" he asked finally of Andy.

"I lived," said Andy, "at the end of Parliament Street and Byrd Avenue."

"It was terrible around there before they started tearing it up, wasn't it?" Arnold's father said, his eyes filled with memories.

Andy pushed the table roughly aside and walked quickly over to the bar.

"He didn't know anyone decent in the whole blooming town," said Arnold's father. "Parliament and Byrd was the section—"

"Please," said Miss Goering. "Look, you've insulted him. What a shame; because neither one of you cares about this sort of thing at all! What nasty little devil got into you both?"

"I don't think he has very good manners, and he is clearly not the type of man I would expect to find you associating with."

Miss Goering was a little peeved with Arnold's father, but instead of saying anything to him she went over to Andy and consoled him.

"Please don't mind him," she said. "He's really a delightful old thing and quite poetic. It's just that he's been through some radical changes in his life, all in the last few days, and I guess he's feeling the strain now."

"Poetic is he?" Andy snapped at her. "He's a pompous old monkey. That's what he is." Andy was really very angry.

"No," said Miss Goering, "he is not a pompous old monkey."

Andy finished his drink and swaggered over to Arnold's father with his hands in his pockets.

"You're a pompous old monkey!" he said to him. "A pompous old good-for-nothing monkey!"

Arnold's father slid out of his seat with his eyes cast downward and walked towards the door.

Miss Goering, who had overheard Andy's remark, hurried after him, but she whispered to Andy as she passed him, that she intended to come right back.

When they were outside they leaned together against a lamp post. Miss Goering could see that Arnold's father was trembling.

"I have never in my life encountered such rudeness," he said. "That man is worse than a gutter puppy."

"Well, I wouldn't worry about it," said Miss Goering. "He was just ill-tempered."

"Ill-tempered?" said Arnold's father. "He's the kind of cheaply dressed brute that is more and more thickly populating the world today."

"Oh, come," said Miss Goering, "that is neither here nor there."

Arnold's father looked at Miss Goering. Her face was very lovely on this particular evening, and he sighed with regret. "I suppose," he said, "that you are deeply disappointed in me in your own particular way, and that you are able to have respect in your heart for him while you are unable to find it within that very same heart for me. Human nature is mysterious and very beautiful, but remember that there are certain infallible signs that I, as an older man, have learned to recognize. I would not trust that man too far. I love you, my dear, with all my heart, you know."

Miss Goering stood in silence.

"You are very close to me," he said after a little while, squeezing her hand.

"Well," she said, "would you care to step back into the saloon or do you feel that you've had enough?"

"It would be literally impossible for me to return to that saloon even should I have the slightest desire to. I think I had better go along. You won't come with me, will you, my dear?"

"I'm very sorry," said Miss Goering, "but unfortunately this was a previous engagement. Would you like me to walk down to the basketball court? Perhaps Arnold will have wearied of his game by this time. If not, you can easily sit and watch the players for a little while."

"Yes, that would be very kind of you," said Arnold's father, in such a sad voice that he almost broke Miss Goering's heart.

Very shortly they arrived at the basketball court. Things had changed quite a bit. Most of the small boys had dropped out of the game and a great many young men and women had taken the place of both the small boys and the guards. The women were screaming with laughter and quite a large crowd had gathered to watch the players. After Miss Goering and Arnold's father had stood there for a minute they realized that Arnold himself was the cause of most of the merriment. He had removed his coat and his sweater and, to their surprise, they saw that he was still wearing his pajama top. He had pulled it outside of his pants in order to appear more ridiculous. They watched him run across the court with the ball in his arms roaring like a lion. When he arrived at a strategic position, however, instead of passing the ball on to another member of his team he merely dropped it on the court between his feet and proceeded to butt one of his opponents in the stomach like a goat. The crowd roared with laughter. The uniformed guards were particularly delighted because it was a pleasant and unexpected break in the night's routine. They were all standing in a row, smiling very broadly.

"I shall try and see if I can find a chair for you," said Miss Goering. She returned shortly and led Arnold's father to a folding chair that one of the guards had obligingly set up right outside of the ticket office. Arnold's father sat down and yawned.

"Good-by," said Miss Goering. "Good-by, darling, and wait here until Arnold has finished his game."

"But wait a moment," said Arnold's father. "When will you return to the island?"

"I might not return," she said. "I might not return right away, but I will see that Miss Gamelon receives enough money to manage the house and the food."

"But I must certainly see you. This is not a very human way to make a departure."

"Well, come along a minute," said Miss Goering, taking hold of his hand and pulling him with difficulty through the crowd over to the sidewalk.

Arnold's father remonstrated that he would not return to the saloon for a million dollars.

"I'm not taking you to the saloon. Don't be silly," she said. "Now, do you see that ice-cream parlor across the street?" She pointed to a little white store almost directly opposite them. "If I don't come back, which is very probable, will you meet me there on Sunday morning? That will be in eight days, at eleven o'clock in the morning."

"I will be there in eight days," said Arnold's father.

WHEN SHE RETURNED with Andy to his apartment that night, she noticed that there were three long-stemmed roses on a table next to the couch.

"Why, what lovely flowers!" she exclaimed. "This reminds me that my mother had once the loveliest garden for miles around her. She won many prizes with her roses."

"Well," said Andy, "no one in my family ever won a prize with a rose, but I bought these for you in case you came."

"I'm deeply touched," said Miss Goering.

MISS GOERING HAD been living with Andy for eight days. He was still very nervous and tense, but he seemed on the whole to be much more optimistic. To Miss Goering's surprise, he had begun on the second day to talk of the business possibilities in town. He surprised her very much too by knowing the names of the leading families of the community and moreover by being familiar with certain details concerning their private lives. On Saturday night he had announced to Miss Goering his intention of having a business conference the next morning with Mr. Bellamy, Mr. Schlaegel, and Mr. Dockerty. These men controlled most of the real estate not only in the town itself but in several neighboring towns. Besides these interests they also had a good many of the farms of the surrounding country. He was terribly excited when he told her his plans, which were mainly to sell the buildings he owned in the city, for which he had already been offered a small sum, and buy a share in their business.

"They're the three smartest men in town," he said, "but they're not gangsters at all. They come from the finest families here and I think it would be nice for you too."

"That is not the kind of thing that interests me in the least," said Miss Goering.

"Well, naturally, I wouldn't expect it to interest you or me," said Andy, "but you've got to admit we're living in the world, unless we want to behave like crazy kids or escaped lunatics or something like that."

For several days it had been quite clear to Miss Goering that Andy was no longer thinking of himself as a bum. This would have pleased her greatly had she been interested in reforming her friends, but unfortunately she was only interested in the course that she was following in order to attain her own salvation. She was fond of Andy, but during the last two nights she had felt an urge to leave him. This was also very much due to the fact that an unfamiliar person had begun to frequent the bar.

This newcomer was of almost mammoth proportions, and both times that she had seen him he had been wearing a tremendous black overcoat well cut and obviously made of very expensive material. She had seen his face only fleetingly once or twice, but what she had seen of it had so frightened her that she had been able to think of very little else for two days now.

This man, they had noticed, drove up to the saloon in a very beautiful big automobile that resembled more a hearse than a private car. Miss Goering had examined it one day when the man was drinking in the saloon. It appeared to be almost brand-new. She and Andy had looked in through the window and had been a little surprised to see a lot of dirty clothes on the floor. Miss Goering was completely preoccupied now with what course to take should the newcomer be willing to make her his mistress for a little while. She was almost sure that he would, because several times she had caught him looking at her in a certain way which she had learned to recognize. Her only hope was that he would disappear before she had the chance to approach him. If he did, she would be exempt and thus able to fritter away some more time with Andy, who now seemed so devoid of anything sinister that she was beginning to scrap with him about small things the way one does with a younger brother.

On Sunday morning Miss Goering woke up to find Andy in his shirt sleeves, dusting off some small tables in the living-room.

"What is it?" she asked him. "Why are you bustling around like a bride?"

"Don't you remember?" he asked, looking hurt. "Today is the big day—the day of the conference. They are coming here bright and early, all three of them. They live like robins, those business men. Couldn't you," he asked her, "couldn't you do something about making this room prettier? You see, they've all got wives, and even if they probably couldn't tell you what the hell they've got in their living-rooms, their wives have all got plenty of money to spend on little ornaments and their eyes are probably used to a certain amount of fuss."

"Well, this room is so hideous, Andy, I don't see that anything would do it any good."

"Yes, I guess it's a pretty bad room. I never used to notice it much." Andy put on a navy-blue suit and combed his hair very neatly, rubbing in a little brilliantine. Then he paced up and down the living-room floor with his hands in his hip pockets. The sun was pouring in through the window, and the radiator was whistling in an annoying manner while it overheated the room as it had done constantly since Miss Goering had arrived.

Mr. Bellamy, Mr. Schlaegel, and Mr. Dockerty had received Andy's note and were on their way up the stairs, having accepted the appointment more out of curiosity and from an old habit of never letting anything slip by than because they actually believed that their visit would prove fruitful. When they smelled the terrible stench of the cheap cooking in the halls, they put their hands over their mouths in order not to laugh too loudly and performed a little mock pantomime of retreating towards the staircase again. They really didn't care very much, however, because it was Sunday and they preferred being together than with their families, so they proceeded to knock on Andy's door. Andy quickly wiped his hands because they were sweaty and ran to open the door. He stood in the doorway and shook hands with each man vigorously before inviting them to come in.

"I'm Andrew McLane," he said to them, "and I'm sorry that we have not met before." He ushered them into the room and all three of them realized at once that it was going to be abominably hot. Mr. Dockerty, the most aggressive of the three men, turned to Andy.

"Would you mind opening the window, fellow?" he said in a loud voice. "It's boiling in here."

"Oh," said Andy blushing, "I should have thought of it." He went over and opened the windows.

"How do you stand it, fellow?" said Mr. Dockerty. "You trying to hatch something in here?"

The three men stood in a little group near the couch and pulled out some cigars, which they examined together and discussed for a minute.

"Two of us are going to sit on this couch, fellow," said Mr. Dockerty, "and Mr. Schlaegel can sit here on this little armchair. Now where are you going to sit?"

Mr. Dockerty had decided almost immediately that Andy was a complete boob and was taking matters into his own hands. This so disconcerted Andy that he stood and stared at the three men without saying a word.

"Come," said Mr. Dockerty, carrying a chair out of a corner of the room and setting it down near the couch, "come, you sit here."

Andy sat down in silence and played with his fingers.

"Tell me," said Mr. Bellamy, who was a little more soft-spoken and genteel than the other two. "Tell me how long you have been living here."

"I have been living here two years," said Andy listlessly. The three men thought about this for a little while.

"Well," said Mr. Bellamy, "and tell us what you have done in these three years."

"Two years," said Andy.

Andy had prepared quite a long story to tell them because he had suspected that they might question him a bit about his personal life in order to make certain what kind of man they were dealing with, and he had decided that it would not be wise to admit that he had done absolutely nothing in the past two years. But he had imagined that the meeting was to be conducted on a much more friendly basis. He had supposed that the men would be delighted to have found someone who was willing to put a little money into their business, and would be more than anxious to believe that he was an upright, hard-working citizen. Now, however, he felt that he was being cross-questioned and made a fool of. He could barely control his desire to bolt out of the room.

"Nothing," he said, avoiding their eyes, "nothing."

"It always amazes me," said Mr. Bellamy, "how people

are able to have leisure time—that is, if they have more leisure time than they need. Now I mean to say that our business has been running for thirty-two years. There hasn't been a day gone by that I haven't had at least thirteen or fourteen things to attend to. That might seem a little exaggerated to you or maybe even very much exaggerated, but it isn't exaggerated, it's true. In the first place I attend personally to every house on our list. I check the plumbing and the drainage and the whatnot. I see whether or not the house is being kept up properly and I also visit it in all kinds of weather to see how it fares during a storm or a blizzard. I know exactly how much coal it takes to heat every house on our list. I talk personally to our clients and I try to influence them on the price they are asking for their house, whether or not they are trying to rent or to sell. For instance, if they are asking a price that I know is too high because I am able to compare it with every price on the market, I try to persuade them to lower their price a little bit so that it will be nearer the norm. If, on the other hand, they are cheating themselves and I know . . ."

The other two men were getting a little bored. One could easily see that Mr. Bellamy was the least important of the three, although he might easily have been the one that accomplished all the tedious work. Mr. Schlaegel interrupted him.

"Well, my man," he said to Andy, "tell us what this is all about. In your letter you stated that you had some suggestions whereby you thought we could profit, as well as yourself, of course."

Andy got up from his chair. It was evident to the men now that he was under a terrific tension, so they were doubly on their guard.

"Why don't you come back some other time?" said Andy very quickly. "Then I will have thought it out more clearly."

"Take your time, take your time, now, fellow," said Mr. Dockerty. "We are all here together and there's no reason why we shouldn't talk it over right away. We don't really live in town, you know. We live twenty minutes out in Fairview. We developed Fairview ourselves, as a matter of fact."

"Well," said Andy, coming back and sitting on the edge of his chair, "I have a little property myself."

"Where's that?" said Mr. Dockerty.

"It's a building, in the city, way down, near the docks." He gave Mr. Dockerty the name of the street and then sat biting his lips. Mr. Dockerty didn't say anything.

"You see," continued Andy, "I thought I might hand my rights to this building over to the corporation in return for an interest in your business—at least a right to work for the firm and get my share out of the selling I do. I wouldn't need to have equal rights with you immediately, naturally, but I thought I'd discuss these details with you later if you were interested."

Mr. Dockerty shut his eyes and then after a little while he addressed himself to Mr. Schlaegel.

"I know the street he is talking about," he said. Mr. Schlaegel shook his head and made a face. Andy looked at his shoes.

"For a long time," said Mr. Dockerty, still addressing Mr. Schlaegel, "for a long time the buildings in that district have been a drag on the market. Even as slums they're pretty bad and the profit from any one of them is just enough to keep body and soul together. That's because, as you remember, Schlaegel, there is no means of transportation at any convenient distance and it's surrounded by fish markets.

"Besides that," went on Mr. Dockerty, turning to Andy, "we have in our charter a clause that prohibits our taking on any more men except on a strict salary basis, and, my friend, there's a list as long as my arm waiting for a job in our offices, if there should be a vacancy. Their tongues are hanging out for any job we can offer them. Fine young men too, the majority of them just out of college, roaring to work, and to put into use every modern trick of selling that they have learned about. I know some of their families personally and I'm sorry I can't help these lads out more than I am able to."

Just then Miss Goering came rushing through the room. "I'm an hour or two late for Arnold's father," she screamed over her shoulder as she went out the door. "I will see you later."

Andy had got up and was facing the window with his back to the three men. His shoulder blades were twitching.

"Was that your wife?" Mr. Dockerty called to him.

Andy did not answer, but in a few seconds Mr. Dockerty repeated his question, mainly because he had a suspicion it had not been Andy's wife and he was anxious to know whether or not he had guessed correctly. He kicked Mr.

Schlaegel's foot with his own and they winked at each other.

"No," said Andy, turning around and revealing his flame-red face. "No, she is not my wife. She's my girl friend. She's been living here with me for a week nearly. Is there anything else you men want to know?"

"Now look here, fellow," said Mr. Dockerty, "there's nothing for you to get excited about. She's a very pretty woman, very pretty, and if you're upset about the little business talk we had together, there's no reason for that either. We explained everything to you clearly, like three pals." Andy looked out of the window.

"You know," said Mr. Dockerty, "there are other jobs you can get that will be far more suited to you and your background and that'll make you lots happier in the end. You ask your girl friend if that isn't so." Still Andy did not answer them.

"There are other jobs," Mr. Dockerty ventured to say again, but since there was still no answer from Andy, he shrugged his shoulders, rose with difficulty from the couch, and straightened his vest and his coat. The others did likewise. Then all three of them politely bade good-by to Andy's back and left the room.

ARNOLD'S FATHER HAD been sitting in the ice-cream parlor one hour and a half when Miss Goering finally came running in. He looked completely forlorn. It had never occurred to him to buy a magazine to read and there had been no one to look at in the ice-cream parlor because it was still morning and people seldom dropped in before afternoon.

"Oh, I can't tell you, my dear, how sorry I am," said Miss Goering, taking both his hands in hers and pressing them to her lips. He was wearing woolen gloves. "I can't tell you how these gloves remind me of my childhood," Miss Goering continued.

"I've been cold these last few days," said Arnold's father, "so Miss Gamelon went into town and bought me these."

"Well, and how is everything going?"

"I will tell you all about that in a little while," said Arnold's father, "but I would like to know if you are all right, my dear woman, and whether or not you intend to return to the island."

"I—I don't think so," said Miss Goering, "not for a long time."

"Well, I must tell you of the many changes that have taken place in our lives, and I hope that you will not think of them as too drastic or sudden or revolutionary, or whatever you may call it."

Miss Goering smiled faintly.

"You see," he continued, "it has been growing colder and colder in the house these last few days. Miss Gamelon has had the sniffles terribly, I must concede, and also, as you know, she's been in a wretched test about the old-fashioned cooking equipment right from the beginning. Now, Arnold doesn't really mind anything if he has enough to eat, but recently Miss Gamelon has refused to set foot in the kitchen."

"Now what on earth has been the outcome of all this? Do hurry up and tell me," Miss Goering urged him.

"I can't go any faster than I'm going," said Arnold's father. "Now, the other day Adele Wyman, an old school friend of Arnold's, met him in town and they had a cup of coffee together. In the course of the conversation Adele mentioned that she was living in a two-family house on the island and that she liked it but she was terribly worried about who was going to move into the other half."

"Well, then, am I to gather that they have moved into this house and are living there?"

"They have moved into that house until you come back," said Arnold's father. "Fortunately, it seemed that you had no lease on the first little house; therefore, since it was the end of the month, they felt free to move out. Miss Gamelon wonders if you will send the rent checks to the new house. Arnold has volunteered to pay the difference in rent, which is very slight."

"No, no, that is not necessary. Is there anything more that is new?" said Miss Goering.

"Well, it might interest you to know," said Arnold's father, "that I have decided to return to my wife and my original house."

"Why?" Miss Goering asked.

"A combination of circumstances, including the fact that I am old and feel like going home."

"Oh my," said Miss Goering, "it's a shame to see things breaking up this way, isn't it?"

"Yes, my dear, it is a pity, but I have come here to ask

you a favor besides having come because I loved you and wanted to say good-by to you."

"I will do anything for you," said Miss Goering, "that I can possibly do."

"Well," said Arnold's father, "I would like you to read over this note that I have written to my wife. I want to send it to her and then I will return on the following day to my house."

"Certainly," said Miss Goering. She noticed there was an envelope on the table in front of Arnold's father. She picked it up.

Dear Ethel [she read],

I hope that you will read this letter with all that indulgence and sympathy which you possess so strongly in your heart.

I can only say that there is, in every man's life, a strong urge to leave his life behind him for a while and seek a new one. If he is living near to the sea, a strong urge to take the next boat and sail away no matter how happy his home or how beloved his wife or mother. It is true also if the man is living near a road that he may feel the strong urge to strap a knapsack on his back and walk away, again leaving a happy home behind him. Very few people follow this urge once they have passed their youth without doing so. But it is my idea that sometimes age affects us like youth, like strong champagne that goes to our heads, and we dare what we have never dared before, perhaps also because we feel that it is our last chance. However, while as youths we might continue in such an adventure, at my age one very quickly finds out that it is a mere chimera and that one has not the strength. Will you take me back?

Your loving husband,
Edgar

"It is simple," said Arnold's father, "and it expresses what I felt."

"Is that really the way you felt?" asked Miss Goering.

"I believe so," said Arnold's father. "It must have been. Of course I did not mention to her anything concerning my sentiments about you, but she will have guessed that, and such things are better left unsaid . . ."

He looked down at his woolen gloves and said no more for a little while. Suddenly he reached in his pocket and pulled out another letter.

"I'm sorry," he said, "I almost forgot. Here is a letter from Arnold."

"Now," said Miss Goering opening the letter, "what can this be about?"

"Surely a lot about nothing and about the trollop he is living with, which is worse than nothing." Miss Goering opened the letter and proceeded to read it aloud:

Dear Christina,

I have told Father to explain to you the reasons for our recent change of domicile. I hope he has done so and that you are satisfied that we have not behaved rashly nor in a manner that you might conclude was inconsiderate. Lucy wants you to send her check to this present address. Father was supposed to tell you so but I thought that perhaps he might forget. Lucy, I am afraid, has been very upset by your present escapade. She is constantly in either a surly or melancholic mood. I had hoped that this condition would ameliorate after we had moved, but she is still subject to long silences and often weeps at night, not to mention the fact that she is exceedingly cranky and has twice had a set-to with Adele, although we have only been here two days. I see in all this that Lucy's nature is really one of extreme delicateness and morbidity and I am fascinated to be by her side. Adele on the other hand has a very equable nature, but she is terribly intellectual and very much interested in every branch of art. We are thinking of starting a magazine together when we are more or less settled. She is a pretty blonde girl.

I miss you terribly, my dear, and I want you to please believe that if I could only somehow reach what was inside of me I would break out of this terrible cocoon I am in. I expect to some day really. I will always remember the story you told me when we first met, in which I always felt was buried some strange significance, although I must admit to you now that I could not explain what. I must go and take Bubbles some hot tea to her room now.

Please, please believe in me.
Love and kisses,
Arnold

"He's a nice man," said Miss Goering. For some reason Arnold's letter made her feel sad, while his father's letter had annoyed and puzzled her.

"Well," said Arnold's father, "I must be leaving now if I want to catch the next ferry."

"Wait," said Miss Goering, "I will accompany you to the dock." She quickly unfastened a rose that she had been wearing on the collar of her coat and pinned it on the old man's lapel.

When they arrived at the dock the gong was being sounded and the ferry was all ready to leave for the island. Miss Goering was relieved to see this, for she had feared a long sentimental scene.

"Well, we made it in the nick of time," said Arnold's father, trying to adopt a casual manner. But Miss Goering could see that his blue eyes were wet with tears . . . She could barely restrain her own tears and she looked away from the ferry up the hill.

"I wonder," said Arnold's father, "if you could lend me fifty cents. I sent all my money to my wife and I didn't think of borrowing enough from Arnold this morning."

She quickly gave him a dollar and they kissed each other good-by. While the ferry pulled out, Miss Goering stood on the dock and waved; he had asked her to do this as a favor to him.

When she returned to the apartment she found it empty, so that she decided to go to the bar and drink, feeling certain that if Andy was not already there, he would arrive sooner or later.

She had been drinking there a few hours and it was beginning to grow dark. Andy had not yet arrived and Miss Goering felt a little relieved. She looked over her shoulder and saw that the heavy-set man who owned the hearse-like car was coming through the door. She shivered involuntarily and smiled sweetly at Frank, the bartender.

"Frank," she said, "don't you ever get a day off?"

"Don't want one."

"Why not?"

"Because I want to keep my nose to the grindstone and do something worth while later on. I don't get much enjoyment out of anything but thinking my own thoughts, anyway."

"I just hate thinking mine, Frank."

"No, that's silly," said Frank.

The big man in the overcoat had just climbed up on a stool and thrown a fifty-cent piece down on the bar. Frank served him his drink. After he had drunk it he turned to Miss Goering.

"Will you have a drink?" he asked her.

Much as she feared him, Miss Goering felt a peculiar thrill at the fact that he had at last spoken to her. She had been expecting it for a few days now, and felt she could not refrain from telling him so.

"Thank you so much," she said in such an ingratiating manner that Frank, who approved little of ladies who spoke to strangers, frowned darkly and moved over to the other end of the bar, where he began to read a magazine. "Thank you so much, I'd be glad to. It might interest you to know that I have imagined our drinking together like this for some time now and I am not at all surprised that you asked me. I had rather imagined that it would happen at this time of day too, and when there was no one else here." The man nodded his head once or twice.

"Well, what do you want to drink?" he asked her. Miss Goering was very disappointed that he had made no direct answer to her remark.

After Frank had served the drink the man snatched it from in front of her.

"Come on," he said, "let's go and sit in a booth."

Miss Goering clambered down from her stool and followed him to the booth that was farthest from the door.

"Well," he said to her after they had been sitting there for a little while, "do you work here?"

"Where?" said Miss Goering.

"Here, in this town."

"No," said Miss Goering.

"Well, then, do you work in another town?"

"No, I don't work."

"Yes, you do. You don't have to try to fool me, because no one ever has."

"I don't understand."

"You work as a prostitute, after a fashion, don't you?"

Miss Goering laughed. "Heavens!" she said. "I certainly never thought I looked like a prostitute merely because I had red hair; perhaps like a derelict or an escaped lunatic, but never a prostitute!"

"You don't look like no derelict or escaped lunatic to me. You look like a prostitute, and that's what you are. I don't mean a real small-time prostitute. I mean a medium one."

"Well, I don't object to prostitutes, but really I assure you I am no such thing."

"I don't believe you."

"But how are we to form any kind of friendship at all," said Miss Goering, "if you don't believe anything I say?"

The man shook his head once more. "I don't believe you when you say you're not a prostitute because I know you're a prostitute."

"All right," said Miss Goering, "I'm tired of arguing." She had noticed that his face, unlike most other faces, seemed not to take on any added life when he was engaged in conversation and she felt that all her presentiments about him had been justified.

He was now running his foot up her leg. She tried to smile at him but she was unable to.

"Come now," she said, "Frank is very apt to see what you are doing from where he is standing behind the bar and I should feel terribly embarrassed."

He seemed to ignore her remark completely and continued to press on her leg more and more vigorously.

"Would you want to come home with me and have a steak dinner?" he asked her. "I'm having steak and onions and coffee. You could stay a few days if everything worked out, or longer. This other little girl, Dorothy, just went away about a week ago."

"I think that would be nice," said Miss Goering.

"Well," he said, "It's almost an hour's drive there in a car. I have to go now to see someone here in town, but I'll be back in half a hour or so; if you want some steak you better be here too."

"All right, I will," said Miss Goering.

He had not been gone more than a few minutes when Andy arrived. He had both hands in his pockets and his coat collar turned up. He was looking down at his feet.

"Lord God Almighty!" Miss Goering said to herself. "I have to break the news to him right away and I have not seen him so dejected in a week."

"What on earth happened to you?" she asked him.

"I have been to a movie, giving myself a little lesson in self-control."

"What does that mean?"

"I mean that I was upset; my soul was turned inside out this morning and I had but two choices, to drink and continue drinking or to go to a movie. I chose the latter."

"But you still look terribly morose."

"I am less morose. I am just showing the results of the terrific fight that I have waged inside of myself, and you know that the face of victory often resembles the face of defeat."

"Victory fades so quickly that it is scarcely apparent and it is always the face of defeat that we are able to see," said Miss Goering. She did not want to tell him, in front of Frank, that she was leaving, because she was certain that Frank would know where she was going. "Andy," she said, "would you mind coming across the street with me, to the ice-cream parlor? I have something that I want to talk to you about."

"All right," said Andy rather more casually than Miss Goering had expected. "But I want to come back right away for a drink."

They went across the street to the little ice-cream parlor and sat down at a table opposite each other. There was no one in the store with the exception of themselves and the boy who served the customers. He nodded at them when they came in.

"Back again?" he said to Miss Goering. "That old man sure waited for you a long time this morning."

"Yes," said Miss Goering, "it was dreadful."

"Well, you gave him a flower, anyway, when you left. He must have been tickled about that."

Miss Goering did not answer him as she had very little time to waste.

"Andy," she said, "I'm going in a few minutes to a place that's about an hour away from here and I probably won't be coming back for quite some time."

Andy seemed to understand the situation immediately. Miss Goering sat back and waited while he pressed his palms tighter and tighter to his temples.

Finally he looked up at her. "You," he said, "as a decent human being, cannot do this to me."

"Well, I'm afraid I can, Andy. I have my own star to follow, you know."

"But do you know," said Andy, "how beautiful and delicate a man's heart is when he is happy for the first time? It is like the thin ice that has imprisoned those beautiful young plants that are released when the ice thaws."

"You have read that in some poem," said Miss Goering.

"Does that make it any the less beautiful?"

"No," said Miss Goering, "I admit that it is a very beautiful thought."

"You don't dare tear the plant up now that you have melted the ice."

"Oh, Andy," said Miss Goering, "you make me sound so dreadful! I am merely working out something for myself."

"You have no right to," said Andy. "You're not alone in the world. You've involved yourself with me!" He was growing more excited perhaps because he realized that it was useless saying anything to Miss Goering at all.

"I'll get down on my knees," said Andy, shaking his fist at her. No sooner had he said this than he was down on his knees near her feet. The waiter was terribly shocked and felt that he had better say something.

"Look, Andy," he said in a very small voice, "Why don't you get up off your knees and think things over?"

"Because," said Andy, raising his own voice more and more, "because she daren't refuse a man who is down on his knees. She daren't! It would be sacrilege."

"I don't see why," said Miss Goering.

"If you refuse," said Andy, "I'll disgrace you, I'll crawl out into the street, I'll put you to shame."

"I really have no sense of shame," said Miss Goering, "and I think your own sense of shame is terribly exaggerated, besides being a terrific sap on your energies. Now I must go, Andy. Please get up."

"You're crazy," said Andy. "You're crazy and monstrous—*really*. Monstrous. You are committing a monstrous act."

"Well," said Miss Goering, "perhaps my maneuvers do seem a little strange, but I have thought for a long time now that often, so very often, heroes who believe themselves to be monsters because they are so far removed from other men turn around much later and see really monstrous acts being committed in the name of something mediocre."

"Lunatic!" Andy yelled at her from his knees. "You're not even a Christian."

Miss Goering hurried out of the ice-cream parlor after having kissed Andy lightly on the head, because she realized that if she did not leave him very quickly she would miss her appointment. As a matter of fact, she had judged correctly, because her friend was just coming out of the saloon when she arrived.

"Are you coming out with me?" he said. "I got through a little sooner than I thought and I decided I wasn't going to wait around, because I didn't think you'd come."

"But," said Miss Goering, "I accepted your invitation. Why didn't you think I'd come?"

"Don't get excited," said the man. "Come on, let's get in the car."

As they drove past the ice-cream parlor on their way out of town, Miss Goering looked through the window to see if she could catch a glimpse of Andy. To her surprise, she saw that the store was filled with people, so that they overflowed into the street and quite crowded the sidewalk, and she was unable really to see into the store at all.

The man was sitting in front with the chauffeur, who was not in uniform, and she was sitting alone in the back seat. This arrangement had surprised her at first, but she was pleased. She understood shortly why he had arranged the seating in this manner. Soon after they had left the town behind them he turned around and said to her:

"I'm going to sleep now. I'm more comfortable up here because I don't bounce around so much. You can talk to the chauffeur if you want."

"I don't think I care to talk with anyone," said Miss Goering.

"Well, do whatever the hell you want," he said. "I don't want to be waked up until those steaks are on the grill." He promptly pulled his hat down over his eyes and went to sleep.

As they drove on, Miss Goering felt sadder and lonelier than she had ever felt before in her life. She missed Andy and Arnold and Miss Gamelon and the old man with all her heart and very soon she was weeping silently in the back of the car. It was only with a tremendous exertion of her will that she refrained from opening the door and leaping out into the road.

They passed through several small towns and at last, just at Miss Goering was dozing off, they arrived in a medium-sized city.

"This is the town we were heading for," said the chauffeur, assuming that Miss Goering had been watching the road impatiently. It was a noisy town and there were many tramways all heading in different directions. Miss Goering was astonished that the noise did not awaken her friend in the front seat. They soon left the center of town, although they were still in the city proper when they drove up in front of an apartment building. The chauffeur had quite a difficult time awakening his employer, but at last he succeeded by yelling the man's own address close to his ear.

Miss Goering was waiting on the sidewalk, standing first on one foot and then on the other. She noticed that there was a little garden that ran the length of one side of the apartment house. It was planted with evergreen trees and bushes, all of small dimensions because it was obvious that both the garden and the apartment house were very new. A string of barbed wire surrounded the garden and there was a dog trying to crawl under it. "I'll go put the car away, Ben," said the chauffeur.

Ben got out of the car and pushed Miss Goering ahead of him into the lobby of the apartment.

"Fake Spanish," Miss Goering said more to herself than to Ben.

"This isn't fake Spanish," he said glumly, "this is real Spanish."

Miss Goering laughed a little. "I don't think so," she said. "I have been to Spain."

"I don't believe you," said Ben. "Anyhow, this is real Spanish, every inch of it."

Miss Goering looked around her at the walls, which were made of yellow stucco and ornamented with niches and clusters of tiny columns.

Together they entered a tiny automatic elevator and Miss Goering's heart nearly failed her. Her companion pressed a button, but the elevator remained stationary.

"I could tear the man to pieces who made this gadget," he said, stamping on the floor.

"Oh, please," said Miss Goering, "please let me out."

He paid no attention to her, but stamped even harder than before, and pressed on the button over and over again as though the fear in her voice had excited him. At last the elevator started to rise. Miss Goering hid her face in her hands. They reached the second floor, where the elevator stopped, and they got out. They waited together in front of one of three doors that opened on a narrow hall.

"Jim has the keys with him," said Ben; "he'll be up in a minute. I hope you understand that we won't go dancing or any nonsense. I can't stand what people call fun."

"Oh, I love all that," said Miss Goering. "Fundamentally I am a light-hearted person. That is, I enjoy all the things that light-hearted people enjoy."

Ben yawned.

"He's never going to listen to me," Miss Goering said to herself.

PRESENTLY THE CHAUFFEUR returned with the keys and let them into the apartment. The living-room was small and unattractive. Someone had left an enormous bundle in the middle of the floor. Through some rents in the paper Miss Goering could see that the bundle contained a pretty pink quilt. She felt a little heartened at the sight of the quilt and asked Ben whether or not he had chosen it himself. Without answering her question he called to the chauffeur, who had gone into the kitchen adjoining the living-room. The door between the two rooms was open, and Miss Goering could see the chauffeur standing next to the sink in his hat and coat and slowly unwrapping the steaks.

"I told you to see that they called for that damn blanket," Ben shouted to him.

"I forgot."

"Then carry one of those reminder pads with you and pull it out of your pocket once in a while. You can buy one at the corner."

Ben threw himself down on the couch next to Miss Goering, who had seated herself, and put his hand on her knee.

"Why? Don't you want the quilt now that you have bought it?" Miss Goering asked him.

"I didn't buy it. That girl who was here with me last week bought it, to throw over us in bed."

"And you don't like the color?"

"I don't like a lot of extra stuff hanging around."

He sat brooding for a few minutes and Miss Goering, whose heart began to beat much too quickly each time that he lapsed into silence, searched her mind for another question to ask.

"You're not fond of discussions," she said to him.

"You mean talking?"

"Yes."

"No, I'm not."

"Why aren't you?"

"You say too much when you talk," he answered absently.

"Well, aren't you anxious to find out about people?"

He shook his head. "I don't need to find out about people, and, what's more important, they don't need to find out about me." He looked at her out of the corner of his eye.

"Well," she said a little breathlessly, "there must be something you like."

"I like women a lot and I like to make money if I can make it quickly." Without warning he jumped to his feet and pulled Miss Goering up with him, grabbing hold of her wrist rather roughly. "While he's finishing the steaks let's go inside for a minute."

"Oh, please," Miss Goering pleaded, "I'm so tired. Let's rest here a little before dinner."

"All right," said Ben. "I'm going to my room and stretch out till the steaks are cooked. I like them overdone."

While he was gone, Miss Goering sat on the couch pulling at her sweating fingers. She was torn between an almost overwhelming desire to bolt out of the room and a sickening compulsion to remain where she was.

"I do hope," she said to herself, "that the steaks will be ready before I have a chance to decide."

However, by the time the chauffeur awakened Ben to announce that the steaks were cooked, Miss Goering had decided that it was absolutely necessary for her to stay.

They sat together around a small folding table and ate in silence. They had barely finished their meal when the telephone rang. Ben answered, and when he had finished his conversation he told Miss Goering and Jim that they were all three of them going into the city. The chauffeur looked at him knowingly.

"It doesn't take long from here," said Ben, pulling on his coat. He turned to Miss Goering. "We are going to a restaurant," he said to her. "You'll sit patient at a separate table while I talk business with some friends. If it gets terribly late you and me will spend the night in the city at a hotel where I always go, downtown. Jim will drive the car back out and sleep here. Now is everything understood by everybody?"

"Perfectly," said Miss Goering, who was naturally delighted that they were leaving the apartment.

THE RESTAURANT WAS NOT very gay. It was in a large square room on the first floor of an old house. Ben led her to a table near the wall and told her to sit down.

"Every now and then you can order something," he said, and went over to three men who were standing at a makeshift bar improvised of thin strips of wood and papier-mâché.

The guests were nearly all men, and Miss Goering noticed that there were no distinguished faces among them, although not one of them was shabbily dressed. The three men to whom Ben was talking were ugly and even brutal-looking. Presently she saw Ben make a sign to a woman who was seated not far from her own table. She went and spoke to him and then walked quickly over to Miss Goering's table.

"He wants you to know he's going to be here a long time, maybe over two hours. I am supposed to get you what you want. Would you like some spaghetti or a sandwich? I'll get you whichever you want."

"No, thank you," said Miss Goering. "But won't you sit down and have a drink with me?"

"To tell you the truth, I won't," said the woman, "although I thank you very much." She hesitated a moment before saying good-by. "Of course, I would like to have you come over to our table and join us, but the situation is hard to explain. Most of us here are close friends, and when we see each other we tell each other everything that has happened."

"I understand," said Miss Goering, who was rather sad to see her leave because she did not fancy sitting alone for two or three hours. Although she was not anxious to be in Ben's company, the suspense of waiting all that time with so little to distract her was almost unbearable. It occurred to her that she might possibly telephone to a friend and ask her to come and have a drink at the restaurant. "Certainly," she thought. "Ben can't object to my having a little chat with another woman." Anna and Mrs. Copperfield were the only two people she knew well enough to invite on such short notice. Of the two she preferred Mrs. Copperfield and thought her the most likely to accept such an invitation. But she was not certain that Mrs. Copperfield had returned yet from her trip through Central America. She called the waiter and requested that he take her to the phone. After asking a few questions he showed her into a drafty hall and called the number for her. She was successful in reaching her friend, who was terribly excited the moment she heard Miss Goering's voice.

"I am flying down immediately," she said to Miss Goering. "I can't tell you how terrific it is to hear from you. I have not been back long, you know, and I don't think I'll stay."

Just as Mrs. Copperfield was telling her this, Ben came into the hall and snatched the receiver from Miss Goering's hand. "What's this about, for Christ's sake?" he demanded.

Miss Goering asked Mrs. Copperfield to hold on a moment. "I am calling a woman friend," she said to Ben, "a woman whom I haven't seen in quite some time. She is a lively person and I thought she might like to come down and have a drink with me. I was growing lonely at my table."

"Hello," Ben shouted into the phone, "are you coming down here?"

"By all means and *tout de suite*," Mrs. Copperfield answered. "I adore her."

Ben seemed satisfied and returned the receiver to Miss Goering without saying a word. Before leaving the hall, however, he announced to Miss Goering that he was not going to take on two women. She nodded and resumed her conversation with Mrs. Copperfield. She told her the address of the restaurant which the waiter had written down for her, and said good-by.

About half an hour later Mrs. Copperfield arrived, accompanied by a woman whom Miss Goering had never seen before.

She was dismayed at the sight of her old friend. She was terribly thin and she appeared to be suffering from a skin eruption. Mrs. Copperfield's friend was fairly attractive, Miss Goering thought, but her hair was far too wiry for her own taste. Both women were dressed expensively and in black.

"There she is," Mrs. Copperfield screamed, grabbing Pacifica by the hand and running over to Miss Goering's table.

"I can't tell you how delighted I am that you called," she said. "You are the one person in the world I wanted to have see me. This is Pacifica. She is with me in my apartment."

Miss Goering asked them to sit down.

"Listen," said Pacifica to Miss Goering, "I have a date with a boy very far uptown. It is wonderful to see you, but he will be very nervous and unhappy. She can talk to you and I'll go and see him now. You are great friends, she told me."

Mrs. Copperfield rose to her feet. "Pacifica," she said, "you must stay here and have drinks first. This is a miracle and you must be in on it."

"It is so late now that I will be in a damned mess if I don't go right away. She would not come here alone," Pacifica said to Miss Goering.

"Remember, you promised to come and get me afterwards," said Mrs. Copperfield. "I will telephone you as soon as Christina is ready to leave."

Pacifica said good-by and hurried out of the room.

"What do you think of her?" Mrs. Copperfield asked Miss Goering, but without waiting for an answer she called for the waiter and ordered two double whiskies. "What do you think of her?" she repeated.

"Where's she from?"

"She is a Spanish girl from Panama, and the most wonderful character that has ever existed. We don't make a move without each other. I am completely satisfied and contented."

"I should say, though, that you are a little run down," said Miss Goering, who was frankly worried about her friend.

"I'll tell you," said Mrs. Copperfield, leaning over the table and suddenly looking very tense. "I am a little worried—not terribly worried, because I shan't allow anything to happen that I don't want to happen—but I am a little worried because Pacifica has met this blond boy who lives way uptown and he has asked her to marry him. He never says anything and he has a very weak character. But I think he has bewitched her because he pays her compliments all the time. I've gone up to his apartment with her, because I won't allow them to be alone, and she has cooked dinner for him twice. He's crazy for Spanish food and eats ravenously of every dish she puts in front of him."

Mrs. Copperfield leaned back and stared intently into Miss Goering's eyes.

"I am taking her back to Panama as soon as I am able to book passage on a boat." She ordered another double whisky. "Well, what do you think of it?" she asked eagerly.

"Perhaps you'd better wait and see whether or not she really wants to marry him."

"Don't be insane," said Mrs. Copperfield. "I can't live without her, not for a minute. I'd go completely to pieces."

"But you have gone to pieces, or do I misjudge you dreadfully?"

"True enough," said Mrs. Copperfield, bringing her fist down on the table and looking very mean. "I have gone to pieces, which is a thing I've wanted to do for years. I know I am as guilty as I can be, but I have my happiness, which I guard like a wolf, and I have authority now and a certain amount of daring, which, if you remember correctly, I never had before."

Mrs. Copperfield was getting drunk and looking more disagreeable.

"I remember," said Miss Goering, "that you used to be somewhat shy, but I dare say very courageous. It would take a good deal of courage to live with a man like Mr. Copperfield, whom I gather you are no longer living with. I've admired you very much indeed. I am not sure that I do now."

"That makes no difference to me," said Mrs. Copperfield. "I feel that you have changed anyway and lost your charm. You seem stodgy to me now and less comforting. You used to be so gracious and understanding; everyone thought you were light in the head, but I thought you were extremely instinctive and gifted with magic powers." She ordered another drink and sat brooding for a moment.

"You will contend," she continued in a very clear voice, "that all people are of equal importance, but although I love Pacifica very much, I think it is obvious that I am more important."

Miss Goering did not feel that she had any right to argue this point with Mrs. Copperfield.

"I understand how you feel," she said, "and perhaps you are right."

"Thank God," said Mrs. Copperfield, and she took Miss Goering's hand in her own.

"Christina," she pleaded, "please don't cross me again, I can't bear it."

Miss Goering hoped that Mrs. Copperfield would now question her concerning her own life. She had a great desire to tell someone everything that had happened during the last year. But Mrs. Copperfield sat gulping down her drink, occasionally spilling a little of it over her chin. She was not even looking at Miss Goering and they sat for ten minutes in silence.

"I think," said Mrs. Copperfield at last, "that I will telephone Pacifica and tell her to call for me in three quarters of an hour."

Miss Goering showed her to the phone and returned to the table. She looked up after a moment and noticed that another man had joined Ben and his friends. When her friend returned from the telephone, Miss Goering saw immediately that something was very much the matter. Mrs. Copperfield fell into her seat.

"She says that she does not know when she is coming down, and if she is not here by the time you feel like leaving, I am to return home with you, or all alone by myself. It's happened to me now, hasn't it? But the beauty of me is that I am only a step from desperation all the time and I am one of the few people I know who could perform an act of violence with the greatest of ease."

She waved her hand over her head.

"Acts of violence are generally performed with ease," said Miss Goering. She was at this point completely disgusted with Mrs. Copperfield, who rose from her seat and walked in a crooked path over to the bar. There she stood taking drink after drink without turning her little head which was almost completely hidden by the enormous fur collar on her coat.

Miss Goering went up to Mrs. Copperfield just once, thinking that she might persuade her friend to return to the table. But Mrs. Copperfield showed a furious tear-stained face to Miss Goering and flung her arm out sideways, striking Miss Goering in the nose with her forearm. Miss Goering returned to her seat and sat nursing her nose.

To her great surprise, about twenty minutes later Pacifica arrived, accompanied by her young man. She introduced him to Miss Goering and then hurried over to the bar. The young man stood with his hands in his pockets and looked around him rather awkwardly.

"Sit down," said Miss Goering. "I thought that Pacifica was not coming."

"She was not coming," he answered very slowly, "but then she decided that she would come because she was worried that her friend would be upset."

"Mrs. Copperfield is a highly strung woman, I am afraid," said Miss Goering.

"I don't know her very well," he answered discreetly.

Pacifica returned from the bar with Mrs. Copperfield, who was now terribly gay and wanted to order drinks for everyone. But neither the boy nor Pacifica would accept her offer. The boy looked very sad and soon excused himself, saying that he had only intended to see Pacifica to the restaurant and then return to his home. Mrs. Copperfield decided to accompany him to the door, patting his hand all the way and stumbling so badly that he was obliged to slip his arm around her waist to keep her from falling. Pacifica, meanwhile, leaned over to Miss Goering.

"It is terrible," she said. "What a baby your friend is! I can't leave her for ten minutes because it almost breaks her heart, and she is such a kind and generous woman, with such a beautiful apartment and such beautiful clothes. What can I do with her? She is like a little baby. I tried to explain it to my young man, but I can't explain it really to anyone."

Mrs. Copperfield returned and suggested that they all go elsewhere to get some food.

"I can't," said Miss Goering, lowering her eyes. "I have an appointment with a gentleman." She would have liked to talk to Pacifica a little longer. In some ways Pacifica reminded her of Miss Gamelon although certainly Pacifica was a much nicer person and more attractive physically. At this moment she noticed that Ben and his friends were putting on their coats and getting ready to leave. She hesitated only a second and then hurriedly said good-by to Pacifica and Mrs. Copperfield. She was just drawing her wrap over her shoulders when, to her surprise, she saw the four men walk very rapidly towards the door, right past her table. Ben made no sign to her.

"He must be coming back," she thought, but she decided to go into the hall. They were not in the hall, so she opened the door and stood on the stoop. From there she saw them all get into Ben's black car. Ben was the last one to get in, and just as he stepped on the running board, he turned his head around and saw Miss Goering.

"Hey," he said, "I forgot about you. I've got to go big distances on some important business. I don't know when I'll be back. Good-by."

He slammed the door behind him and they drove off. Miss Goering began to descend the stone steps. The long staircase seemed short to her, like a dream that is remembered long after it has been dreamed.

She stood on the street and waited to be overcome with joy and relief. But soon she was aware of a new sadness within herself. Hope, she felt, had discarded a childish form forever.

"Certainly I am nearer to becoming a saint," reflected Miss Goering, "but is it possible that a part of me hidden from my sight is piling sin upon sin as fast as Mrs. Copperfield?" This latter possibility Miss Goering thought to be of considerable interest but of no great importance.

Jane Bowles: a memoir

by Truman Capote

Truman Capote with Jane and Paul Bowles

This memoir of Jane Bowles was written as an introduction to her *Collected Works* (1966)

It must be seven or eight years since I last saw that modern legend named Jane Bowles; nor have I heard from her, at least not directly. Yet I am sure she is unchanged; indeed, I am told by recent travelers to North Africa who have seen or sat with her in some dim casbah café that this is true, and that Jane, with her dahlia-head of cropped curly hair, her tilted nose and mischief-shiny, just a trifle mad eyes, her very original voice (a husky soprano), her boyish clothes and schoolgirl's figure and slightly limping walk, is more or less the same as when I first knew her more than twenty years ago: even then she had seemed the eternal urchin, appealing as the most appealing of non-adults, yet with some substance cooler than blood invading her veins, and with a wit, an eccentric wisdom no child, not the strangest wunderkind, ever possessed.

When I first met Mrs. Bowles (1944? 1945?) she was already, within certain worlds, a celebrated figure: though only in her twenties, she had published a most individual and much remarked novel, *Two Serious Ladies*; she had married the gifted composer and writer Paul Bowles and was, together with her husband, a tenant in a glamorous boardinghouse established on Brooklyn Heights by the late George Davis. Among the Bowles' fellow boarders were Richard and Ellen Wright, W. H. Auden, Benjamin Britten, Oliver Smith, Carson McCullers, Gypsy Rose Lee, and (I seem to remember) a trainer of chimpanzees who lived there with one of his star performers. Anyway, it was one hell of a household. But even amid such a forceful assembly, Mrs. Bowles, by virtue of her talent and the strange visions it enclosed, and because of her personality's startling blend of playful-puppy candor and feline sophistication, remained an imposing, stage-front presence.

Jane Bowles is an authoritative linguist; she speaks, with the greatest precision, French and Spanish and Arabic—perhaps this is why the dialogue of her stories sounds, or sounds to me, as though it has been translated into English from some delightful combination of other tongues. Moreover, these languages are self-learned, the product of Mrs. Bowles' nomadic nature: from New York she wandered on to and all over Europe, traveled away from there and the impending war to Central America and Mexico, then alighted awhile in the historic ménage on Brooklyn Heights. Since 1947 she has been almost continuously resident abroad; in Paris or Ceylon, but largely in Tangiers—in fact, both Jane and Paul Bowles may now safely be described as permanent Tangerinos, so total has their adherence become to that steep, shadowy-white seaport.

Tangiers is composed of two mismatching parts, one of them a dull modern area stuffed with office buildings and tall gloomy dwellings, and the other a casbah descending through a medieval puzzlement of alleys and alcoves and *kif*-odored, mint-scented piazzas down to the crawling with sailors, shiphornhollering port. The Bowles have established themselves in both sectors—have a sterilized, *tout confort* apartment in the newer quarter, and also a refuge hidden away in the darker Arab neighborhood: a native house that must be one of the city's tiniest habitations—ceilings so low that one has almost literally to move on hands and knees from room to room; but the rooms themselves are like a charming series of postcard-sized Vuillards—Moorish cushions spilling over Moorish-patterned carpets, all cozy as a raspberry tart and illuminated by intricate lanterns and windows that allow the light of sea skies and views that encompass minarets and ships and the blue-washed rooftops of native tenements receding like a ghostly staircase to the clamorous shoreline. Or that is how I remember it on the occasion of a single visit made at sunset on an evening, oh, fifteen years ago.

A line from Edith Sitwell: *Jane, Jane, the morning light creaks down again*—. This from a poem I've always liked, without, as so often with the particular author, altogether understanding it. Unless "morning light" is an image signifying memory (?). My own most satisfying memories of Jane Bowles revolve around a month spent in side-by-side rooms in a pleasantly shabby hotel on the rue du Bac during an icy Paris winter—January, 1951. Many a cold evening was spent in Jane's snug room (fat with books and papers and foodstuffs and a snappy white Pekingese puppy bought from a Spanish sailor); long evenings spent listening to a phonograph and drinking warm applejack while Jane built sloppy, marvelous stews atop an electric burner: she is a good cook, yessir, and kind of a glutton, as one might suspect from her stories, which abound in accounts of eating and its artifacts. Cooking is but one of her extracurricular gifts; she is also a spookily accurate mimic and can re-create with nostalgic admiration the voices of certain singers—Helen Morgan, for example, and her close friend Libby Holman.

Years afterward I wrote a story called *Among the Paths to Eden*, in which, without realizing it, I attributed to the heroine several of Jane Bowles' characteristics: the stiff-legged limp, her spectacles, her brilliant and poignant abilities as a mimic ("She waited, as though listening for music to cue her; then, *'Don't ever leave me, now that you're here! Here is where you belong. Everything seems so right when you're near. When you're away it's all wrong.'* And Mr. Belli was shocked, for what he was hearing was exactly Helen Morgan's voice, and the voice, with its vulnerable sweetness, refinement, its tender quaver toppling high notes, seemed not to be borrowed, but Mary O'Meaghan's own, a natural expression of some secluded identity"). I did not have Mrs. Bowles in mind when I invented Mary O'Meaghan—a character she in no essential way resembles; but it is a measure of the potent impression Jane has always made on me that some fragment of her should emerge in this manner.

During that winter Jane was working on *In the Summer House*, the play that was later so sensitively produced in New York. I'm not all that keen on the theater: cannot sit through most plays once; nevertheless, I saw *In the Summer House* three times, and not out of loyalty to the author, but because it had a thorny wit, the flavor of a newly tasted, refreshingly bitter beverage—the same qualities that had initially attracted me to Mrs. Bowles' novel, *Two Serious Ladies*.

My only complaint against Mrs. Bowles is not that her work lacks quality, merely quantity. The volume in hand [*The Collected Works of Jane Bowles*] constitutes her entire shelf, so to say. And grateful as we are to have it, one could wish that there was more. Once, while discussing a colleague, someone more facile than either of us, Jane said: "But it's so easy for him. He has only to turn his hand. Just turn his hand." Actually, writing is never easy: in case anyone doesn't know, it's the hardest work around; and for Jane I think it is difficult to the point of true pain. And why not?—when both her language and her themes are sought after along tortured paths and in stony quarries: the never-realized relationships between her people, the mental and physical discomforts with which she surrounds and saturates them—every room an atrocity, every urban landscape a creation of neon-dourness.

And yet, though the tragic view is central to her vision, Jane Bowles is a very funny writer, a humorist of sorts—but not, by the way, of the Black School. Black Comedy, as its perpetrators label it, is, when successful, all lovely artifice and lacking any hint of compassion. "Camp Cataract," to my mind the most complete of Mrs. Bowles' stories and the one most representative of her work, is a rending sample of controlled compassion: a comic tale of doom that has at its heart, and as its heart, the subtlest comprehension of eccentricity and human apartness. This story alone would require that we accord Jane Bowles high esteem.

A note on books by and about Jane Bowles

Everything Is Nice: Jane Bowles's Collected Stories (Sort Of Books; forthcoming). This new edition features the collection of stories published, in Jane Bowles's lifetime, as *Plain Pleasures*, together with a dozen 'fragments' edited by Paul Bowles. These include 'Señorita Córdoba' (the 'Third Serious Lady' excised from the original draft of *Two Serious Ladies*) and sections of her unfinished novels, *Going to Massachusetts* and *Out In the World*. The book also includes her play, *In the Summer House*.

Out in the World: Selected Letters of Jane Bowles 1935–70 (Black Sparrow Press). As her editor Millicent Dillon writes, 'these letters are exercises in emotional accuracy – little essays in which Jane Bowles explained her joys, doubts, and obesssions to herself and to her correspondents, including her husband, Paul Bowles.'

A Little Original Sin: The Life and Work of Jane Bowles by Millicent Dillon (Black Sparrow Press/Virago Press). This is the definitive biography, written in the late 1970s with the co-operation of Paul Bowles and Jane's friends.